Also in this series:

When trouble hits too close to home...

Savannah Martin has always been a good girl, doing what was expected and fully expecting life to fall into place in its turn. But when her perfect husband turns out to be a lying, cheating slimeball—and bad in bed to boot—Savannah kicks the jerk to the curb and embarks on life on her own terms. With a new apartment, a new career, and a brand new outlook on life, she's all set to take the world by storm. If only the world would stop throwing her curveballs...

Savannah's late. The kind of late that comes with midnight feedings and the pitter-patter of little feet. And while it's a circumstance that should make everyone happy—now she can finally settle down and marry Todd Satterfield, the way everyone's been hoping and praying—it isn't Todd's baby. And Rafe Collier, whose baby it is, didn't sign on for fatherhood. Savannah hasn't seen him or heard from him for two months. So what's a girl to do? Keep the baby and become a single mother, or terminate the pregnancy and pretend it never happened?

Add in the murder of Savannah's sister-in-law—Dix's wife Sheila—the trial of a murderess Todd's prosecuting—a woman who just happens to be Sheila's friend Marley—and the disappearance of Rafe's twelve year old son David—the kid he never knew he had!—and things get complicated fast. And there is worse to come: When Rafe comes back to Nashville to help look for David, and learns that Savannah's pregnant, things do not work out the way Savannah hopes. In the end, she's left with nothing she wanted and a whole lot of trouble she didn't, and for once, Rafe's not there to save the day.

CLOSE TO HOME

Jenna Bennett

CLOSE TO HOME
SAVANNAH MARTIN MYSTERY #4

Interior design: April Martinez, GraphicFantastic.com

ISBN: 978-0-9899434-1-3

MAGPIE INK

One

When Rafe Collier came back from the dead, I was late.

Not the kind of late that mother always drummed into me is rude and inconsiderate, because it makes other people feel I don't value their time or consider them as important as myself. In mother's book of Southern etiquette, making someone wait is a sin of equal magnitude with eating dessert on a date or wearing white shoes after Labor Day.

I wasn't that kind of late. In fact, if mother had realized what kind of late I was, she might well have disowned me.

Rafe wasn't that kind of dead, either. I knew that. (Except for eight pretty bad hours when I'd thought he'd really died, before I realized it was all part of a big, elaborate hoax the Nashville PD and the Tennessee Bureau of Investigation had cooked up.)

See, earlier this fall, someone had sent a contract killer named Jorge Pena after Rafe. Jorge was very good at his job—this was per Rafe, whose opinion I tended to trust on things like that—and when word came down from the Sweetwater sheriff that Rafe was dead, I'd believed it. It wasn't until eight hours later—eight horrible, interminable hours—that I learned the truth: Rafe wasn't dead, Jorge was. The powers that be (and they didn't include Sheriff Satterfield in Sweetwater) had decided that Rafe should take Jorge's place, to try to figure out who was paying Jorge to kill him. The fact that there was a slight resemblance between them—both tall, dark and dangerous—only helped with the illusion. Rafe had left Nashville for parts unknown six weeks ago, and while he was away, I'd realized I was late.

As in, I should have gotten my period, and didn't.

Yes, I was *that* kind of late. The kind that results in morning sickness and the pitter-patter of little feet.

"I have a problem," I told Dix.

"I'm sorry to hear that," my brother answered, his voice as clear in my ear as if he were sitting right next to me instead of a couple of counties over. "What's *your* problem?"

The emphasis told me I wasn't the only one with problems. Maybe our sister Catherine had called him to moan and groan. Or maybe Todd had. Dix's best friend, assistant D.A. Todd Satterfield, had probably called to whine about me, and about the fact that I hadn't yet accepted his proposal of marriage.

Or maybe something was going on with Dix himself. Although what kind of problem could Dix possibly have, with his perfect wife, his perfect children, and his perfect career?

Still, I've been trained well. I asked. Making sure my voice was sympathetic. "What's wrong?"

"Nothing you can help me with right now. Except maybe by giving me a distraction. What sort of problem, sis?"

"I'm..." I cleared my throat, "...pregnant."

Dix was quiet for a second. "I'm sorry," he said. "I could have sworn I heard you say you're pregnant."

I didn't answer.

"You did say you're pregnant."

He waited. When I still didn't speak, he added, "Well, that did it. I'm distracted. Are you sure?"

Of course I was sure. It wasn't the kind of thing I'd toss around if I weren't. I'd bought six different over-the-counter pregnancy tests, all different brands, two of each so as to safeguard myself against any mistakes, and all six had come out positive, one after the other. I was definitely pregnant.

"Well, are congratulations in order?" Dix asked. "If you don't mind my saying so, you don't sound happy."

"I'm not sure how I feel." Other than scared out of my mind.

"Because of the..." he lowered his voice, "miscarriage?"

I'd had a miscarriage some three years ago, while I'd been married to Bradley Ferguson. I had told Catherine about it, and she had told mom, and at some point I guess someone had told Dix. It wasn't me. It's not the sort of thing you discuss with your brother. "How do you know about that?"

"Catherine told Sheila." His voice changed subtly on his wife's name, but I didn't pursue it. In retrospect I realize I should have, but at the time I had other things on my mind.

"That's part of it," I answered. "It was not a good experience."

Understatement of the year. Bradley and I had lasted less than two years before we called it quits, so I guess it had been for the best really, but at the time it had been difficult.

"This'll make Todd happy, anyway," Dix said, trying to look on the bright side. "Now you'll have to marry him."

I didn't answer. Couldn't bring myself to come right out and say it. "*It isn't Todd's baby.*"

And then I didn't have to. When I didn't say anything, Dix read my silence. His voice changed. "Oh, sis. What have you done?"

"Something stupid?" I don't know why I posed it as a question. I'd been stupid, no doubt about it.

"I'd say. You slept with him? And you didn't make sure you were protected? What were you thinking?"

"That's kind of the problem," I muttered. "I wasn't."

I'd been feeling. Needing. Enjoying. But not thinking. Too wrapped up in the moment, I hadn't given the possibility of getting pregnant a thought until I didn't get my period on time. And Dix was right. I'd been an idiot. It had been bad enough to sleep with Rafe in the first place, when I knew we'd never have any kind of real relationship, but to do it without protection...!

"That's obvious," Dix said.

My voice was tiny. "So what do I do now?"

"You're asking me?" I could picture him, running his fingers through his sandy blond hair, making it stand straight up. Fisting his hands in it in frustration and yanking. "All right. You don't have many options that I can see. There's not much chance you can pass this kid off as Todd's..."

"No." Any baby Rafe and I made would have its father's dark hair, dark eyes, and golden skin. My blonde and blue-eyed fairness might lighten things up a little, like a liberal dash of milk in coffee, but we're still talking café au lait, not plain vanilla. And since Todd is as fair-haired and blue-eyed as I am, there was no way we'd be able to explain something like that away. Or like he'd want to.

"God, sis," Dix said, as if he were looking at the picture in my mind and freaking out all over again, "what were you thinking?"

The thing is, the picture was beautiful. A little baby... girl? boy?... with big dark eyes, thick black lashes, and a big toothless smile, holding on to my finger—

"Obviously marrying him is out," Dix said, popping the bubble.

I nodded. Yes, and not only because he hadn't asked. He probably didn't want to. No, scratch that—he *definitely* didn't want to. He'd been upfront about it. He wanted me in his bed, but he didn't want a relationship. Not that he'd said so, but surely if he had,

I would have heard something from him at least once in the past six weeks. The whole experience must not have been as mind-blowing for him as it had been for me. He'd achieved his goal of bedding Savannah Martin, and now he was on to the next woman. While I was here, barefoot—I was painting my toenails—and pregnant. Damn him.

"And I can't imagine you want to be a single mother," Dix continued, twisting the knife.

I shook my head again. I knew he couldn't see me, but I couldn't help the kneejerk reaction.

"So I guess that leaves the two As. Adoption or abortion."

And there it was. Carrying the baby to term and giving it away to someone else, or getting rid of it now, before it developed into a real problem.

There were issues inherent in these scenarios too, of course. While healthy white newborns are a hot commodity on the adoption market, this baby wouldn't precisely be white. LaDonna Collier had been a blue-eyed blonde like me, but Rafe's father had been black, and Rafe looked, if not specifically African-American, at least far from Caucasian, which might make things more difficult. Although not impossible. There was sure to be someone out there who'd be happy to have Rafe's baby. Someone who'd love it and take care of it. A mixed couple, maybe, who couldn't conceive. Or just someone braver than me, who wouldn't care what people thought. After all, any baby of Rafe's would be beautiful. Couldn't help but be. And having gone through a miscarriage myself, I had all the sympathy in the world for people who couldn't conceive. But if I carried the baby for nine months and then gave birth to it, would I be able to give it up? Or would I get attached, in spite of my fears?

And as for deliberately terminating the pregnancy, I wasn't sure I could do that, either. It'd be the easiest solution, certainly, it was just—

"Did you tell him?" Dix interrupted my train of thought.

God, no. "I just realized it a few days ago." And although I could have gotten hold of him if I really wanted to, through Detective Grimaldi with the Nashville police, I wasn't yet sure I wanted him to know.

"I don't suppose it would have mattered," Dix said judiciously. "After all, there's nothing he could have done about it. Your body, your choice. Although if he'd told his grandmother..."

"What do you mean, there's nothing he can do?" He could do a hell of a lot, as far as I was concerned.

Dix was silent for a moment. "Who are we talking about here, sis?"

I took the phone away from my ear to stare at it, and put it back. "What do you mean, who are we talking about? Who do you think we're talking about? Rafe, of course."

"Right," Dix said. "Rafe Collier. Isn't he dead?"

Oh... shit.

"Darn," I said faintly.

"He's not dead? Sis?"

I drew breath and blew it out, thinking about knocking my head against the coffee table. Stupid, stupid, stupid...

Well, the cat was out of the bag now. Lying wouldn't do any good; besides, Dix could always tell when I did. I might as well tell the truth. And beg him not to pass it on.

"No, he isn't dead. He's undercover. But you can't tell anyone, Dix. You've got to promise me that you won't. If word gets out that he survived that nutcase they sent to kill him, they'll just send someone else. And I don't want him to die."

My voice shook. I could still remember that horrible feeling I got when Dix told me that Todd had told him that the sheriff had said that Rafe was dead. No doubt Dix remembered, as well.

He was silent for a moment. "Are you in love with this guy, sis?"

"Of course not," I said, grabbing a strand of hair and twirling it around my finger.

"You're blushing."

"No, I'm not." And even if I were, he couldn't possibly tell from two counties away.

"Is your finger turning blue?"

"Why would my finger be turning blue?" I unwound the hair and inspected the finger. Not blue.

"You always play with your hair when you're lying," Dix said.

"I'm not lying." I leaned back on the sofa pretending I hadn't been doing exactly what he'd accused me of doing. "God, Dix, have you lost your mind? How could you possibly think I'd fall in love with Rafe Collier? Mother would kill me!"

"You forget," Dix said, "I saw your face last month, when you thought he'd died. And don't bother trying to tell me that you knew, at that point, that he was just faking it, because I won't believe you. You thought he was dead, and you had a meltdown."

"It wasn't a meltdown." I'd kept myself from becoming a blubbering mess, and as far as I was concerned, that was a major achievement, when all I'd wanted to do was break down in hysterics.

"You also told me you'd fallen for him."

"A little. I said a little. And that was when I thought he was dead."

"Right," Dix said. "Relax, sis. It's not like I'm going to tell anyone. This isn't something I'd want to get around."

"Thank you."

"I'm not doing it for you," Dix said. "You're up there in Nashville. You can turn off your phone. I live with these people. And if word got out that you're pregnant, and with Rafe Collier's baby—oh, and by the way, he's not really dead after all, so guess what, he'll be around, practically part of the family—can you imagine the flak I'd get?"

I could imagine, only too well. I suppressed a shudder.

"So no," Dix said, "until you figure out what you're going to do, I won't be saying a word to anyone. And when you do figure it out, assuming there's anything to tell at that point, *you're* telling them."

Fair enough.

"So Collier doesn't know." Dix picked up the conversation where we'd left off several tangents ago.

I shook my head, although he couldn't see it. "He left that same night. And I haven't heard from him since."

"He seduced you and left town and he didn't even leave a number? I'm gonna kill him."

"Please don't." And not just because if he tried, chances were Rafe would kill Dix instead. "It's not his fault."

"Whose fault is it?"

I sighed. "It's mine. I should have been more careful. He was always upfront about what he wanted, and it wasn't anything permanent."

"I should hope not," Dix said darkly, "because if he offers to marry you, I want you to say no."

I couldn't help it, I giggled. Weakly, but it was a giggle. "I don't think you have to worry about that."

God, could you picture it? Rafe Collier facing mother over the Thanksgiving Day turkey for the next thirty years...?

And then, to my absolute mortification, the giggle turned to a sob, and then another. "I don't know what to do, Dix. I can't keep the baby—what will people think?—but I don't think I can give it away, either. Not after carrying it for nine months. I'll get attached, you know I will. And aborting it—just because I'm too much of a coward to keep it—seems wrong."

"Maybe you should talk to him," Dix said.

It was the last thing I expected him to say, and for a second I just sat there, stunned. Then—

"Are you crazy? I can't tell him! What if he says he wants me to keep it?"

"He can't force you," Dix pointed out. "It's your body."

"But it's his baby." Our baby. And God, the thought of that—! "He has the right..."

"He doesn't have the right to tell you what to do. Legally—"

I interrupted him. Mother taught me that interrupting is wrong, but I couldn't keep it in. "Legally, schmegally. Come on, Dix. Morally and ethically, he has the right to an opinion. And I have an obligation to take what he says into account."

"I always suspected Bradley Ferguson wasn't the only reason you dropped out of law school," Dix grumbled. "With an attitude like that, you'd never make it as a lawyer. Legally, it's your body and you can do what you want with it."

"But here in the real world, I offered him my body, and he put a baby inside it, and that means he gets a say in what happens to that baby."

"If you tell him," Dix said.

"Right. If I tell him."

"And right now he's gone. Any idea when he's coming back?"

"None." Could be tomorrow, could be never. He'd already been gone longer than he thought he'd be. Before he left, he'd told me he expected it to take a few weeks, maybe a month at the most. It had been almost two.

"Then I suggest you think fast," Dix said. "How far along are you? No more than two months, right? You'll start showing in another month or two, if you haven't terminated by then, and I think you owe your family an explanation before it gets to that point. Not to mention Todd."

Todd. My brother's best friend, the man who wanted to marry me. The idea of having to face Todd and tell him I was pregnant—and with Rafe Collier's baby!—made my head hurt. For that reason alone, it was tempting to end the pregnancy now.

And mother... how could I face my mother and tell her how far I'd strayed from the straight and narrow? She'd be disappointed in me, and that disappointment would cut deeper than any harsh words she could ever use.

Yet at the same time, a small, rebellious part of me said, *it was my life, wasn't it?* I'd spent the first twenty five years of it doing everything

I was told. First by mother and dad, then by Bradley. I'd thought, if I toed the line and did everything perfectly, that I'd have the life I'd always dreamed of. That was until I realized that Bradley had been unfaithful, and that my perfect husband was far from perfect, and my perfect marriage was a shambles. So I'd dumped Bradley and gone out on my own instead. Refusing to run home to Sweetwater with my tail between my legs, determined to make it on my own terms. And now look where I was. But at least this mess was of my own making and no one else's. There was something to be said for that.

"I have to go," Dix said, as the sound of breaking glass came through the phone. "Sheila's out, and it sounds like one of the kids just destroyed something. Call me back if you want to talk more, OK?"

"Sure."

"Later, though. Right now I've got to take care of this."

He hung up before I had the chance to say goodbye and to thank him for the help he'd given me. I disconnected too, and curled up on the sofa to contemplate my future and my choices.

Two

I've visited the same OB/GYN my entire adult life, ever since I was twelve and got my first period. Doctor Denise Seaver practices in Columbia, Tennessee, twenty minutes from where I grew up in Sweetwater. When I moved to Nashville, I still made the trip south twice a year to see Dr. Seaver, and when I was married to Bradley and had my miscarriage, she was the one who saw me through it. I trust her. But I had to think long and hard about whether to visit Dr. Seaver with this pregnancy. On the one hand, she knew me. She knew my history and what I'd had to deal with in the past, and there was comfort in that.

On the other hand, she knew me. The same way she knew my mother and my sister and my sister-in-law, my Aunt Regina—my father's sister—and my mother's best friend Audrey, and at least half the other female population of Sweetwater. Todd's late mother Pauline had probably gone to Dr. Seaver with her female problems. Rafe's mother LaDonna might have done the same. Dr. Seaver knew us all, intimately. She knew I'd been a virgin until I entered college, and she knew I hadn't been sexually active since Bradley and I got divorced.

She'd asked me repeatedly over the past two years whether I wanted a prescription for birth control pills, and I'd always given her the same answer: "There's no need for that."

I realize that my sex life, real or imagined, is no business of Dr. Seaver's—or of anyone else's, for that matter. I'm a consenting adult, and if I want to sleep around, I can. Not that I do. It had happened once in two years, so it's not as if I'm promiscuous. But Dr. Seaver didn't know that, and I knew what she'd be thinking when she found out. Margaret Anne Martin's perfect youngest daughter isn't supposed to get pregnant out of wedlock. The good doctor would be shocked. And then she'd probably be on the phone with my mother.

"Nonsense," Dix said. "There's such a thing as doctor-patient confidentiality, you know."

It was a few days later. He had cleaned up whatever mess had resulted from the glass I'd heard breaking last time we were on the phone together, and when he hadn't heard from me for the next couple of days, he'd called back. One of the questions he'd asked—right after inquiring whether I'd made a decision one way or the other—was whether I'd been to see a doctor about my options.

"Well, why not?" he'd said when I replied in the negative. "You know you're going to need one. Either you're having the baby, and you'll need someone to deliver it, or you're not having the baby, and you'll need someone to terminate the pregnancy."

He was right, but at the moment I stayed busy pretending that if I didn't deal with the issue, it didn't exist. And I didn't want him to ruin my comfortable fantasy, so I tried to derail him. "Could you possibly talk a little louder? Just in case Sheila didn't hear you?"

"She isn't here," Dix said. "It's just me and the girls, and they're in bed. Don't try to change the subject, sis. You need to go see a doctor. If you're keeping the baby, you'll need prenatal vitamins and regular check-ups. I've been through this twice with Sheila; I remember the drill."

Of course he did. And because he was putting me on the spot, I did the same to him. "Speaking of that, are you two going to have any more? Hannah's three, isn't she? You'd better hurry; you aren't getting any younger."

"You sound like mother," Dix said. "But for your information, probably not. At least not anytime soon."

"Something wrong?"

"Nothing you can help with. To get back to what I was saying, if you decide not to have the baby, you don't have all the time in the world to get rid of it, you know. That window closes after a while."

"I don't know which doctor to go to. I don't have one here in Nashville." And the indignity of going to one of the clinics, like some vapid teenager who'd had no idea that sex could lead to pregnancy, was just too embarrassing to contemplate.

"Go to Dr. Seaver in Columbia," Dix said. "Just like you've always done."

"What if she tells mom?"

And that's when Dix reminded me that there's such a thing as doctor-patient confidentiality.

"I know that," I said. "I studied law too, for a couple of semesters. But you know how that kind of thing goes out the window where mother is concerned. I'm sure she has Denise Seaver just as firmly wrapped around her finger as she has the rest of us. They've known each other forever."

"It's the law," Dix said. "She can't tell mom, no matter how much mom whines and begs. It's illegal. You're not underage."

"Mom thinks so."

"Mom's wrong," Dix said. "The circumstances of how you got yourself into this mess is none of Dr. Seaver's business, anyway. You don't have to give her any of the details."

I hadn't planned to. The way my family—and the population of Sweetwater in general—feels about Rafe Collier, I planned to keep his name out of the story for as long as I could.

"What if meet someone I know?"

"Just tell them you're there for your annual checkup. It's not like they'll know the difference." He hung up without waiting for an answer.

And that was how I came to be in Dr. Seaver's office a couple of days later.

I'll spare you the details. Peeing in a cup and pelvic exams make for poor narrative. Let's just skip to the part where I was dressed again, and sitting on the examining table waiting to discuss my situation with the doctor.

"You're pregnant," Denise Seaver said when she came back into the room. Somehow she managed to sound surprised.

"I told you I was." Six home pregnancy tests don't lie.

"I thought you must have made a mistake." She seated herself on the stool by the wall, still holding the folder with the results of my various tests and examinations, and crossed her ankles.

"Obviously not," I said. Calmly, as if the implication that I'd done something surprising, even shocking, didn't sting at all.

She nodded. "You're about eight weeks along."

"Seven weeks, four days."

She looked up at that. "You know exactly when you conceived?"

"I'm not in the habit of doing this. It happened once. I'm not likely to forget."

To be honest, I wished I remembered it a little less well. Or at least part of me did. The well-brought-up part that was horrified at what I had done, and which couldn't quite believe that it had happened.

The other, less well-brought-up part liked to take out the memories and dwell on them in the darkness of night, when I lay in bed alone, with nothing but silence and worries to keep me company, snuggled into Rafe's T-shirt that still smelled faintly of him.

Dix was right: I had fallen for Rafe, maybe more than just a little, and the fact that he'd headed into what I knew was a dangerous situation, one he might not come out of unscathed, gave me plenty of cause to worry. He might be hurt. He might even be dead. I had to believe, for my own sanity, that Detective Grimaldi would contact me if something happened to him. She hadn't, which had to mean, I told myself, that he was safe and still in one piece. But there were times when it was comforting to picture him being alive, and that invariably led to memories of warm skin under my hands, and hard muscles sliding against my body.

Yes, I knew precisely how many weeks and days it had been since that night. I could have given Dr. Seaver the hours and minutes too, had she asked.

"I guess I can take it you're not in a relationship with the father of the baby, then?"

I blinked, caught between answering the question because she was the doctor, and questioning her need to ask. Added to that was the fact that it wasn't an easy question to answer.

"It's complicated," I said eventually.

Dr. Seaver looked at me. "Either you're in a relationship or you're not."

Not necessarily. Rafe and I had a relationship, certainly, but I had no idea how to describe it. Friendship, with a healthy dose of sexual attraction thrown in for good measure, and a lot more trust on my part than I'd found it easy to give to anyone before. And that was before we had sex.

"Let's start with something simpler," Dr. Seaver said. "The father of the baby... do you know who he is?"

I sat up straight, stung. "Of course! It wasn't a one night stand, for God's sake. I didn't go out to a bar to pick up a guy I didn't know and took him home with me."

"Excellent," Dr. Seaver said and made a note in her folder. "So you're involved?"

"We're..." Yes, I guess it would be accurate to say we were involved. Sort of. Except what sort of involvement was still up in the air, and besides, he'd been gone for seven weeks, and I didn't know whether he was dead or alive. "Friends," I said.

Dr. Seaver arched her brows. "Friends with benefits?"

"God, no!" That sounded so tawdry. "I've known him for a while, and there's always been…" I hesitated, casting around for the right word, "…something there, I guess, but I never considered acting on it. And then this happened."

"And since then?"

"He's been away on business," I said firmly. Everyone in Sweetwater knew that Rafe was supposed to be dead—everyone in Sweetwater had rejoiced, in their own quiet way—and in this, at least, I could make it sound like I was talking about someone else. Not that Dr. Seaver would have any reason to think I was talking about Rafe. He's not the kind of man anyone in Sweetwater would expect me to associate with. No one but my family knew we had any contact at all these days.

My family and the Satterfields.

And Cletus Johnson, one of Bob Satterfield's deputies. His wife Marquita had been working for Rafe until she was killed two months ago.

Oh, and Yvonne McCoy, an old friend of Rafe's from school. She knew, too.

And then there were the waitresses and everyone else who'd been at Beulah's Meat'n Three the morning the two of us had bumped into one another there…

Yes, much better to divert attention from Rafe. Too many people had seen us together, and I certainly didn't want anyone to jump to the conclusion that my visit to the OB/GYN had anything at all to do with Rafe Collier.

"So you'll be raising this baby by yourself?" Dr. Seaver asked.

"That's… something I wanted to talk to you about."

She blinked. Dr. Seaver is around mother's age, mid fifties, and unlike mother she looks every inch of it. She's a little plump, mostly gray, and has an avuncular manner. Very earth-motherly. The loose-fitting dress under the white lab coat looked like it was sewn from home-woven material, and she had plastic clogs on her feet, with pink ankle socks. "Yes?"

"I'm not sure I want... I mean, I don't feel like I'd be able to... I don't know if..."

Either way I tried to articulate it, my feelings didn't make me sound like a very nice person. *I'm not sure I want this baby, because my family is going to give me hell about its father, and I don't know if I can handle bringing it up on my own with no support from anyone.*

It made me sound so selfish. Like I'd had my fun but now I didn't want to deal with the consequences.

Dr. Seaver must have heard it before. "Facing life as a single parent is never easy," she said. "There are options."

"Adoption and abortion."

I'd thought about little else since I'd talked to Dix last week. And I was no closer to making a decision about what I wanted to do. Carrying the baby to term and then giving it away would be hard, and I'd still have to explain to my family—and possibly Rafe—what was going on. Once I started looking pregnant, he'd certainly ask. That's if he ever got back to Nashville, of course. The only way I could avoid any of the explanations was by terminating the pregnancy before I started showing. That was probably what I ought to do. I just couldn't bring myself to do it. Not quite yet.

"You have some time to think about it," Dr. Seaver said. There was no accusation in her voice, which I appreciated. "While you decide what to do, you should start taking prenatal vitamins. If you do decide to carry the baby to term, you'll be glad you did."

I nodded.

"I'll also give you a prescription for mifepristone. That's the abortion pill. If you decide you'd prefer to end the pregnancy within the next week, you can take it. If you do, I need you back in the office within three days of taking it to make sure that everything worked out as planned and the pregnancy has ended. After the middle of next week, that option is off the table and you'll have to have an in-clinic abortion. I'd like to see you back here in four weeks. If you don't take the pill but you decide you'd like to schedule an abortion procedure before then, call and I'll make an appointment for you with a facility in Nashville."

I nodded. Each mention of the word abortion hit me like a tiny pebble, stinging just a little, with the accumulation turning into a sort of dull overall pain.

"Make an appointment at the desk on your way out," Dr. Seaver said, getting to her feet. "Here," she pulled a business card out of her pocket and handed it to me, "this has my private number on it. If you want to discuss the options in more detail, give me a call."

"Thank you." I pocketed it, reflecting that my voice sounded faint, strangely distant.

She put a comforting hand on my shoulder as she herded me toward the door and the hallway beyond. "It'll be all right, Savannah. You'll get through this. I believe in you."

I managed a smile. She might believe in me, but I wasn't sure I did.

I was standing at the nurse's desk making my appointment for next month and carefully keeping my eyes off the tiny newborns in their carriers, when the door to the outside opened and a woman came through. She was about an inch shorter than me, slender and elegant, with a sleek blonde pageboy haircut cupping her jaw and big, brown eyes in a pointed pixie face.

My first reaction was to run and hide.

I disregarded it almost immediately, although I did make a deal with myself to strangle Dix at the first opportunity that presented itself. If Sheila was here, it could only be because my brother had spilled the beans. Damn him.

And if she knew what was going on, it wasn't like hiding would do me any good. I put the best face I could on it. "Sheila."

She jumped, and for a second she looked as unpleasantly surprised as I'd felt upon seeing her. "Savannah."

"Dix didn't tell me you were going to be here," I said, since it was rather obvious she wasn't there to see me.

She smiled. It almost looked painful. "It must have slipped his mind. What are you doing here?"

"Annual checkup. You?"

"The same."

I nodded. "I can wait for you, if you want. We could have lunch or something."

"Oh," Sheila said, sounding less than thrilled about the idea, "that's not necessary. I'm sure you want to get back to Nashville as soon as possible."

"I can take time out to have lunch with my only sister-in-law." I smiled.

It's not like I'm setting the real estate world on fire up there in Nashville. We were close to Thanksgiving now, and the upcoming holiday season had put even more of a crimp in what was already a slow economy. I'd managed to pull down a couple of commissions since getting my real estate license back in the summer, just enough to keep food on the table and the wolf from the door, but there wasn't anything pressing that I needed to get back to. Not in the next few hours.

"I'm sorry," Sheila said, "but I've already made plans for lunch. With a friend."

"Oh," I said. "OK. Maybe I'll run down to Sweetwater instead, see if Catherine is free for lunch. Or mom. Since I'm down here anyway."

"Sure." She leaned in and gave me air kisses on both cheeks. I returned the favor, and then hightailed it out the door while Sheila turned to the nurse behind the counter and gave her name. I couldn't help but notice that she spoke in a low voice, almost a whisper, as if she were trying to make sure no one in the waiting room would know who she was.

Sweetwater is located about twenty minutes southeast of Columbia, down the Pulaski highway. It's a nice little town, full of well-to-do people and old houses. The Martin mansion, my childhood home, is the oldest of them all: an 1839 red brick antebellum construction with tall, two-story pillars, sitting on a little knoll just outside Sweetwater proper. Rafe once likened it to a mausoleum, and as I passed by on my way into town, I could see his point. It did look forbidding sitting there among the bare trees. Especially, I imagined, to a boy who had grown up in the Bog, the trailer park on the other side of town.

Once upon a time, all the land surrounding the mansion belonged to the Martin family. These days, there's just a couple of acres left, with a few old outbuildings from the glory days and a whole lot of grass and flowers. Everything else is sold off. And there are new subdivisions cropping up all the time, all over town. The city limits are spreading in every direction, north toward Columbia and south toward Pulaski. In another ten years, Columbia will probably become a suburb of Nashville, and it won't be long after that, that Sweetwater gets gobbled up, too. One day, we'll all live in cities.

Not that I mind subdivisions, of course. I'm a realtor; they're my bread and butter. And most of my family lives in subdivisions. Mother is still in the mansion, but Catherine and Jonathan and their three kids live in a subdivision called Summer Point, while Dix and Sheila and the girls are in Copper Creek.

My entire family, save for mother, Sheila and I, are lawyers. Dad was a lawyer, and his dad before him. My great-grandfather founded the family firm, on the square in Sweetwater. When Catherine married Jonathan McCall, whom she met in law school, his name was added to the front window in gold letters. Martin and McCall, attorneys at law. Catherine still has a license, and she keeps it current, but these days she spends most of her time at home with the children. Martin and McCall is Dix and Jonathan, for the most part.

When I walked through the door a few minutes before noon, Jonathan was manning the front desk in the lobby.

My brother-in-law is a Yankee from Massachusetts, a bit of an anomaly here where most people can trace their ancestry back to the War Against Northern Aggression. Mother and dad gave him a difficult time when he first started dating Catherine, but after he proved himself to be a gentleman in spite of his unfortunate origin, he was accepted with open arms. It wasn't his fault that he'd been born above the Mason-Dixon line, and his Boston Brahmin family turned out to be just as old-fashioned and uptight as ours. He and Catherine are a match made in heaven.

It helps that he's good looking, in that tall and skinny, pale Northern way. Dark hair, brown eyes, pointy nose, narrow face. Sort of aristocratic. The total opposite of Dix, who's about average height, fair haired, blue eyed, and a little stocky. Not overweight, just sort of square. He appeared in the door to his office approximately five seconds after I'd walked into the lobby, just as soon as he heard my voice saying hello to Jonathan.

"What are you doing here?" he demanded.

"Goodness," I said, blinking, "is that a way to greet your favorite sister?"

"I thought Catherine was your favorite," Jonathan said.

"She is. Believe me." Dix scowled. "Savannah?"

When his eyes dipped down to my stomach for just a second, I scowled back. "Dix." It wasn't like there was anything to see there. Not yet, anyway.

"What are you doing here?"

"I had an appointment," I said, "in Columbia. I thought you might want to have some lunch. Both of you. Either of you."

They exchanged a glance. "Are you buying?" Jonathan wanted to know.

"Are you crazy?" I answered. "I can hardly feed myself. And what would your wife say if she knew you let me pick up the tab for lunch?"

"She'd never let me hear the end of it," Jonathan said. "You two go ahead. I'm waiting for a phone call."

"Don't you have a cell phone?"

He did. "But I also have a lot of paperwork I have to refer to, and it's easier to keep it here. You can bring me something back, if you don't mind."

"What do you want?"

"That depends on where you're going," Jonathan said.

"Café on the Square?" Dix suggested. It was the closest place to get something to eat; just a few doors down from the law office. It was also a favorite hangout of mother's, not to mention of mother's best friend Audrey, who owned a boutique on the town square. The last time I'd had lunch at the café, I'd been with both of them. I wondered what my chances were of meeting both or either today.

"We could go to Beulah's," I said.

Dix and Jonathan exchanged another look. "Why would you drive all the way to Beulah's Meat'n Three when you can eat at the café?" Jonathan wanted to know, and turned to Dix. "Bring me back a roast beef on rye and a bag of chips."

"Will do." Dix disappeared into his office just long enough to fetch his jacket. He was in the process of shrugging into it when he came back through the door. "Ready, Savannah?"

"Whenever you are," I said, and let myself be ushered back out of the office and down the sidewalk to the café on the square.

Three

I got lucky. The café was mercifully free of people I knew, and Dix and I were able to snag the last table for two in a quiet corner. We arrived just as the previous occupants got up to leave, and we swooped in and sat down even as the waitress was clearing off used flatware and her tip. Five minutes later, we were munching rolls and waiting for our food to finish prepping. Cobb salad for me, turkey on whole wheat for Dix.

"So what's up?" my brother asked, watching me demolish a roll as though I hadn't eaten for days.

I glanced up. "Nothing. Why would something be up?"

"You didn't say anything about coming to Sweetwater."

"I was in Columbia. To see Dr. Seaver. I figured I was so close I might as well come down."

"That's true, I guess," Dix said.

"And besides, I saw Sheila at the doctor's office. I asked her to have lunch with me, and she said no. So I figured I'd ask you instead."

His brow clouded. "Sheila was at the doctor's office?"

I reached for another roll. Usually I avoid having one, let alone two, but I was starving. "Didn't you know?"

He shook his head. "She hasn't said anything about it."

"Any chance you're pregnant again?"

"None," Dix said.

I blinked. He sounded so definite. "You're not... you know...?"

"Not for a while."

It was difficult to know what to say to that, so I said nothing. After a longish pause, he added, "She had a miscarriage about four months ago."

"I didn't know that."

"It wasn't the first," Dix said. "She had another last year. We knew it could happen again, so we didn't say anything to anyone when she got pregnant this last time."

No sense in getting everyone's hopes up only to dash them, I supposed.

"Ever since then, she hardly ever goes to bed when I do anymore. The only reason I know she's been there, is because her side of the bed's been slept in. And she's always up before me, too. I think she's afraid, you know?"

I nodded. "It's hard, losing a baby. Maybe not as much for the father—" at least Bradley hadn't seemed to understand my sense of loss, "but our bodies change, and we actually feel the difference, long before anything's visible on the outside."

"I tried to be sensitive," Dix said. "And I haven't been pressuring her."

"I'm sure you haven't. Maybe she's ready to try again, and she wanted to check with the doctor that it would be OK." That might make my brother happy, anyway. Men seem to like regularity in that aspect of their lives.

"Maybe," Dix said. "Don't you think you ought to slow down a little, sis?"

I pulled my hand back from the basket of rolls. Two were probably enough, anyway. "I can't help it. I'm hungry all the time. And I feel like I could sleep twelve hours a night."

"You may as well," Dix said. "If you go through with this, it's the last sleep you'll get in a long time."

I shook my head. "I can't go through with it. What would mother say?"

"You should have thought about that before you slept with him," Dix said.

"I did. It was worth it."

"Too much information," Dix said. "Listen, Savannah. If you want to keep this baby, and you want to raise it on your own, I'll do my best to support you. You're my sister, and I love you. I'm not saying it'll be easy, or that mom won't have all sorts of fits, but she'll come around eventually. She dotes on her grandchildren."

"Your children and Catherine's don't have Rafe Collier for a father."

"No," Dix admitted. "But it isn't your baby's fault who its father is. And it'll help that everyone thinks he's dead."

Great. So if I could deal with the stigma and the stares, my baby might eventually be accepted by my relatives. Although my baby's father was better off dead. "You know, there are times when I hate our family."

"You don't mean that," Dix said.

"Not really, no. But this would be a lot easier if I had the kind of family who adored me and thought I could do no wrong. Or if I'd had a couple of older siblings who hadn't done everything perfectly in their lives. You and Catherine are a lot to live up to."

"Catherine married Jonathan," Dix said. "A damn Yankee."

"But she's a lawyer. And she has three perfect children. And Jonathan turned out to be pretty perfect, too, in spite of being from Boston. And you married Sheila, mother's ideal of a daughter-in-law. Sheila will be just like mom in thirty years."

"Hopefully not just like her," Dix said, and leaned back as the waitress moved in to put his sandwich in front of him. I smiled appreciatively as she came around the table with my salad.

I had just lifted my fork to dig in when I heard a voice I knew. The very last voice I wanted to hear, if I had thought about it.

No, it wasn't mother's voice, or even her friend Audrey's. It wasn't my aunt Regina's or my sister Catherine's. It was worse. Much worse.

"Savannah!" Todd said, surprise laced through every syllable. "Dix."

I closed my eyes for a second. When I opened them, Dix was looking at me with concern. I pasted on a smile, the same bright, polite, social smile mother drilled into me when I was but a wee little Southern Belle in the making, and turned on my chair. "Todd! How delightful to see you!"

Todd Satterfield is the assistant district attorney for Maury county. He works out of the courthouse in Columbia, twenty minutes away. The fact that I might run into him down here hadn't even crossed my mind.

Dix stood up, and the two men shook hands and slapped backs with every evidence of pleasure. They've been friends since elementary school, and if they're not as close now as they used to be, what with Sheila and the kids placing more demands on Dix's time, they're still plenty close enough.

Todd and I used to be close, too. We were boyfriend/girlfriend his last year of high school, my sophomore year, and before he left for college, he asked me to marry him. I was sixteen at the time, and thought he was joking. Two years later, I went off to finishing school in Charleston and then university in Nashville, and at twenty three I dropped out to marry Bradley Ferguson. Shortly after that, Todd married a girl named Jolynn Lowry; mother says because she looked like me. Two years later I divorced Bradley, and it wasn't but a few months later that Todd divorced Jolynn. Now he wants to try again. He proposed to me back in September, and I think he was pretty sure I'd say yes. It must have come as quite a shock when I didn't.

That was the night I ended up in Rafe's bed. I'd known that Todd was thinking of asking me to marry him, and there was even a part of me that wanted him to, because by getting myself engaged, I thought maybe I'd be able to exorcise those conflicting feelings I had for Rafe. But when I was sitting there across the table from Todd, faced with the actual question and the look in his eyes, I couldn't bring myself to say yes. So I'd told him I had to think about it. And then I got in my car to go back to the Martin mansion for the night, and instead had found myself driving until I reached Nashville and Rafe. And the rest is history, except it was history that had come back to bite me in the butt.

"I didn't know you were coming to Sweetwater," Todd said now.

"I had an appointment in Columbia. I thought I'd see if Dix was free for lunch."

"You want to join us?" Dix asked. He probably meant it sincerely. But we were sitting at a table for two, and there was no way to squeeze in another chair, let alone another place setting. Todd shook his head.

"I'm meeting dad. He's over there." He gestured to the other side of the café. I looked over and saw the grizzled Sweetwater sheriff raising a hand to us from a table by the opposite wall. I waved back, wondering when on earth he'd arrived and what he might have heard before we realized he was there. If he'd caught any part of our conversation, this could get ugly in a hurry.

"We'll be going over the Cartwright trial," Todd added.

Dix nodded, like he knew what Todd was talking about. I didn't. "The what?"

"It happened a couple of years ago," Todd said. "That was before I came to work here, so I'm meeting with dad to go over some of the details. When I get Marley Cartwright up on the stand, I want to be able to nail her."

"Who's Marley Cartwright and what did she do?"

"Killed her baby," Todd said. "Then she dumped the body somewhere and told everyone the baby was kidnapped. There was a big to-do for days, trying to find any trace of him."

"Sheila was fit to be tied," Dix added. "She knew Marley. They'd been in exercise classes together, or something. Hannah was less than a year old when little Oliver was born, and I guess Sheila thought it might have been Hannah."

I shuddered. I could imagine the fear such news might strike into a mother's heart. Sweetwater is such a small place; nobody expects something like that to take place here. "So what happened? They found the baby?"

Dix and Todd both shook their heads. "The baby's gone," Todd said. "She never admitted doing anything to him. Her husband wasn't around when whatever it was happened."

"And what did she say that was?"

"The baby was asleep in the swing on the back deck. Marley went inside to take a shower. When she came out a couple of minutes later, he was gone."

"But you don't believe her?"

"She did something to him," Todd said. "And then she hid the body somewhere until she could get rid of it. At first everyone thought she might be telling the truth, that someone had kidnapped him. Every available volunteer scoured the neighborhood for hours. The police interviewed witnesses and watched security tapes of any unfamiliar cars that had been in the area. A couple of days went by. Plenty of time for Marley to dump the body and clean the house from top to bottom to get rid of any evidence."

"She did that?"

"Top to bottom," Todd nodded. "Floors, walls, ceilings. By the time dad started to suspect her, there wasn't a speck of physical evidence left in the house."

"Sounds like a simple case, then."

I'd come up against a few murder cases of my own in recent months—it had been quite the season on Nashville realtors earlier in the fall; two of my coworkers had died, as well as my close friend Lila, who also was an agent—and they'd all been a lot more complicated than this.

Both the men shook their heads. "There's no body," Dix said.

Todd added, "That's why I want all the ammunition I can get. Dad worked the case, and I'm hoping he can tell me something that isn't in the official statements. Some insignificant little detail that might rattle her."

I nodded. Now that they had reminded me, I did recall having heard about the disappearance of Oliver Cartwright, but it had been just after Bradley and I divorced, and I'd had other things on my mind than the disappearance of a baby I didn't know, even if it was in my old hometown. I didn't remember hearing that the investigation had turned from abduction to murder, though. But if Marley Cartwright had harmed her son, I hoped Todd nailed her to the wall.

"Are you staying the night?" he wanted to know.

I shook my head. "I'm driving back to Nashville after lunch."

Todd looked disappointed. "I thought maybe I could talk you into having dinner with me at the Wayside Inn tonight."

"I'm sorry," I said. "But I really have to get back. Work, you know."

"I understand." He thought for a second. "How about tomorrow? If I drove up to Nashville, would you go to dinner then?"

Dix looked at me. I avoided his eyes.

Todd had reiterated his offer of marriage several times in the past two months. At this point, he couldn't think of any logical reason why I'd keep turning him down. Like everyone else in Sweetwater—with the exception of Dix, now—Todd thought that Rafe was dead, and since he'd always suspected that I had a soft spot for Rafe, and that Rafe was the reason I didn't want to marry him, he was quietly thrilled at the turn of events.

I was fairly certain I'd be faced with another proposal if I went out with him tomorrow night, and I was tired of telling him to hold on, I needed more time. But by the same token, I didn't want to hurt his feelings by refusing to go out with him. He couldn't help the fact that he was ready to get married and I wasn't. It wasn't his fault that he was everything I should want in a man, but nothing I wanted.

So I said the only thing I could say. "Of course, Todd."

"I'll pick you up at seven," Todd said, with a smile that was just as much relieved as exultant. I smiled back, feeling my heart dropping all the way down to my toes.

"You're not being fair to him," Dix said when Todd had sat down across from his father, all the way on the other side of the restaurant.

I sighed. "Don't you think I know that? It's not like I enjoy hurting his feelings, Dix. I like Todd. I'm just not ready to marry him."

"So tell him so," Dix said. "It'll be quicker and cleaner than stringing him along like this, hoping he'll get the message and stop proposing. Just say no and get it over with. He's a big boy. He can handle it."

"I can't just say no! Mother would kill me."

"Mother will have to handle it. Just because she's dating Bob Satterfield, doesn't mean you have to marry his son."

I put down my fork. The food that had looked and smelled so good before Todd showed up, suddenly tasted like ashes in my mouth. "There's more to it than that, and you know it. Mother always wanted me to marry Todd. She and Pauline probably planned it when we were in the cradle, like Sleeping Beauty's mother and what's-her-name. She could hardly even wait for me to divorce Bradley properly before she started pushing Todd at me again."

"She only wants what's best for you," Dix said.

"She wants what *she* thinks is best for me. She doesn't care what *I* want!"

In my excitement, I raised my voice, and both Satterfields glanced our way. I flushed and moderated my tone. "You know it's true, Dix. Mother treats me like a child, like she has to constantly remind me of the proper thing to do, just in case I've forgotten. As if I ever could, with the childhood I had."

Dix shrugged.

"Let's talk about something else," I said. "I haven't wanted to bring it up while you thought that Rafe was dead, but I've been wondering whether you ever made any headway on finding that boy in the picture?"

I didn't have to explain to Dix which boy in which picture. Seven weeks ago, on the night when Jorge Pena died and Rafe got shot, a woman named Elspeth Caulfield also died. She was someone we'd all gone to school with. She was a year older than me, a year younger than Dix, and she'd once had a one night stand with Rafe. A one night stand which, according to Todd, had resulted in a pregnancy. Either that, or a nervous breakdown. I'd been inclined to believe in the breakdown, since I—and more importantly, Rafe—had never heard a word about a child. But I'd had to revise my stance when her will stated that she wanted everything she owned to go to her son. Since no one knew she had a son, and since Martin and McCall were her attorneys, Dix had gone to her house to look for information. And since that was the same morning he'd had to tell me that Rafe was dead, he took me with him, and I was the one who found the photograph in Elspeth's bedside table. A boy, maybe nine or ten years old, with Rafe's dark eyes and bright grin. A boy none of us had known existed until then.

The photograph had had no name attached, no identifying characteristics, and Elspeth's house was filled to the brim with paperwork. She'd been a writer, and writers love their paper. I knew Dix had been looking for the boy ever since, between other work he had to do, but I hadn't wanted to question him about it, since I didn't want to give him the idea that A) Rafe was still alive and, B) I was still thinking about him.

But now, of course, both of those were out on the table, and Dix knew exactly why I was asking.

"Did you show him the picture before he left?" he wanted to know.

I nodded. It had taken some doing, since the TBI, especially, didn't want anyone to make the connection that Jorge Pena was dead and Rafe was taking his place. Rafe had to cut all contact with me, with his grandmother, and with anyone else he might know in Nashville. But I couldn't let him leave without telling him that he had a son. Or that he might have a son, since we didn't know that the boy in the picture wasn't just some kid Elspeth had seen on a trip to the grocery store and had glommed onto because he looked so much like Rafe. She'd been crazy enough to do something like that. For all I knew, she could have imagined the whole pregnancy and birth and relationship, when she'd never really been pregnant at all.

If it hadn't been for the photograph, that's what I would have assumed had happened. Now I wasn't sure.

"What did he say?"

I shook off the thoughts. "What do you think he said? He was shocked. He'd had no idea she was pregnant. She didn't tell him."

"But he thinks the kid's his?"

"With the resemblance it's hard to deny," I said. "Do you have any idea who he is?"

Dix shook his head. "I've been able to go through most of the paperwork in Elspeth's house, but there's nothing there. No name or address, no other photos, no adoption paperwork. Her Rolodex and Christmas card list seem to be all writers. I don't think she had much of a social life. I contacted her literary agent in New York, but the woman had no idea about Elspeth's personal life. We don't even know when this child was born, and even if we did, there would likely be too many babies born on that day in the U.S. for us to be able to pinpoint who he was. I've checked Elspeth's medical records, but they don't go back that far."

"If her parents were trying to hide the fact that she had a baby, they probably wouldn't involve a doctor or a hospital anyway. Her father was a preacher in some fundamentalist church, wasn't he? Maybe they shipped her off to Utah or Arizona, to have the baby the old-fashioned way. With pain and suffering."

"If so," Dix said, "we have no hope of finding him. Whoever took him in got him at birth, and probably just registered him with the state as their own."

"Is that possible?"

"It's illegal," Dix said, "but those communes take some liberties with both the truth and the law, from what I understand. And honestly, it wouldn't be hard to do, even here. The hospital files the birth certificate with the Department of Health. All they'd have to do is put the wrong names on it."

"The boy didn't look like his parents were in a commune. He was dressed in normal clothes, and there was a nice car behind him and houses in the background."

"I haven't really examined the photo that closely," Dix said. "Maybe I should. Maybe there's something there that would help."

"He was wearing what looked like part of a school uniform. A shirt with some kind of logo on the chest. I only have the picture I took to show to Rafe—" I rooted in my bag for my cell phone, "and I doubt it's clear enough, but if you look at the photograph itself, maybe you can make out the logo. If you can match it to a school, you might be able to find him that way. Here."

I scrolled through my photographs to the picture I'd taken of the photo from Elspeth's bedroom, and handed the phone across the table. Dix peered at it.

"Too blurry. But there's definitely something there. And if I look at the photograph, or I have the photograph enlarged, you're right; I might be able to match it to a school. Good call."

He handed the phone back. I looked at the screen for a second—the familiarity of the boy's smile and his dancing dark eyes tugging at me—before I put it back in my bag. "Where's the original? Still at Elspeth's house?"

"At the office," Dix said. "Let me get the check and order Jonathan's sandwich, and then we can go back. If I could find this kid and settle the Caulfield estate, at least that would be one thing off my mind." He caught the eye of the waitress, who bustled over, pulling her order pad out of her pocket as she went.

Four

I got back to Nashville in time to stop by the office before it closed for the day.

When I first got my real estate license, I went to work for Walker Lamont Realty, a mile or two from my apartment on East Main Street. After Walker killed several people and went to prison, Timothy Briggs took over as head broker, and the name of the company changed to Lamont, Briggs & Associates, to remove some of the stigma of Walker's name. By now, that had become LB&A, and I was on my third set of new business cards. If I knew Tim—and I did—it wouldn't be long before the L disappeared altogether, and we'd be Timothy Briggs and Minions.

Nothing else had changed. We were still located in the same building just down the street from the FinBar in the heart of East Nashville, and my office was still a converted broom closet off the lobby, where Brittany, the dippy twenty two year old blonde receptionist, answered the phone between polishing her nails, updating her Facebook, and tweeting.

I have nothing against blondes. I am one myself, and I'm certainly not stupid. Brittany isn't either. She's just young, and doesn't care about much except Devon, her musician boyfriend. When I walked in, she looked up from a catalogue she was perusing with Heidi Hoppenfeldt, Tim's assistant. Once she'd ascertained that I wasn't anyone important, she looked down again, without greeting me.

"Hello to you too," I said. Heidi must have misunderstood and thought I said 'you two,' because she addressed me quite civilly.

"Hi, Savannah."

Heidi is about my age, and about twice my size, with lots of frizzy brown hair and a penchant for leaving crumbs on her voluminous chest. One of those girls about whom it is said, "She's got such a pretty face." Followed, at least here in the South, by 'bless her heart,' the obligatory disclaimer for when you're pointing out something not so complimentary about someone. *She must have gained a hundred pounds carrying that baby. Bless her heart.*

Pregnancy weight wasn't Heidi's problem. She was single, unattached, childless... she just liked to eat. The afternoon snack must have consisted of Fritos, judging from the residue on the front of the green sweater.

"Hi, yourself," I said, heading for the mail slots on the wall. "Anything exciting going on?"

"We're looking at a maternity catalogue," Heidi said.

For a second, my heart stood still. I hadn't told anyone I worked with about the pregnancy. But last Monday I'd had to excuse myself in the middle of the weekly sales meeting to run to the bathroom after someone brought in sausage biscuits and the odor turned my stomach. Had they caught on to what was wrong?

"Is somebody pregnant?"

I held my breath while I waited for Brittany to give me her patented 'you're such an idiot' look. When it didn't happen, I started breathing again.

"My sister," Heidi said. "It's her birthday next month, and I want to buy her a gift."

"That's nice. When is she due?" There was nothing interesting in the mail, just a bunch of circulars and postcards about other people's listings. I wandered around the desk to peer over Heidi's shoulder and Brittany's head at the catalogue.

"March," Heidi said. "It's a boy."

My due date was in July. But it was much too early to know whether I was carrying a boy or a girl yet. "Congratulations. You'll be an aunt. Is it your first time?"

Heidi nodded, her round face beaming.

"It's better when you can give them back to their parents," Brittany said with a toss of her ponytail. Heidi and I both looked at her. She shrugged. "Well, it is. And who wants to look like that, anyway?"

She used one poison-green fingernail to indicate a rather stunning model-type, rail thin except for her breasts and what looked like a basketball in her stomach, in a beautiful sheath-dress. She was almost glowing with health, and I imagined many women would have killed to look like that. Heidi's expression was wistful.

"What do you mean?" I said. "She's gorgeous."

"She's fat," Brittany said.

"She's pregnant. It isn't the same thing."

Brittany shrugged. "Her body'll never be the same again. From now on, she'll have stretch marks and saggy boobs and maybe even a pouch." She shuddered.

"You're thinking of kangaroos," I said, although I've been brought up to eat like a bird to maintain that Scarlett O'Hara wasp waist myself. Not that I've got one. Or was likely to keep even the waist I had for much longer. I'd already noticed certain of my clothes getting a little tight around the middle. If I wasn't careful with what I put in my mouth, someone would guess my secret before I had decided what to do. And then it would be too late. At least too late to make the situation go away without anyone being the wiser.

Brittany shrugged. "Why don't you buy her a necklace," she suggested. "Something to distract people from her stomach."

"I think when women are pregnant, they want people to notice their stomachs," Heidi said, but she didn't sound sure. Either way, she removed the catalogue from Brittany's desk preparatory to going back to her own office.

"Wait a second. Before you go..." I put the mail down and rooted around in my bag, "has either one of you seen this before?"

I pulled out a sheet of paper and held it in front of them.

"What is it?" Brittany said, her head tilted.

I looked at it, too. Wasn't it obvious? "It's half a monogram or logo. I copied it from a photograph. It was on someone's shirt pocket. But the picture cut off without showing it all."

"So what are you trying to do?" Brittany asked, leaning back on her chair and crossing one skinny leg over the other.

I held the paper in front of Heidi while at the same time addressing Brittany. "I'm trying to figure out what the logo is and where it belongs. I think it's a school. Could be anywhere."

"That should be easy," Brittany said.

"Could be BGA," Heidi suggested, tilting her head. "Battleground Academy. Or MBA, Montgomery Bell Academy. Or FRA. Franklin Road Academy."

"Nashville private schools?" Very snobby ones, from what I knew of them.

Heidi nodded. "The last letter looks like an A. Many private schools are called Something Academy."

The almost half a letter I could see at the end of the monogram did look like an A. The two preceding letters, however, might be almost anything at all. For all I knew, the letters might be L, B, and A, for Lamont, Briggs, and Associates. The configuration worked.

"That's a start, anyway. Thanks."

"Glad to help," Heidi said and marched down the hallway with her catalogue, the hem of her skirt flouncing around her thick calves.

I headed in the opposite direction, into my little cubby, where I opened the drawer in the desk and dug out a biscotti to nibble while I waited for the laptop to boot up. I had taken to keeping snacks in the desk for emergencies. It had been almost four hours since lunch, and I was ready to chew the wallpaper. If I didn't watch out, I reminded myself—as I bit into the biscotti, scattering crumbs—I'd end up looking like Heidi, as broad as I was tall and wearing the remains of my food.

A Google search for schools with the word 'academy' in their names netted me such a glut of results I might as well not have bothered. There were thousands across the country, and I had no way of knowing where the photograph of Elspeth's son—if he was Elspeth's son—had been taken. Since it was all I could do, I forced myself to focus my attention on the local schools and on ignoring the others.

There were quite a few local academies in addition to the ones Heidi had mentioned. Davidson Academy, St. Bernard Academy, Smithson Craighead Academy. St. Cecilia's Academy for girls. And that was without counting the academies in surrounding counties.

But the internet made everything easier. All the schools had websites, and most showed their logos. Several had photographs of students wearing school shirts. I narrowed down the logo in the picture to either St. Bernard's Academy or MBA. If the boy was local, he'd be at one of those. Or he'd be at one of a thousand schools somewhere in the rest of the big place that's the United States of America.

School was out for the day, so there wasn't anything else I could do tonight, but I made a note of where each school was located and determined to go there tomorrow, to see if anyone could identify the boy. That done, I headed home to cook myself dinner and crawl into bed. The baby wasn't any bigger than a blueberry, or so Dr. Seaver had told me, but so much went into creating it that I felt exhausted all the time. I nodded off over my latest romance purchase before the clock even struck eight o'clock, and I slept dreamlessly until morning.

Since I hadn't had time to think about much of anything last night before falling asleep, I thought now, lying in bed. The first few minutes of the day were usually nice, at least as long as I lay still. It was when I got up and started to move around, that the nausea started.

The tiny life inside me was seven weeks old, going on eight. It was basically a blob right now, but it would turn into a baby. A baby that would most likely look a whole lot like its father. A baby that might reasonably expect to inherit a chunk of his personality, as well. But while the idea of having a small version of Rafe in my life didn't fill me with the kind of dread that perhaps it should—he'd been a real hellion as a child, from what I knew about it—there was a bit of apprehension and not a little worry mixed in regarding the possibility.

All right, so Dix was on my side. That was one point in my favor. Catherine loved me; she'd probably support me too. Jonathan was slightly less hidebound than the rest of the family, so he might not be shocked out of his wits if Savannah had a 'colored' baby. Sheila... well, Sheila was almost as uptight as mother, but she was Dix's wife, and if Dix sided with me, there wasn't much Sheila could do about it if she wanted to stay on her husband's good side.

Not that that seemed to matter a whole lot to her at the moment, actually. I couldn't believe that she hadn't even told my brother that she was going to the OB/GYN. What if she really was pregnant? Didn't he have the right to know?

Doesn't Rafe have a right to know? a tiny voice asked in the back of my head. I ignored it.

Todd would be devastated by the situation, of course. And not just devastated, but insulted and angry. His father would be insulted and angry on Todd's behalf, and he'd be shocked and dismayed right along with mother. Sheriff Satterfield had never liked Rafe. Whenever something went wrong anywhere in Maury County, the sheriff tended to blame Rafe for it. Not totally surprisingly, since for a few years at least, whenever something went wrong anywhere in Maury County, it was usually Rafe's fault.

And Sheriff Satterfield wasn't the only person in Sweetwater who felt that way. There was Todd, of course, who loathed Rafe, but there was also everyone else in town, who had spent years lamenting LaDonna Collier's colored boy and the trouble he caused. Rafe had told me once that when he went to prison at eighteen, it was partly because he'd been so sick of everyone waiting for him to screw up that he'd figured he might as well just give them what they wanted and be done with it. If I had Rafe's baby, everybody in town would be whispering.

Could I handle the stares and whispers? The pointed fingers? The fact that everyone would know what I'd done, and with whom?

On the other hand, if I didn't have the baby, no one would know anything. Dix wouldn't tell anyone, not if I begged him not to. I wouldn't have to tell my family. No one would stare or whisper. And Rafe wouldn't have to know.

Rafe...

I missed him. More than I thought I would. More that I'd thought possible. He'd gone away before, and I'd missed him then too, but this was different. This time, it was like a part of me was gone.

I hadn't been entirely truthful with Dix on the phone last week. I'd admitted that I'd fallen for Rafe just a little, but the truth was, I'd done a lot more than that. And I had a sneaking suspicion that Dix already knew it. He knows me, so he knows I'm not promiscuous, and I'm pretty sure he had figured out that I wouldn't have sex with just anyone. If I'd gone to bed with Rafe, it would be because I'd fallen in love with him.

God help me.

That may have been the thought that caused me to jump out of bed and run to the commode. On the other hand, it might just have been past time for the tiny blueberry to make his or her presence known.

After purging, I sipped ginger ale and nibbled on dry saltines while I got ready for the day. I was still determined to do something to hunt down Elspeth's heir, who might also be Rafe's son, today. It wasn't long before I was in my car—a pale blue Volvo which was the only thing I'd salvaged from my marriage to Bradley, save a small chunk of change and my self-respect—and on my way across town to St. Bernard Academy.

Opened in the wake of the War Between the States by the Sisters of Mercy, St. Bernard is a Catholic school which caters to both boys and girls from elementary through junior high. I turned off 21st Avenue just south of Hillsboro Village, and drove up the long, tree-lined drive toward the lovely old brick building. No sooner had I parked in the lot than the front door opened and a nun followed by a line of children came down the stairs onto the lawn. All except the nun were dressed in gray sweatpants and identical red hooded sweaters with the letters SBA on the chest. And the letter formation didn't look anything like the one I'd seen in the photograph of the boy we thought might be Elspeth's son. The letters in the picture were spiky; these were squared.

Nonetheless, I climbed out of the Volvo and approached the group. "Excuse me."

"Yes?" The nun looked up and all the little boys and girls peered at me curiously.

"I'm looking for a boy. I think he may be a student here." I pulled out the photograph I'd taken the liberty of borrowing from Dix's office yesterday. "Do you know him?"

The nun looked me over, thoroughly, before turning her attention to the picture. "I'm afraid not," she said after a moment.

"Are you sure?"

"I'm positive. I've taught at St. Bernard Academy for over twenty years. I've seen every boy and girl who came through the doors in that time. And he isn't one of them. Sorry I can't help you." She turned to the children, and clapped her hands briskly.

"That's OK," I said to the back of her wimple, and headed for my car.

There was a chance she'd been lying, of course—she probably wasn't supposed to give out information about their students—but I hadn't gotten the impression that she was. Scratching St Bernard off my mental list, at least for the time being, I put the car back in gear and headed down Blair Boulevard toward West End instead, in the direction of Montgomery Bell Academy. If I didn't find what I was looking for there, I could always come back.

MBA is a Nashville institution. It opened its doors in September 1867, the same year as St. Bernard. It's namesake, Montgomery Bell, was a Pennsylvanian who came to Dickson County around the year 1800 and purchased the Cumberland iron furnace from James Robertson, one of the founders of Nashville. Mr. Bell did well, and when he died in 1855, he left twenty thousand dollars—a considerable sum in those days, and one I personally wouldn't scoff at right now—to the University of Nashville. The money was invested, and by 1867, the investment had grown to forty-six thousand dollars, which was used to open Montgomery Bell Academy.

Today MBA is one of the top college prep schools in the country, and boasts around 700 students, all male. I parked the car in the parking lot outside the old stone building and stepped out onto the asphalt, surrounded by boys.

The first thing I noticed was that the Montgomery Bell students did not wear uniform shirts. They wore khaki pants, white or blue oxford shirts, and blue blazers. And ties. The ties seemed to be the only way they could express individuality, since everything else was the same. I saw conservative stripes, polkadots, paisley prints, and one lovely tie dye. I thought that was as good as it was going to get, until Bugs Bunny came along.

The office was located on the first floor, just around the corner from the entrance. It was manned by your typical Southern matriarch:

around fifty, with soft blonde hair shellacked into place, wearing a designer suit with real pearls. I knew the type. My mother is one of them. Sheila will turn into another. If I'm not careful, I will, too.

When I walked in, she smiled graciously, but I knew that could turn at any moment. "May I help you, young lady?"

I smiled back, trying to stay on her good side for as long as I could. "I'm hoping you can. I'm looking for this boy." I dug out the photograph again, and put it on the desk in front of her. She looked down.

A second later she looked up, all the warmth gone from her eyes. "May I ask who you are?"

"Savannah Martin," I said, thinking better of extending a hand to shake. "Martin and McCall, attorneys at law." I laid a business card I'd also liberated from Dix's office on the desk. To clinch things I pulled out my wallet and showed her my driver's license. With any luck, she'd never realize that I wasn't actually affiliated with Martin and McCall. Legally speaking.

She glanced at it. "And what is this in reference to?"

"I'm afraid I'm not at liberty to discuss details. Client confidentiality, you know. Other than to say that we're trying to trace the heirs to a woman who died in Sweetwater a few months ago."

"I'm sorry," the dragon said, sounding not sorry at all, "but we at Montgomery Bell Academy are not in a position to be able to share our students' private information with anyone. Not without a court order. Do you have one?"

I shook my head. "Bet I could get one, though. I have a friend at the courthouse in Columbia."

Of course, Todd probably wouldn't feel inclined to help me track down Rafe Collier's son. But Dix and Jonathan might know people at the courthouse that they could tag too, if it came to that.

"In that case, I'm afraid this conversation is over," the dragon said, lifting the photograph between two fingers, as though it contained contaminants, and extending it to me.

I took it. "Can you at least confirm that he's a student here? That way I'll have something to take back to my boss. He's going to need that before he puts the wheels in motion for a court order."

She hesitated. "I'm afraid I'm unable to do even that, Miss Martin. We have a policy to never discuss our students with outsiders. Whether they're students here or not."

"Well, would you mind if I had a look around?"

"I'm afraid not. If I have to have security escort you off the premises, I will."

She sounded like she meant it.

"Fine," I said. And reverted to good manners in time to add, "Thank you for your time," before I walked out the door.

Outside in the hallway I stopped to glance around, while I slid the photograph into my bag again, careful not to bend it.

Just my luck, though: where there had been lots of boys around earlier, now there was no one. There were, however, photographs lining the walls. The orchestra, the drama department, the various sports teams: football and basketball, tennis and lacrosse. And some of the boys in the pictures were wearing shirts with logos. Logos that looked familiar.

I was peering intently at the faces of the boys who played baseball when I heard the sound of a throat clearing behind me. When I turned around, I came face to face with the school secretary again. "Miss Martin."

"Sorry," I said. "I was just..."

"I believe I know what you were doing, Miss Martin." She glanced at the picture I'd been examining, but it didn't contain the boy I was looking for, and she took hold of my sleeve. "If you'll come along quietly, please. Do not make me call security to have you escorted out."

She towed me toward the front door. My mother brought me up to be respectful of my elders, so I followed without demur. When she had pushed me through the door into the fresh air, I headed for my car without further resistance.

As soon as I got there, I pulled out my cell phone and scrolled through my contacts until I found the number I was looking for. Once I had, I dialed, and leaned back to wait.

As I should have expected, I was rerouted to voice mail. It was the middle of the school day, and the girl I was calling was sixteen. Obviously, Harpeth Hall—the girl equivalent of Montgomery Bell Academy—did not allow their students to answer their cell phones during the school day.

"This is Alex," came the familiar voice. "I'm in class. Leave me a message and I'll call you back."

I waited for the tone, then introduced myself and told Alexandra Puckett to give me a call when she could.

Alexandra was Brenda Puckett's daughter. Brenda used to be a coworker of mine, until our boss, Walker Lamont, slit her throat and left her to bleed out on Rafe's grandmother's floor. It's a long story. In the course of it, Alexandra and I had met, and had struck up a sort of unlikely friendship. She missed her mother, I'd found her mother, and she was under the mistaken impression that we had unsuitable boyfriends in common. At the time, Alexandra was dating a young black man named Maurice, whom Brenda abhorred. I wasn't dating Rafe—I'd never dated Rafe; as I'd tried to tell Dr. Seaver, our relationship was complicated—but we were seeing a fair amount of each other, and he was every bit as unsuitable as Maurice Washington.

At any rate, Alexandra and I had gotten somewhat close. At least until Steven Puckett's new girlfriend, Maybelle, had warned me off. She'd been trying to establish friendly relations with Alexandra, and it hadn't been easy when the girl missed her mother and was resentful of anyone trying to take Brenda's place. The fact that she liked me, and didn't like Maybelle, didn't help, and so Maybelle told me I needed to leave Alexandra alone for a while. I'd told Alexandra what Maybelle said, of course, since any loyalty I felt was to Alexandra and not Maybelle, but since she was sixteen and I was twenty seven, it wasn't like we'd ever be BFFs anyway. She called me once in a while, to update me on what was going on in her life and to ask about Rafe, whom she had a schoolgirl crush on, but I hadn't actually seen her in a while.

You may be wondering just exactly why I was calling Alexandra.

Well, the picture of the MBA baseball players in the hallway hadn't included the boy from Elspeth's picture. It had, however, included another boy I recognized. Austin Puckett, Alexandra's little brother, was around twelve, and if he went to MBA, there was a good chance he'd recognize the boy in the picture, and that he could even give me a name and address.

Five

Alexandra called back, but not until late. By then, I was sitting down to dinner with Todd.

He came to pick me up at seven, just as he said he would, and as usual, we'd ended up at Fidelio's Restaurant off Murphy Road in West Nashville. Todd likes it there, and somehow he's gotten it into his head that it's 'our' place. I wish he hadn't, because my ex-husband used to take me there, and it brings back bad memories. But of course I've been too well brought up to complain, so I grin and bear it. It helps that the food is outstanding, and well beyond anything I can afford to buy myself these days.

What didn't help was that I was wearing the same dress I had worn the last time I'd been here with Rafe. A black wrap-dress with a deep V-neck and a sash that tied on the side, it was forgiving of my slightly expanded waistline. I'd tried on several others, slinky cocktail dresses of the type I usually wear when I go out with Todd, but they'd all made me feel like I couldn't breathe, and I thought it best not to tempt fate. Besides, I probably looked like I was poured into them. And I certainly didn't want to risk Todd noticing that I'd gained a little weight.

As usual, he attempted to order for me. I usually let him, but this time I put my foot down. Gently, of course. But there was no sense in letting him pay through the nose for a glass of wine I couldn't drink, was there? So when he told the waiter to bring me a glass of Sauvignon Blanc, I shook my head. "Not tonight, thanks. Just water for me, please."

The waiter nodded.

"Are you sure, Savannah?" Todd said.

"Positive. I'm not in the mood tonight." I smiled, to take some of the sting out.

Todd nodded, giving the waiter the go-ahead to do as I said, but when he turned back to me, he was frowning. "Are you feeling all right?"

"Of course," I said. "Why wouldn't I be?"

"You always enjoy a glass of Sauvignon Blanc with dinner."

"I know I do. But I don't have to have a glass of wine to enjoy myself. And I promise I'll enjoy the food."

I would, too. I was starving. Hopefully Todd wouldn't be too shocked when he saw me tuck into dinner. Usually I nibble delicately, as befits a Southern Belle, and I leave at least half on my plate, but there was no way I'd be able to refrain from eating everything tonight. I'd do good not to lick the empty plate afterwards.

Luckily the waiter brought some Italian bread along with Todd's wine and my water, and I grabbed a slice and began stuffing pieces in my mouth. Todd watched me, concerned. "Are you sure you're feeling all right, Savannah?"

"I'm fine," I said. "Just hungry. I skipped lunch."

"I see." Todd watched me chew. "Were you working?"

"I was actually helping Dix with something. Tracking down an heir."

"How did it go?" Todd asked, interested. Perhaps he was hoping that I would come to my senses and finish law school and come back to Sweetwater to work for the family firm. Little did he know what I'd actually been doing. And I wasn't about to tell him.

"I haven't found the person yet, but I made a step in the right direction."

"Excellent," Todd said jovially.

I reached for another chunk of bread. "What about you? How did the appointment with your dad go yesterday? Did he remember anything helpful about the Cartwright case?"

Todd grimaced. "Unfortunately not. It was a total waste of time. Except for having seen you, of course."

"Spending time with your dad must have been nice, too."

"I live in the same house with my dad," Todd said with a shrug. "I see him all the time."

That he did. I wondered if Todd had given any thought to where we'd live if I ever took him up on his proposal of marriage. It wasn't like I could move into the foursquare in Sweetwater with him and Bob Satterfield.

But maybe he planned to kick Bob out, in the hope that mom would take him in, and then we'd have the house to ourselves.

I used to say that if I ever got remarried, I'd marry Todd. He was everything I'd been brought up to desire in a mate: successful, handsome, reasonably wealthy, and Southern. The current situation had put a crimp in that whole scenario, of course, but it wasn't that I didn't like Todd. We'd always gotten along well, even if I'd originally started dating him back in high school because Dix was going out with my best friend Charlotte, and it would make everyone happy if we hooked up. Mother had never given up hope that I'd marry Todd. When Bradley proposed, she gave us her blessing, but she never let me forget that I could have had Todd instead.

The problem—one of them, anyway—was that he was too much like Bradley for comfort.

Oh, not that I thought Todd would ever cheat on me. He loved me. If I agreed to marry him, it really would make him the happiest man in the world, and he'd never, ever stray. He'd always stay with me, always cherish me, always put me on a pedestal and worship at my feet... and why did that sound like more of a prison sentence than a recipe for a happy marriage?

Before I could take this depressing train of thought any further, my phone rang, and I excused myself to answer it. "This is Savannah."

"Hi!" said a familiar voice, "this is Alex!"

I smiled. It was impossible not to, in the face of so much enthusiasm. "Hi, Alex."

"I'm so sorry it took me so long to get back to you. I didn't pick up my messages for a while, and then I had to wait until I was out of the house to call. Didn't want to do it in front of Maybelle."

So Maybelle was still around. Part of me had hoped that Steven would wise up and kick her to the curb once he got over the grief of losing Brenda. That he'd see what a barracuda she was. But no, Maybelle must have dug in deeply enough that he couldn't.

I'd always liked Steven Puckett. Not in any romantic way, just as one person to another. He'd suffered a horrible loss when Brenda was killed—he'd seemed to genuinely like her, poor sap, in spite of having been kept firmly under her fat thumb for twenty years—and I had hoped good things might come his way in the aftermath of the murder.

Instead, Maybelle had gotten her claws into him before Brenda was even in the ground. Maybe he was just the kind of man who was attracted to, and attractive to, managing women.

"So where are you now?" I asked, just a little worried. One night a few months ago, I'd had to venture into one of the less desirable neighborhoods on Nashville's east side to rescue Alexandra from a party at Maurice Washington's house. I hoped she hadn't gotten herself into some sort of crazy situation again. Todd wouldn't be nearly as effective a backup as Rafe had been.

"Just over at a friend's house. Lynn and Heather and I are watching a movie."

"That's nice," I said, smiling apologetically at Todd, who watched me like a hawk from across the table.

"Nothing else to do tonight. So why did you call?"

"I need a favor," I said.

"What?" It wasn't an exclamation, just a request for information.

"Your brother goes to MBA, right?"

"Sure."

"Do you think he'd mind looking at a photograph and telling me if he knows the boy? I'm trying to track him down."

"Why?"

"It's a long story," I said. "And confidential. But it has to do with a will and a woman who died a couple of months ago."

"My mom?"

Lord, no. "Not at all. It has nothing whatsoever to do with your mom. Or anyone else you know. I'm doing this for my brother. He's an attorney in Sweetwater. The woman who died lived there, too."

"Oh," Alexandra said. "Sure. When do you want to do it?"

"When do you think he'll be available?"

"He has a game tomorrow morning," Alexandra said. "Afternoon, maybe? Or Sunday?"

"Either one of those would be fine." I'd prefer it to be sooner, although I'd take what I could get. "I have to sit an open house for Tim on Sunday afternoon, but before or after would be all right. Or Saturday. I don't have anything scheduled then. Why don't you give me a call after you've spoken to Austin?"

"Sure, Savannah," Alexandra said, and hung up before I could say thanks, let alone goodbye. I was shaking my head as I tucked the phone away in my purse.

"Who's Alex?" Todd wanted to know.

I glanced at him. "Just a girl I met a couple of months ago."

"Alex is a girl?"

"Sure. Alexandra Puckett." And that right there was one of

Todd's more annoying character traits. He tends to be jealous, for no good reason.

All right, so sometimes he has reason. But he'd been fixated on Rafe long before anything actually happened between us, too.

This time it was the waiter who derailed my train of thought. A plate of steaming Chicken Marsala appeared in front of me, and the delicious smell found its way into my nostrils. My stomach rumbled, and Todd glanced up. I smiled sweetly. He smiled back, as the waiter put his own plate of Veal Piccata in front of him.

For the next few minutes we ate. Todd attempted to engage me in genteel conversation, but after the second time he had to wait for me to swallow before I could answer him, he must have given up, because he let me finish in peace. He did look somewhat taken aback at my hunger, and when I was finished, he glanced at my empty plate. "You really were hungry, weren't you?"

There was a faint note of resentment in his voice.

"Sorry," I said. "I guess I was."

I waited for him to make some joke about women and dieting, but he didn't. Of course not. He's much too much the Southern gentleman to draw attention to a woman's weight.

"Dessert?"

He asked every time, and I always said no. This time I was tempted to tell him yes, because I still had a bit of room, and the Fidelio cheesecake was out of this world. If I couldn't enjoy cheesecake when I was pregnant, when could I?

But of course I couldn't. Todd would wonder why I was eating enough for two, and from there he might guess that I actually *was* eating for two. Or mother might, once he told her that I'd behaved like a swine at dinner. She taught me better than that. So I shook my head. It was just as well, really. Once I stopped being pregnant, either in the next couple of weeks or seven months from now, I'd have to trim back down anyway, and it would be easier if I didn't gain too much weight.

And besides, the longer I stayed slim, the longer before anyone would guess my secret.

"Coffee?" Todd said.

"Better not." Caffeine was something else I'd cut back on since learning I was pregnant. I didn't exactly know why, since I was pretty sure I wasn't going to be carrying this baby to term, but it seemed like the right thing to do.

"Have you had problems sleeping?" Todd asked, frowning.

I blinked, and then realized he'd handed me a perfect excuse. "That's right. Between finding Brenda Puckett's body back in August, and Lila dying in September, and that whole incident with Perry Fortunato—" who'd had me tied to a bed ready to do unspeakable things to me before strangling me; Todd's face darkened at the reminder, "I sometimes have nightmares. It's better if I don't drink coffee before bed."

"You had coffee last time we went out," Todd said.

"It's something new I'm trying." I was getting pretty good at this lying business. Even if I found my hand sneaking up to my hair to play with a tendril. Hopefully Todd wasn't as adept at reading me as my brother was.

"I'm sorry," he said, and sounded sincere, too. That didn't stop him from ordering a piece of cheesecake for himself, and devouring it, right in front of me, with every sign of enjoyment. Any guilt I'd felt evaporated as I tried to content myself with nibbling on a dry piece of bread left over from dinner.

So far he hadn't tried to propose, and I'd allowed myself to believe I might get through a meal without having to refuse him again. I should have known better.

Although I will say for him that he waited until we were alone, instead of proposing in public, the way he did the first time. I guess maybe he was expecting another refusal, and he wanted to save himself at least that little bit of embarrassment. To be honest, I couldn't figure out why he didn't just stop proposing altogether. But

I guess I ought to give him points for persistence as well as for having a hopeful attitude.

Anyway, he waited until we were back at my apartment and I'd invited him to come in for a few minutes before he had to drive back to Sweetwater. He'd said yes to a glass of sweet tea, and while I was in the kitchen fetching it, like a good little Southern-wife-in-training, he'd wandered over to my dining room table and laptop and to the picture of Elspeth's son—or who we assumed was Elspeth's son—lying there. When I came back into the living room, he had it in his hand.

"Where did this come from?"

I bristled at the tone of his voice—suspicion mixed with accusation and distrust—but I did my best not to let it show. "What do you mean?"

"What are you doing with a picture of Rafe Collier as a boy?"

"I'm not." I handed him his iced tea with one hand while I took the photograph out of his hand with the other, laying it facedown on the table.

"What do you mean?" Todd said, promptly picking it up again. "This is Rafe Collier."

"No, it isn't." I retrieved the photo once more, and this time held onto it. "This is the boy I'm helping Dix track down. If you look at the car in the background, you can see that this picture was taken sometime in the last couple of years. Chrysler didn't start making those cars until recently."

Todd held out a hand, and I put the photo back into it. He examined it again, and admitted, grudgingly, that I was right. "This is Elspeth Caulfield's son, isn't it?"

"That's the assumption." If she'd had a son and wasn't just confused.

"Always knew there was something to those stories," Todd said with a sort of gloomy satisfaction. "You can't look at this and deny that, Savannah."

"Deny what? That Rafe and Elspeth had a fling in high school? No one's ever tried to deny it." Rafe certainly hadn't. It wasn't something he'd volunteered, I'd had to ask, but when I did, he was upfront about what had happened. And I believed him when he said he never knew there'd been a baby.

Todd looked down at the picture again. "I guess he got adopted?"

"So we assume. He certainly didn't live with Elspeth, and Rafe never heard of him. Until Dix found the will, no one knew Elspeth had a child."

"Dix hasn't been able to trace him?"

I shook my head. "That why I'm trying to find him through the logo on his shirt. If he *is* Elspeth's son, he inherits her house and any money she may have had."

That was if his adoptive parents allowed it. It all depended on the kind of relationship the boy had had with his biological mother. It could have been a closed, or even secret adoption, and the boy had no idea he was even adopted. That would explain why Dix hadn't had any luck finding any information through legal channels.

Although that left the question of the photograph. Elspeth had gotten it from somewhere, but there was no way to know whether she'd taken it herself, whether she'd hired someone to track the boy down, or whether it had been an open adoption and she'd been in the boy's life all along, as his loving 'aunt' or his mother's good friend. Watching as another woman loved and cared for and openly claimed her son.

"That must have been incredibly hard."

"Excuse me?" Todd said.

I realized I'd spoken out loud. "Oh, nothing. I was just wondering whether Elspeth stayed in contact with him through the years. It must have been difficult to watch her son being raised by someone else."

"It wasn't like she could have kept him," Todd said reasonably.

"I imagine she could have if she'd wanted to."

"She was seventeen."

"Lots of girls have babies when they're young. Look at LaDonna Collier." Rafe's mother had been fourteen when she got herself in the family way; fifteen when Rafe was born.

"I'm not sure LaDonna Collier is the example you should be using here, Savannah," Todd said.

It seemed like a pretty good example to me, and I said so. "They lived in the same area, with the same kind of people and the same prejudices. LaDonna was even younger than Elspeth when she got pregnant, and her father was a horrible racist; it's hard to imagine that Elspeth's parents could have been any worse. Yet LaDonna managed to keep Rafe, and to raise him to be a pretty decent human being."

"That's spurious," Todd said, reminding me that I should know better than to argue with a trial lawyer. "Rafe Collier was not a decent human being. He was a criminal. And a man who abandoned his pregnant girlfriend and his child."

I could feel my eyes narrow. "First of all, Elspeth was not his girlfriend, she was someone who took advantage of him when he was drunk. Second, he didn't abandon her, he went to prison." All right, so maybe that wasn't actually a point in his favor. Neither of my points were, come to think of it. "And I told you, he never knew about the baby."

"Or so he said," Todd said.

"So he said, and I believe him."

We stared at one another for a moment in silence before Todd straightened. "Your loyalty is admirable, Savannah, if misplaced."

I shrugged.

"I don't suppose it matters now, anyway," Todd added. "They're both dead. That's a good thing. It will make it easier for the parents when you find him."

I found I had no response to that. It was a wrinkle I hadn't foreseen. Elspeth was dead, yes. But Rafe wasn't. Not technically. When we found this boy, assuming Austin Puckett recognized the picture and actually knew the boy's name, did we let his parents know that the boy's biological father was still alive? And that he hadn't given consent to the adoption?

In light of my own predicament I'd done a little bit of research, and I knew that both birth parents have to give consent to adoption unless one of them has given up parental rights. The reasons for giving up parental rights would be through abandonment, failure to support the child, abuse or neglect, or mental incompetence, usually. Rafe hadn't done that. Mentally he was just fine, and the abandonment and failure to support the baby hadn't been his fault; he was in prison and no one told him he had a baby to support.

Not that I thought he'd want to challenge the adoption. He knew he wasn't in a position to take care of a child. But he might want to get to know his son. Having grown up without a father himself, I knew he felt strongly about being there for any children he made. It was the main reason he'd never had any. Or at least none he knew about.

But that touched on my own problem, and I didn't want to think about it right now. So I forced myself to focus on Todd again. He was watching me with concern, so I may have checked out for a few seconds. "Is everything all right, Savannah?"

"Everything's fine," I said. "I was just thinking about children. Having them and giving them up and adopting them."

Todd reached out and took my hand. "We can make our own children, Savannah."

No, we couldn't. Not right now, anyway. Not ever, if I had Rafe's baby and kept it. Dix and I had already discussed how I couldn't pass it off as Todd's, and I couldn't imagine he'd be open to marrying me and raising it as his own.

"Would you ever do that?"

"Do what?" Todd said, still holding my hand. A small wrinkle had formed between his sandy brows.

"Adopt a baby. One that looked like this." I held up the photograph.

Todd dropped my hand and took a step back. "I hardly think that'd be fair to either of us, Savannah."

"Either of who?"

"The parents or the child," Todd clarified. "He'd be better off with his own kind, don't you think?"

His own kind. "I suppose," I said.

Todd fumbled for my hands again. Both of them this time. I had to drop the photograph on the floor. "I love you, Savannah. Will you marry me and have my children?" His blue eyes were sincere, and I felt like a heel.

"I can't. I'm sorry, Todd, but I just can't."

Todd sighed and dropped my hands. "I understand."

No, he didn't. But I wasn't up to explaining. "Thank you."

"I'll just keep asking. One of these days you'll change your mind." He smiled.

I smiled back. "It might be better if you didn't, Todd. At least for a little while. When I told you I needed more time, I meant more time than the two weeks between every time we go on a date."

Todd looked like I'd kicked him, but he recovered himself. "If that's what you want."

"Thank you." Impulsively I went up on my toes to kiss his cheek. He turned his head at the last second and I ended up kissing him on the lips instead. The kiss lasted a little longer than I'd intended, and when it was over, Todd's eyes held a look of suppressed triumph.

By the time he had gone, I was ready to fall into bed and sleep for twelve hours, but I made myself get on the phone with my brother. Things tended to be a little hectic in the morning, what with the morning sickness and getting up and dressed and to the office, and I wanted to get Dix and the news out of the way before I went to bed. So I pulled out my cell phone and dialed, after kicking off my shoes and curling up on the sofa.

The phone rang once, and then was answered. "Sheila?"

"Sorry," I said. "It's Savannah."

"Oh." Dix took a breath. I could hear the girls squabbling in the background. "What's going on?"

"Nothing. I just came home from a date with Todd and figured I'd call you."

"What did he do?" Dix asked, resigned.

"Nothing. I mean, he proposed again, but I'm not calling about that. I think I may have found Elspeth's son. Or at least I've found a lead."

"Tell me about it," Dix said, and I imagined him leaning back and getting comfortable.

"Well, I looked up private schools in Nashville I thought might match the logo on the boy's shirt. There were a few possibilities, so I drove around to them this morning. One of them is Montgomery Bell Academy."

"I've heard of that," Dix said. "Mom wanted to send me there, didn't she?"

"I wouldn't be surprised if she did. It's a very good school. Very expensive, too. And quite a long way from Sweetwater."

"That's why I didn't end up there," Dix said. "Mom didn't feel like getting up at four every morning to drive me to Nashville."

"Well, I talked to the school secretary. And she said that she couldn't help me. She wouldn't even confirm that the boy is a student there. Not without a court order, she said. But I think he must be. Her demeanor was very cold, and she couldn't wait to get rid of me. Even threatened me with security if I didn't leave."

"I can get a court order," Dix said.

"I figured you could. But before you do that, I'm going to show the picture to a boy I know. He goes to MBA, and he might be able to give us a name."

"Sounds great," Dix said, and muttered something to the effect that at least one thing was going his way today.

"What's wrong?" I asked. "Did you and Sheila have a fight?"

"Of course not."

Of course not. My perfect brother would never argue with his perfect wife. How could I even suggest such a thing?

"It's just that when I called, you thought I was Sheila. I thought maybe you'd argued and she left."

"No," Dix said. "She dropped off the girls at school and mothers-day-out this morning, and I haven't seen her since. She hasn't called or anything."

"That's weird," I said. "Have you called the police?"

"I told Todd's dad. But there's nothing he can do until she's been gone for twenty four hours." He sounded dissatisfied, but not actually worried.

"I'm sure she just lost track of time. Maybe she went out with a friend? You know how girls are when we get together."

"Gabbling geese," Dix said. "Let me know what you find out about the boy in the photo, sis. Any decisions about your situation yet?"

"No. I still don't know what to do." Although the conversation with Todd had at least clarified one thing: I couldn't have my cake and eat it too. Marrying Todd and keeping the baby was out of the question. Not that I hadn't known it all along.

"Have you spoken to Collier?"

"I haven't even tried to find him. If I decide to end the pregnancy, he never has to know it even happened."

"Right," Dix said, but he didn't sound happy. "Listen, Savannah, I have to go. I think I hear a car. It's probably Sheila."

"Fine. You know where to find me if you want to talk more. I'll give you a call after I've shown Austin the picture."

"Thanks," Dix said, and hung up. I dragged myself off the sofa and to bed.

IT FELT LIKE I HAD JUST closed my eyes, but when I woke up the next morning, a glance at the clock showed me I'd slept for nine hours. Even with that, I knew I would have stayed in bed longer if someone hadn't been knocking on the front door. It wasn't loud, nobody was hammering and demanding to be let in, but the knocking was insistent, and I had the impression it had been going on for a while. Grumbling, I swung my feet over the side of the bed and stuffed them into fuzzy slippers. I grabbed the negligee that matched my lacy nightgown from behind the door and shrugged it on while I stumbled into the living room and down the hall, fighting back nausea with every step.

"Hold on, I'm coming!"

There was a part of me that thought it might be Rafe outside the door. I don't get many visitors. My family is all in Sweetwater, my ex-husband is busy with his new wife, and I don't have many friends. Lila was my closest girlfriend in Nashville, and she was murdered a couple of months ago. And I'm not close enough to my colleagues that any of them are likely to come knocking on my door at seven thirty in the morning on a Saturday. Alexandra Puckett might, but I wasn't sure she knew where I lived. But Rafe knows where to find me, and he isn't the type to bother with a phone call to announce his arrival. If he got back to Nashville overnight, and if I meant anything to him at all, he might have stopped by to tell me he was here, and safe. My heart was beating double time when I unhooked the security chain and pulled the door open.

And then I felt that same heart rocket to a stop in my chest when I came face to face with Detective Tamara Grimaldi of the Metropolitan Nashville Police Department. The same Tamara Grimaldi that Rafe had told me to contact if I needed to get in touch with him. The Tamara Grimaldi who knew where Rafe was and what was going on with him.

I felt my hand close convulsively around the door handle as the smile froze on my face. Detective Grimaldi's dark eyes were hooded and her face was grim. "Ms. Martin," she said; we haven't really progressed to first names yet, "I'm afraid I have some bad news—"

And that was all I heard before everything went black and I fell to the floor in a dead faint.

Six

When I woke up, I was flat on my back on the sofa, and the front door was closed and locked. Detective Grimaldi was sitting in the chair on the other side of the table, one leg crossed over the other, dressed in her customary pantsuit and low-heeled boots. She must have dragged me here after I fainted. And then she'd gone to the refrigerator. On the table next to me was a small dish with a handful of saltines and a glass of what I could only assume was ginger ale. It looked like ginger ale.

"You scared the crap out of me," the detective said when she saw my eyes were open.

"You scared the crap out of me too," I retorted.

"I'm sorry. I guess my first words should have been, 'he's fine.'"

There was no need to specify who 'he' was. I felt myself starting to breathe again. "Really?"

"As far as I know. I haven't heard anything to the contrary."

I moved to sit up, my head still spinning. "When I saw you standing there, I thought..."

There was no need to finish that sentence, either. We both knew that I thought she'd come to tell me that Rafe was dead.

"I check in with Mr. Craig every week, and the last time I spoke to him, everything was normal. He'd tell me if it wasn't."

I nodded. Wendell Craig is—in the parlance of the TBI—Rafe's handler. His contact while he's undercover. And since he's spent most of the past ten years undercover, he and Wendell have a strong relationship. Wendell would know if anything was going on, and I thought I could trust Wendell to tell Tamara Grimaldi the truth.

"Something you want to tell me, Ms. Martin?" Grimaldi added as I reached out a hand for the ginger ale.

"About...? Oh. I don't imagine I have to, do I?" Not if she'd figured out that I needed saltines and ginger ale. There was really only one thing that would cause that reaction, and bad news wasn't it.

"I thought you said Mrs. Jenkins was mistaken."

"What?" It took me a second to catch up. Put it down to low blood sugar.

Mrs. Jenkins is Rafe's grandmother. She's in her seventies and struggles with dementia, and about half the time, she loses track of time and thinks that Rafe is his father, Tyrell, and I'm LaDonna Collier, pregnant with Rafe. She keeps asking me how the baby is doing and telling me to take care of her grandson. Detective Grimaldi was with me once when Mrs. J lost her grip on reality, and I had to explain that Mrs. Jenkins was old and confused. Now it seemed the detective had decided to give me hard time about it.

"Does he know?" was the next thing she asked. There was no need for specification now either. And because she already knew I'd slept with Rafe, I didn't bother trying to pretend it might be someone else's baby.

"How could he?" I put the glass down and lifted a saltine. "He's been gone. I haven't seen him or heard from him. That was the rule, right? No contact? If I'd tried to get in touch with him, you'd have known. He said to go through you."

"Do you want me to tell him?" Her dark eyes were steady. I came close to choking on the cracker.

"God, no. Please don't. I don't want him to know yet. Not until I figure out what to do."

She was silent for a moment, and then she leaned forward and put something on the table between us. "I found this in the kitchen."

It was the abortion pill Dr. Seaver had given me. Every time I went into the kitchen for something, I picked it up and contemplated it. So far I'd always put it back down again. I drew in a lungful of breath, but let it out without speaking.

"You haven't taken it," Grimaldi said.

I shook my head. When she didn't comment, I added, "I had a miscarriage once. A spontaneous one. While I was married to Bradley. It was awful."

She nodded.

"I don't know what to do."

"Do you want to talk about it?"

I shook my head. I was all talked out. It wasn't like I could say anything different to Detective Grimaldi, or like I'd hear anything different from her, than I'd already told or heard from Dix. I knew my options, and no one but me could make this decision. "I'm sure you didn't come her to talk about my personal problems. What can I do for you, Detective? If you're not here to tell me that Rafe's dead, what the matter?"

Tamara Grimaldi made a face as she dug in her pocket. An iPhone came out, and she manipulated buttons and icons. After a few seconds she looked up at me. "I'm sorry to do this. Especially under the circumstances. If I'd known..."

"It's all right. Just give it to me." My heart was beating hard. If it wasn't Rafe, then it was someone else I knew. Detective Grimaldi wouldn't come here unless it was serious.

She put the phone in my hand and watched my face. I looked down at the display and felt my vision tunneling again. "Oh, my God."

"You know her?"

"Of course I know her." I swallowed. "It's Sheila. My sister-in-law."

I MADE IT TO THE BATHROOM just in time, and rid myself of the ginger ale and crackers. This time I didn't blame the pregnancy. When I came back out, pale and shaky, Detective Grimaldi was standing at the balcony doors, the phone to her ear. "In about an hour," I heard her say. "Yes, of course. I'll see you then."

She turned when she heard me open the door. "Everything all right?"

I waved a limp hand. "Nothing seven months and delivery won't take care of. I do this every day."

"If it's bad, there's medicine you can take for nausea, you know."

"It isn't bad. It's just morning sickness. This was worse because of..." I stopped and swallowed, feeling my stomach riot again. The sight of Sheila's pale and sunken face, even on the tiny iPhone screen, seemed burned into my brain. "Have you called Dix?"

"Dix?"

"My brother. Sheila's husband."

Detective Grimaldi shook her head, her short dark curls bouncing. "I came here first. I'm sorry."

"It's all right. I'd rather know. This way I can prepare Dix."

Grimaldi opened her mouth, maybe to say that it was her job to notify next of kin, and then closed it again.

"I spoke to him last night," I said. "He was concerned, because she'd gone out and wasn't back by the time the kids were supposed to go to bed. But then he heard a car outside and told me had to go, because he thought it was her. I can't let him hear it from the police. Please let me talk to him first."

I was already dialing when she nodded.

When he answered the phone, my brother sounded even more frazzled than last night, but at least he'd taken the time to look at the display this time, and knew who I was. "Hi, Savannah. I can't stay on long. Sheila didn't come home last night, and I don't want to tie up the line in case she calls."

"She isn't going to call," trembled on the tip of my tongue, but I bit it back. There were kinder, gentler ways of telling him the news. "That's why I'm calling," I said instead.

"That's nice, but really..."

"Wait, Dix."

I paused to make sure he'd stopped, and not just for breath, before I went on. "I'm really sorry, but something's happened to Sheila."

"What?" Unlike Alexandra's what, this wasn't a request for information. It was an exclamation of disbelief and fear.

I gentled my tone. "My friend Tamara Grimaldi is here. She works for the Nashville PD..."

"You've told me about her," Dix said, his voice somehow faint even though it hadn't diminished in volume. "She works homicide."

"I'm going to let you talk to her, OK?" I handed the phone over to Grimaldi, who put it to her ear.

"Mr. Martin? I'm so sorry to be the bearer of bad news."

Dix's voice quacked, but I couldn't hear what he said. Grimaldi continued, "I'll need you to drive up to Nashville, all right? She's at the medical examiner's office right now. Your sister will be able to do the formal identification, but I'm sure you'll want to see her for yourself."

Dix's voice sounded again. I shook my head and headed for the bedroom to get dressed for the day.

"What happened?" I asked twenty minutes later, when we were in the car on our way to the M.E.'s office in Inglewood. It had taken me a little time to get ready, since I'd had a hard time finding something to wear. I didn't think it would be right to dress up—skirt and blouse and high heels—especially since I wouldn't be going to the office afterwards, but my pitifully small selection of casual clothes proved to pinch. My favorite pair of jeans—one of only two I owned—had gotten too tight around the waist. It wasn't by much—I could still get the button closed—but they hurt. I ended up pulling on a pair of leggings and an oversized sweater instead, and dressing the ensemble up with high heeled boots, earrings, and a necklace. I've had it drilled into me from an early age not to go outside the front door looking less than my best. The fact that I didn't spend fifteen minutes on my face was a concession in itself. I did put on mascara and lipstick; without it, I literally looked like death warmed over.

Tamara Grimaldi glanced at me. She was driving the unmarked SUV, I was sitting in the passenger seat. "She was found late last night. By the showboat."

The Cumberland River runs straight through downtown Nashville, and it's full of boats. Barges carrying things like sand and gravel and containers up and down the river; small fishing and pleasure boats, and one old-fashioned paddle wheeler that belongs to the Opryland Hotel. It's called the General Jackson—after Andrew—and it's something like a floating dinner theatre.

"She drowned?"

"We haven't confirmed that yet," Grimaldi said. "There's a compression on the back of her skull that may have come pre- or post-mortem. We'll know more after the autopsy. The M.E. will look for cause of death and anything unusual."

The saltines and ginger ale threatened to make a repeat performance. I swallowed. "Don't mention the autopsy again. Please."

"Sorry." She signaled to turn the car onto the ramp for Ellington Parkway North. "I caught the case. We fished her out and brought her to the morgue, but there was no identification in her pockets and her prints aren't in the IAFIS."

"Excuse me?"

"The Integrated Automated Fingerprint Identification System. IAFIS."

Right. "So how did you know to come to me?"

"Someone found her car this morning," Grimaldi said. "In a parking lot near the river."

"Was her purse still in it?" And her identification?

Grimaldi shook her head. "Purse was gone. I had to run the registration on the car. When I found out her last name was Martin and she had an address in Sweetwater, I thought you might know her. I didn't expect it to be your sister-in-law, though. I thought maybe a cousin a few times removed, or something. Sorry."

"It's all right. What happened?"

"So far we have no idea," Grimaldi said. "With her purse gone, it looks like perhaps robbery. Then again, someone could easily have taken her car, with the keys in it, and they didn't. So perhaps the motive wasn't robbery after all."

"What was she doing there? In the parking lot?"

"That's something else we'll have to find out. I'll check whether anyone who works there has any connection with your sister-in-law, but on the face of it, the business doesn't enter into it. They're not open at night. Once I track down whoever was the last man out last night, I'll ask whether the car was in the parking lot at that time."

"She could have gotten lost, I suppose," I said.

"Her car had a GPS system."

"What do you think she was doing there, then?"

"I have no idea. Any chance she could be looking to score?"

"What does that mean?" If it meant that Sheila was looking for sex, I doubted it. If she didn't sleep with my brother, surely she wasn't sleeping with anyone else either.

"Buy drugs," Grimaldi said.

I shook my head in automatic rejection. "No way."

"How can you be sure?"

"We're a close knit family."

She just looked at me, and I added, "Yes, I'm here in Nashville, so I don't see her that often. But the rest of them live within a few minutes of one another. Dix and Jonathan work together. Abigail and Hannah—Dix and Sheila's daughters—spend a lot of time with Catherine and Jonathan's kids. If my sister-in-law had a drug habit, I think someone would have noticed."

"Most likely," Grimaldi admitted. "But not necessarily. Especially if it hasn't been going on long. Do you know if your sister-in-law's personality has changed recently?"

I bit my lip. "Dix said she had a miscarriage four or five months ago. Since then, she's been different. They're not as close anymore, and she doesn't want to... you know..."

Grimaldi nodded. She's used to my Southern Belle sensibilities. "I'll have to ask him for the details, I suppose. One of the aspects of my job I really don't enjoy."

She turned the SUV off the parkway and onto the exit ramp. To the right, behind a clump of trees, I saw the tall antennae of the Tennessee Bureau of Investigations reach toward the sky. The medical examiner's office is just down the road from TBI headquarters a quarter mile or so.

I'd been here once before. It was back in early September, and I'd been showing someone a house in Inglewood (Gary Lee and Charlene Hodges, who had finally closed on their townhouse a few weeks ago; my first real estate commission!) when I got a call from Tamara Grimaldi telling me to hotfoot it over to Gass Boulevard. When I got there, I realized she'd asked me to meet her at the morgue. And then she sprung it on me that my friend Lila Vaughn had been strangled. I didn't have good feelings about the place.

Last time I was here she had taken me up to an office on the second floor, and had shown me photographs. I wasn't kin to Lila, and had no real business looking at her. This time we went down, into the basement. To where the corpses were.

I'd never been downstairs before, and although I'd seen more than my fair share of dead bodies in the past few months, it wasn't like I was used to death. My hands were shaking when we walked along the hallway toward the viewing room, and my stomach was roiling unpleasantly.

"There are three coolers," Detective Grimaldi explained, probably in an effort to keep my thoughts occupied more than because she thought I needed, or wanted, to know. "One for new bodies awaiting autopsy. One for bodies that have been autopsied and are awaiting pickup from the funeral directors, and one for decomposing bodies."

"Is there a soda machine?"

She looked over at me. "Feeling queasy?"

"It's the talk of autopsies and decomposing bodies." Coupled with the fact that it was still early and I was pregnant.

"I'll get you a Coke." She detoured. "Just sit over there for a minute." She waved a hand toward a sofa against the wall. I waited there until she came back, Coke in hand. I didn't even say anything about the fact that she'd gotten me the real thing, not the diet. Now was not the time to quibble about a few extra calories.

"Ready?" She waited until I had opened the can and taken a sip, and then she guided me toward the closest door. It had a plaque with a number one on it.

Inside the small room was a gurney, pared down and almost skeletal compared to the cushy ones you see in hospitals. No need to make these patients comfortable, I guess. A still form lay on it, covered with a sheet.

"Over there." Grimaldi waved me to one side of the gurney while she went to the other. I clutched my soda can, feeling the cold seeping into my fingers as I waited for her to fold back the sheet.

I guess I thought, or at least hoped, there might be some mistake. I'd seen the picture, so I knew it was her, but until I actually saw the body, there was some little part of me that clung to the hope that it might not be Sheila. When Tamara Grimaldi turned back the sheet and I looked down into my sister-in-law's face, it was still a shock, even though I'd been prepared.

She looked pale and very still, her eyes sunken and her lips slack. If she'd had make-up on when they found her—and I couldn't imagine she'd left home without it—someone had cleaned it off. Her eyelashes were soft and fair against her skin, almost invisible, and her lips were pale and seemed thinner than usual.

"You OK?" Detective Grimaldi's voice reached me from far away. I nodded. "It's her?"

"Oh, yes. But you knew that."

"It's good to get an official identification," Grimaldi said, pulling the sheet up over Sheila's face again. "Let's go sit in the lobby until your brother gets here."

I nodded, and let myself be steered out of the viewing room and down the hallway and up in the elevator to the lobby. We settled into a small grouping of sofa and chairs where I'd found Tamara Grimaldi waiting for me the first time I'd been here. For a few minutes neither of us spoke. I was sipping my Coke, trying to settle my stomach while bringing some sort of order to my rampaging thoughts. It was like herding cats. Meanwhile, Detective Grimaldi must have been thinking about what would be happening later.

"Tell me about your brother," she said.

"Dix?"

"Do you have any other brothers?"

I shook my head. "It's just the three of us. I'm twenty seven, Dix is... he's thirty by now, he just had a birthday; and Catherine is thirty one. She'll be thirty two in the spring."

"He's a lawyer, right?"

I nodded. "They all are. Martin and McCall, in Sweetwater. Dixon Calvert Martin and Jonathan McCall. Catherine's husband."

"Dixon Calvert Martin?"

"The Calverts are an old Georgia family," I said. "My grandmother was Catherine Calvert. My mother was a Dixon before she married my dad. This is the South. Everything that goes around, comes around."

"So who are you named for?"

I grimaced. "My mother's home town. And it could have been worse. She could have been born in Augusta. Or Alma."

"Or Hortense," the detective said. "How long had your brother and Sheila been married?"

I thought back. "Seven years, give or take. They met in college and got married while Dix was in law school. They have two daughters. Abigail is five and Hannah is three." They were beautiful children, and they'd be devastated to lose their mother. Sheila was a stay-at-home mom who'd never used her nursing degree for anything. Once she married Dix and started a family, that was it. She spent all her time with Abby and Hannah.

"Any problems you know of?"

"None aside from what I told you," I said. "According to Dix, they've been trying for a couple of years for another baby, and they've had two miscarriages. Sheila's been reluctant to try again. It makes sense that she'd be scared."

Tamara Grimaldi nodded.

"Both my siblings married well. I did too, for that matter. Until Bradley turned out to be a lying, cheating scumbag. But you already know about that."

"Of course," Grimaldi said blandly.

"Catherine and Jonathan met in law school, at Vanderbilt. So did Sheila and Dix, except Sheila was attending the nursing school instead."

"What about you and Bradley?"

"We met at Vanderbilt too. It's family tradition. Catherine is the eldest, she went first. Then Dix, then I. Jonathan was the only spouse my parents objected to. He's a Yankee, you know. From Boston. But they never had a problem with Sheila or Bradley. Sheila's..." I swallowed and corrected myself. "Sheila was perfect. A Southern Belle, born and bred in Virginia. Beautiful, polished, lovely. Never a hair out of place. Always the consummate daughter-in-law. She was more like mother than either Catherine or I could ever hope to be."

Dix and the girls wouldn't be the only ones devastated. Mother had loved her like her own, and this would hurt her terribly.

"Were you close?" Tamara Grimaldi asked.

I shook my head. "Not really. She and Dix met while I lived in Charleston—I did a year of finishing school there before college—and by the time they got married, I'd met Bradley and spent all my time with him." He'd been my date to the wedding. Todd had been best man, and he hadn't been happy, I remembered. "When Dix finished law school, he and Sheila settled in Sweetwater, while Bradley and I stayed in Nashville. Sheila and I got along just fine, but I wouldn't say we were best friends or anything. She was probably closer to Catherine and mom."

"Can you think of anyone else she might have been close to? Any other friends she had?"

"She went to the gym. Took aerobics classes or something like that. She probably has friends among Abby's and Hannah's friends' mothers. But you'd have to ask Dix about it. I didn't know her as well as maybe I should have. And now I never will."

My voice was shaking by the time I got to the end of the sentence.

Tamara Grimaldi must have realized that my sanity was hanging by a shred, because she thanked me for the information without pushing for more, and then started taking and making phone calls. Left to my own devices, I stayed on the sofa until the doors to the outside opened, and Dix came through. The woman he held the door for was my sister Catherine.

I don't know why I was surprised to see her. It made sense that she'd be here, actually, if I'd only stopped to think about it. Dix wouldn't bring the girls, not to the morgue to identify their mother's body, so he'd have had to leave them somewhere while he drove to Nashville. And he wouldn't have called mother, because he wouldn't want to tell her about Sheila until there was absolutely no doubt. Catherine and Jonathan have three kids of their own, and being together would make all five of them happy and above all, occupied.

But of course Catherine would refuse to stay home once she learned what had happened. She'd leave Jonathan to take care of the kids, and insist on driving to Nashville with Dix. She's fiercely loyal, both to him and to me. I'd have done the same thing in her position. So really, I should have expected her.

Catherine is four years older than me, and while Dix and I take after mother's family, the Calverts, Catherine takes after the Martins. Dix and I are taller and fair; Catherine is short and dark and just a little plump, after carrying and giving birth to three children. Mother doesn't give her a hard time about it, partly because Catherine is married, to a man who clearly adores her and who couldn't care less whether she weighs fifteen pounds more or less, and partly because Catherine is just built differently from mom and me.

Her personality is different, too. Mother brought me up to be your stereotypical Southern Belle: sweet, docile, pliant—at least on the outside—and I swear she did the same to Catherine, but it doesn't seem to have stuck. Maybe it's Jonathan's influence, but Catherine is nowhere near as sweet and docile as I am. When I divorced Bradley, it was Catherine who represented me, and who insisted on taking him for a good chunk of change and the Volvo. I just wanted out of the marriage, and I would have paid him to leave if I'd had any money to pay him with, while Catherine wanted to shout his infamy from the rooftops.

She was the one who took charge now too, while Dix just looked lost. "Savannah."

"Catherine." We embraced cautiously.

"Are you all right? You look pale."

She looked me up and down. I folded my arms self consciously over my stomach. "This isn't a pleasant situation."

"You got that right," Catherine said, and looked past me to Detective Grimaldi. "Is that your friend?"

I nodded. "Tamara Grimaldi, Metro Nashville PD. This is my sister Catherine and my brother Dix."

"Nice to meet you both. Sorry for the circumstances." Detective Grimaldi shook hands with them both before focusing on Dix. "Why don't we get this done as quickly as possible, Mr. Martin? If you'll come with me, please."

Dix nodded. So far he hadn't said a word. Catherine and I exchanged a look before joining the procession toward the elevator.

I won't bother to give a blow by blow account of what happened downstairs. We went inside the same viewing room as before, and flanked the gurney. Dix obviously felt the same way I did—that even thought I'd identified her, there might be a chance I was wrong and it wasn't really Sheila—and although he was prepared, the sight of her came as a shock. For a second he reeled, as if from a punch in the gut, and Catherine and I both had to grab hold of him. Unlike me, he reached out and touched Sheila's cheek, and then jerked his hand back when he realized she was cold to the touch. There were tears in his eyes when we rode the elevator back upstairs again, but he held it together until we were back in the lobby. Then he turned to Detective Grimaldi.

"What happened?"

Grimaldi told him the same things she'd told me, and got the same reaction.

"Absolutely not. Not Sheila. I'd have noticed."

"The autopsy will tell us for sure," Grimaldi said, her voice unusually gentle. "In the meantime, I need you to tell me everything that happened yesterday, and everything you know about your wife's friends and interests."

"Sure," Dix said listlessly. Tamara Grimaldi reached out and put a hand on his arm. He didn't know it, but I'd seen enough of her to know it was an almost unprecedented show of sympathy.

"I'll figure out what happened to your wife, Mr. Martin. I promise."

Dix swallowed and nodded. My heart broke.

Seven

Dix and Catherine drove back to Sweetwater around noon. By then, both had been interviewed by Detective Grimaldi and had told her everything they knew. It wasn't much, since Sheila hadn't told either of them that she was going to Nashville, let alone what she was doing there. When Grimaldi asked whether Sheila had friends in Nashville, we all drew a blank.

After they were done in interview, we went and grabbed a quick bite to eat at a downtown restaurant. It was a quiet meal. Dix didn't eat much, and also didn't speak unless one of us asked him a direct question. He seemed to be in shock. Catherine and I did our best to make sure he ate, but it was difficult to force food down his throat when he kept saying, numbly, that he wasn't hungry. In spite of my current predicament, I didn't have much appetite myself. Talking about Sheila would only serve to upset him, so I didn't bring her up, yet at the same time she was the only thing on any of our minds, so we couldn't really focus on anything else.

When I had waved them off, with Catherine at the wheel—a silent concession to just how upset Dix was; under normal circumstances he'd never have let anyone else drive—I went back inside police headquarters and upstairs to Detective Grimaldi's office. "They've left. I guess I'm going, too."

She looked up from the pile of paperwork on her desk. "They didn't take you home?"

"Why would they... Oh."

I'd driven to the medical examiner's office with her, and into downtown with them. Now I was stuck without a car.

Grimaldi sighed. "Give me a couple of minutes, and I'll take you home."

I shook my head. "I'd rather you spend the time trying to figure out what happened to Sheila."

"How do you plan to get home? Taxi? Bus?"

"I'll walk," I said.

"Across the bridge?"

Police headquarters are in downtown, just across the Cumberland River from East Nashville. My apartment was less than two miles away, straight down the road. It wasn't a very pleasant walk: along a busy four-lane road, across the bridge, past a trailer plaza and a few seedy motels, and through an underpass for the interstate before coming out in a still slightly rough residential-slash-industrial area. But it was also high noon, bright and sunny, and it wasn't like anything was likely to happen to me along the way.

"Sure," I said. "Why not?"

"No reason," the detective answered with a shrug. "I just didn't think you'd be the type."

"I'm usually not. But I'm eating everything in sight and gaining weight quicker than I want to. Maybe some exercise will help."

Tamara Grimaldi leaned back on her chair and contemplated me. "When do you plan to tell him?"

I tried to convey an insouciance I didn't feel. "That depends."

"On what? Whether you take the pill or not?" The abortion pill she'd found in my apartment.

"And on whether he comes back. And how he acts when he does." But mostly on whether I decided to stay pregnant. "If I go ahead and... um... terminate, I probably won't ever tell him. It'll be a moot point by then, and not something he needs to know."

Her eyebrows rose.

"Well, it isn't," I said defensively. "Is it?"

"You're asking me?"

I shrugged.

"Then yes. I think it's something he needs to know."

"Why?"

"Isn't it his choice, too? I don't know him well—certainly not as well as you..."

She'd better not, I thought, and then I bit down on the moment of jealousy.

"...but he strikes me as someone who hasn't had a whole lot of good happen in his life. Mostly it's been one damn thing after another, as they say."

They did say that. And it was true that Rafe hadn't had an easy life. What's more, it was getting more complicated all the time.

"A baby might be just what he needs," Grimaldi said.

"He's not going to want a baby."

She cocked her head. "How do you know?"

"He told me. He's made sure not to have any kids because he can't be there for them."

"What if he could be there for this one?"

Rafe Collier facing mother across the Thanksgiving turkey...

"I've got to go," I said. Grimaldi blinked, but didn't question my sudden need for speed.

"Walk carefully," she said.

"I'll call you tomorrow."

She opened her mouth and I added, "I know you're not supposed to tell me what's going on with an open case, but Sheila was family. I'm not asking for anything privileged, just updates. OK?"

"OK," Tamara Grimaldi said. I thanked her and headed out.

THE WALK ACROSS THE RIVER, under the interstate and home, was everything I expected it to be and more. I was approached by several homeless people asking for handouts. I was propositioned by a slouching African-American youth whose pants would have been around his ankles if he hadn't had a tight grip on them. A middle aged portly gentleman in a Chrysler, who looked like an accountant, seemed to think I was a prostitute, because he sidled up alongside me and flicked the lock on his door to signal that I was welcome to get in. I ignored him the same way I ignored everyone else.

Halfway across the bridge I stopped, stepped up to the railing, and peered down into the muddy water far below.

What a horrible day it had turned out to be. Not that I hadn't known it would be from the second I'd seen Tamara Grimaldi outside my door this morning. Even if the news she brought hadn't been as bad as I originally feared.

That thought immediately filled me with guilt. What kind of person was I, to be relieved that it was 'just' my sister-in-law who was dead? Instead of a man I shouldn't care about, but whom I had nonetheless allowed to take up much too much real estate in my thoughts and my heart.

Ruthlessly, I wrenched my thoughts away from Rafe. I'd spent enough time thinking about him; right now, I needed to focus on my family.

Was it possible that Sheila had had a secret life none of us had known about? That she'd been using drugs and had come to Nashville, to a deserted parking lot by the river, to buy more?

Pushing off from the railing and continuing down the other side of the bridge, I reflected that it was difficult to imagine. Surely the others—surely Dix—would have noticed, if something like that was going on?

But Dix had noticed, hadn't he? Not drug use, certainly, but that Sheila had changed in past few months.

I thought back. The last time I'd seen her had been at Dix's birthday at the end of October. Five weeks ago. And she'd seemed completely normal then. Busy, of course. The party was at their house, a big brick McMansion in Copper Creek, and the whole family had been there, including Bob Satterfield and Todd.

Sheila had worn a short-sleeved blouse with ruffles, and if there had been track marks in her arms, I sure hadn't noticed. I hadn't noticed anything else wrong, either.

Come to think of it, that wasn't actually the last time I'd seen her. She'd been at Dr. Seaver's office two days ago. Was that something I should have shared with the detective, in case it had something to do with what Sheila was doing in Nashville yesterday?

It probably was. But when I dug in my purse for my phone and couldn't find it, I realized I must have left it at home in my hurry to get out of the apartment and up to the morgue earlier. So much for that idea. I'd call her when I got home instead.

Or maybe what I should do was call Dr. Seaver first. There was that pesky doctor-patient confidentiality thing to get around, but if I pretended that I actually knew something about what was going on, maybe Dr. Seaver would open up and let something slip. Especially if I shared a little something private myself. There's nothing quite like the mutual sharing of secrets to build instant rapport. That way I'd have some solid to share with Grimaldi when I called her.

Well-pleased with my decision, I ignored the panhandler who was calling to me from the other side of the street, and hustled up Main Street toward my building in the distance.

Once I got upstairs I found my cell phone lying in the middle of the dining room table, and when I turned it on, I realized I had missed a call from Alexandra Puckett. I'd forgotten all about her and Austin and Elspeth's heir in the stress of the morning.

"Hi, Savannah," the voice message said. "We have to go to Cookeville with my dad and Maybelle today, so we can't meet you. I'll give you a call tomorrow, OK?" She hung up. Her voice still changed when she said Maybelle's name, as if she screwed up her face as she said it.

So much for that. Still, it wasn't as if I didn't have plenty of other things to occupy my time. I dug out the card Dr. Seaver had given me the other day and dialed the doctor's private number.

It took a minute, but then her voice answered. "This is Denise."

"Dr. Seaver? This is Savannah Martin."

There was a beat. When her voice came back, it was warm and friendly. "Savannah! I'm glad you called. Have you made a decision about what you want to do?"

"Not exactly," I said apologetically. "It's a tough decision, you know."

"I know." I heard rustling, as if she were moving around. "Let me just find somewhere to sit down, and we can talk for a while." I heard the sound of a door close, and then her voice again. "So what's going on?"

"It's kind of a long story," I hedged, trying to calculate how I might best approach getting the information I was after. I didn't want to tell her any more about my own situation than I had to, but at the same time I realized that the best way to get her to open up would be to share first. And she *was* supposed to keep anything I told her in confidence. I didn't have to worry about her getting on the phone with mother once I hung up.

"Why don't you start at the beginning?" Dr. Seaver suggested.

The beginning. That would be my freshman year of high school. Not likely.

"The father of the baby is someone I met a couple of months ago in Nashville." True, for the most part.

"Yes?" Dr. Seaver said.

"He's the kind of man my mother always warned me about. You know the type. No culture, no breeding, and no manners."

And also no hang-ups about mine. That was precisely what I liked about him. I didn't have to pretend with Rafe. Didn't have to worry about being on my best behavior or weigh every word before I spoke, just so I wouldn't offend him or ruin my image of the perfect Southern Belle. I could say anything, do anything, and know it wouldn't make him think any less of me. He'd already seen, done, and heard worse. A lot worse.

"I knew I should stay away from him," I said, "but things just sort of happened, you know? We kept getting thrown together even when I wasn't looking for him. And now here I am. Pregnant."

"Where is he now?" Dr. Seaver asked.

"I don't know. He left town two months ago. I haven't heard from him since."

To be honest, I felt a little guilty throwing Rafe under the bus. The way I described it, I made him sound like a heartless bastard who'd disappeared without a word, when that wasn't the case at all. He'd taken the time to say a proper goodbye, in spite of risking his cover by doing so. And I did understand why he couldn't communicate with me while he was away.

"Do you know how to get in touch with him?" Dr. Seaver asked. "Does he have family you can contact?"

"He has a grandmother, but I don't know where she is." Long before anyone came up with the plan that forced him to leave town again, while Jorge was still gunning for him, Rafe had arranged for Mrs. Jenkins to go to a safe-house somewhere. I hadn't asked where and he hadn't told me, but hopefully it was somewhere where she was happy, because when she isn't, and when she gets confused, she wanders the streets looking for her house. I made a mental note to ask Detective Grimaldi.

"So there's no one who can help you with the baby," Dr. Seaver said. "What about your family?"

"Mother would have a fit. Catherine and Dix would most likely be supportive, but they're here in Sweetwater. I live in Nashville. And with what's going on with Sheila..."

"What's going on with Sheila?" Dr. Seaver said, right on cue.

"Didn't you hear? She's dead."

"Dead?" Dr. Seaver repeated blankly.

"The police called this morning. Apparently it was a robbery gone wrong. Her purse and phone are missing."

"Oh, dear," Dr. Seaver said.

"The police think it might be drug related. I tried to tell them that my sister-in-law doesn't use drugs, but I don't think they believed me. I guess maybe nobody wants to believe that their relatives do anything wrong."

When she didn't speak, I added, "Maybe you can talk to them. You were her doctor, right? You can tell them that she didn't use drugs."

"How do you know that?" Dr. Seaver said.

I blinked. "That you're her doctor? I saw her at your office a few days ago, when I was there."

"You did?"

"We met in the lobby. Talked a couple of minutes before I had to leave. You'd know if she was into drugs, wouldn't you?"

"I would hope so," Dr. Seaver said. "But let's get back to you, Savannah. As I understand your options, you can either become a single mother or you can take the pill I gave you and have an abortion."

"That's about it," I admitted, reluctant to give up on the discussion about Sheila but recognizing I wasn't likely to get any information. "And I'm not real thrilled about either alternative."

"Have you considered adoption? White newborns are the top choice for most adoptive parents."

Operative word there: white.

"I'm not sure I could carry the baby to term and give birth to it and then give it up. I'm pretty sure I'd get attached along the way."

Truth be told, I was a tiny bit attached already. Or at least reluctant to pop the pill she'd handed over so easily.

"I understand," Dr. Seaver said. "You're an adult, and probably capable of providing for a child on your own, even if the father is a non-entity. It's not as if you're a teenager anymore."

"No..." My mind derailed for a second. "Dr. Seaver? Was Elspeth Caulfield a patient of yours?"

"Elspeth Caulfield?" Dr. Seaver repeated cautiously.

"I went to high school with her. She died a couple of months ago. According to her will she had a son." Our conversation was privileged; I figured I was safe in sharing this piece of equally privileged information from Elspeth's will. Especially because there was a chance Dr. Seaver might actually know something. She'd been my gynecologist twelve years ago, so it was possible she might have been Elspeth's as well. "None of us know anything about him, not even Dix, and Martin and McCall are the executors for Elspeth's estate."

"I see," Dr. Seaver said.

"Dix has been trying to trace him, but so far he hasn't had any luck." It was just as well not to mention the possible lead I'd dug up, since I had no idea whether it would turn into anything. "I don't suppose she was your patient back then, was she? You were practicing twelve years ago. Would you have any idea whether she had a child and what happened to it?"

"I'm afraid that's privileged information," Dr. Seaver said slowly.

"Of course. But I'm sure you can understand that it would be helpful for Dix to know whether there actually was a child, or whether Elspeth was just confused. If there wasn't, he can stop wasting his time looking for it."

Dr. Seaver was silent. After a minute, she said, "Elspeth *was* pregnant. But her child was stillborn. If she said otherwise, she must have been confused. As you said yourself, women get attached during pregnancy, and when something goes wrong they can get mixed up."

Delusional. Which Elspeth had certainly been. The boy in the photograph must be someone with just a passing resemblance to Rafe, then. Elspeth had seen him somewhere, on some trip to Nashville sometime, and had fixated on him as her lost baby.

"If you'll have your brother get in touch with me," Dr. Seaver said, "I'll be happy to tell him everything I know. Within boundaries of doctor-patient confidentiality, of course."

"I'll do that," I said. Although not right now. Dix had enough on his mind.

"As far as your situation goes, I can't tell you what to do, Savannah. It's a decision you'll have to make for yourself. Being a single parent can be difficult, and abortion, though it may seem like the easy choice, always comes with repercussions."

I nodded, although I knew she couldn't see me.

"Why don't you think about it some more," Dr. Seaver suggested, and continued before I had a chance to open my mouth, "and when you make your decision, let me know what it is."

She hung up without giving me time to answer.

Eight

I often sign up to host an open house on Sunday afternoons. Since I don't have any listings of my own, it's always someone else's. Usually Tim's, since he's the big producer in the office.

This week, it was a townhouse in Green Hills, one of the more affluent parts of town. It happened to be the same neighborhood where I'd spent two years with Bradley before we got divorced. In fact, the townhouse was in the same small enclave as our old home, which I drove past on my way to Tim's listing.

I hadn't contacted my brother to tell him anything about my conversation with Dr. Seaver. There wasn't a whole lot there I figured he needed to know. I had spoken to Tamara Grimaldi, but she hadn't had much progress to report. The medical examiner didn't work weekends, so the autopsy wouldn't take place until Monday, and aside from that, the case was moving forward at a snail's pace. All the fingerprints in the car had been matched to Sheila, and there was no evidence that anyone else had been in the car with her. Her purse and phone were still missing, and until the service provider opened for business tomorrow, there was no way to get a record of her calls.

Tamara Grimaldi sounded frustrated, although she did perk up a little when I told her about my visit to the OB/GYN last week, and how I'd seen Sheila there. The perk went away when I explained that I'd contacted Dr. Seaver yesterday. I had to sit through a lecture on why I shouldn't meddle in her—Tamara's—investigations before she let me go with a grudging, "I suppose there's no harm done. She would have found out what happened anyway. I'll give her a call and get the details."

"You're welcome," I said.

Halfway through the open house, my phone rang, and when I picked it up, it turned out to be Alexandra Puckett. I hadn't even thought about her since yesterday. "Savannah? We're back in Nashville. Where are you?"

"Sitting an open house in Green Hills," I said, "but..."

"What's the address?"

I gave it to her. "But Alexandra, listen—"

"Tell me later," Alexandra said, and hung up. I thought briefly about calling her back, to say that there was no longer any need for me to identify the boy in the picture, but then I decided I may as well just let her and Austin look at the photograph. Even if the boy wasn't Elspeth's son, he looked enough like Rafe to be his, so maybe Rafe had knocked up another girl I didn't know about. The way we kept piling up, it was a miracle he didn't have offspring littered all over the Southeast.

They arrived thirty minutes later, in Alexandra's little red Mazda that Brenda had bought her for her sixteenth birthday. Alexandra had cut her hair since the last time I saw her—where it used to hang halfway down her back, now it barely brushed her shoulders—but she still wore enough makeup to shame a hooker. I suspected she did it at least partly to drive Maybelle crazy; her stepmother-to-be was extremely particular about propriety, rather funny for someone who'd gotten herself engaged to the grieving widower before his wife was even cold.

Today, Alexandra was dressed in skintight jeans and a sweater that didn't quite meet the top of her pants. A navel ring glittered in her belly button. Austin's hair was longer than before, hanging like a curtain on either side of his face, and he peered out furtively, like a shy animal in the underbrush. Like last time I'd seen him, at Brenda's funeral, he was dressed in oversized clothes that dwarfed his still-boyish frame.

Alexandra peered around the entrance foyer, hands on her hips, while she blew a big pink bubblegum bubble. "Nice place," she said when she'd popped it, and sucked the gum back into her mouth.

I shrugged. It had the exact same setup as my old townhouse, and being here brought back memories. Most of them bad, but some—the early ones—a little nostalgic, as well.

"So where's this picture you want Austin to look at?"

I hadn't brought it. It was sitting at home, on my dining room table, where I'd put it after Todd's and my discussion the other night.

Alexandra rolled her eyes when I said so.

"I don't think he's the boy I'm looking for after all," I explained. "Although I do have a copy on my phone." It wasn't a great copy, but it might be good enough. "Hold on a second."

I fished out the phone, manipulated buttons, and handed it to Austin, who bent his head over it, his long dark hair falling to cover his face.

"That's David," he said after a second.

"Really?"

He glanced up. "He's in my year. I see him every day."

"Do you know his last name?"

I received another of those 'all adults are idiots' looks. "Flannery." Anticipating my next question, he added, "He lives in West Meade. I've been to his house a couple times."

"What are his parents like?"

He shrugged and handed the phone back. "Nice. His dad has something to do with money. Financial planning or something. His mom works for her church, I think."

"Does David have siblings?"

"Not that I know of," Austin said and stuck his hands in his pockets.

"Well, is he nice? Do you get along?"

"Sure." Another shrug.

"Let me see." Alexandra held out a hand for the phone. She took one look at the photograph and giggled. "Bet I know whose kid this is!"

Austin turned to his sister. "What?"

"He looks just like Savannah's boyfriend."

"He's not my boyfriend," I said automatically.

Austin stared at me. "You're banging David's dad?!"

"Of course not! I've never even met David's dad. This is someone else."

"Who?"

"You don't know him," Alexandra said. "I met him just after mom died. He and Savannah were the ones who found her."

"Oh, that guy? I saw him on TV." Austin took the phone back from Alexandra and looked at the picture of David again. "Yeah, I can see that, I guess."

"So," Alexandra said, "how *is* Rafe, anyway?"

I swallowed. I'd been dreading this. "Dead."

"What?" She looked stricken.

"He died two months ago. A man named Jorge Pena shot him."

"Oh my God." There were tears in her eyes, and I felt horrible about having to lie to her. She was just a girl, and it was only a few months since she'd lost her mother. And it would probably have been safe to tell her the truth. It was unlikely that Alexandra knew anyone who knew Rafe. Still, I wasn't willing to bet Rafe's life on it.

"I'm sorry," I said, my voice convincingly sad.

"Me too." Alexandra sniffled, and then flung herself around my neck. Austin shuffled his feet awkwardly and looked down. I patted Alexandra on the back and let her cry on my pink cardigan.

Just when I thought the embarrassment couldn't get any worse, the front door opened and three women came in. Three young, attractive, well-to-do women, wearing the kinds of clothes I can't afford anymore; one of whom was my ex-husband's new wife, Shelby Ferguson.

And if that wasn't bad enough, Shelby was in the same boat I was. But where I just looked thick around the middle, like I'd gained a few pounds since Bradley dumped me, Shelby looked like she was expecting. Dressed in designer jeans and a striped sweater that draped becomingly over her baby bump, she glowed with health. Unlike me, she must be over her morning sickness.

And of course she recognized me as quickly as I recognized her. Her new collagen lips curved in a stiff smile. "Savannah. I didn't expect to see you here."

"Likewise," I said, while Alexandra straightened up and wiped her eyes with the back of her hand. The crying jag had left a black spot on my shoulder where her mascara had bled. "How are you?"

Shelby smiled, sort of triumphantly. "Wonderful. Expecting, as you can see." She put a hand on her belly.

"I can see that," I nodded, resisting the temptation to say something snide. "And Bradley? Has he made partner yet?" Probably not, if they were still living in the same 1200 square foot townhouse.

She made a moue, but declined the bait. "Brad's just like any expectant father. Giddy."

"Good for you." He hadn't been giddy when I was expecting. Then again, he'd probably realized by then I was the wrong woman. He'd certainly already been working with Shelby, although whether he'd been sleeping with her yet I wasn't sure.

And at this point I really couldn't care less. It was all in the past, and I wouldn't take Bradley back if he begged. No, the thing that bothered me at the moment wasn't that my ex-husband had cheated or that he'd left me for someone else, it was that she was pregnant and delighted while I was pregnant and in such a quandary that I didn't know whether to keep the baby or not.

I forced a professional smile. "I'm sure you're familiar with the setup here. Living room, dining room and kitchen on the first floor, two bedrooms and a full bath on the second. Look around as much as you want." I turned back to Alexandra, who looked raccoon-like with her smudged makeup. "There are tissues in the half bath. Back there." I pointed. "Why don't you go get cleaned up."

Alexandra nodded and scurried down the hall. Shelby sent her a curious glance but didn't comment. Followed by her two girlfriends, who were eyeing me with interest, they headed into the kitchen. After a moment, I heard giggles and Shelby's lowered voice. I thought I heard the word 'chunky,' but I can't be entirely sure.

"Who was that?" Austin wanted to know.

I turned to him. "My ex-husband's new wife. We got divorced two years ago."

He nodded. "You're prettier."

"Thank you."

He shrugged. "D'you think my dad and Maybelle will have kids?"

"I doubt it," I said. "I think Maybelle's probably too old." She must be over forty, so chances were she wouldn't risk a pregnancy at her age.

"Good," Austin said and turned to Alexandra as she came back down the hallway, the excess eye-makeup cleaned off. "Ready to go?"

She nodded. "Will you be OK, Savannah?"

"I'll be fine," I said. "It's just Shelby. Listen." I addressed Austin. "Do me a favor and don't tell David that I asked about him, OK? His parents may not want him to know anything about it, and that's their decision."

"Whatever," Austin said with a shrug. The two of them left, and ten minutes later, so did Shelby and her friends. They weren't actually interested in buying the townhouse; they were just curious about how their neighbors lived, and taking the opportunity to find out.

"Give Bradley my regards," I called after them as they walked out. "Tell him congratulations."

Shelby said, somewhat reluctantly, that she would. I grinned.

I spent the little bit of time that was left of the open house pulling up the White Pages on my phone. West Meade is a well-to-do area on the west side of Nashville, and since I was already halfway there, I figured I might as well swing by before heading east, for home. When I struck out—there are so many people foregoing landlines for cell phones these days—I did what I should have done all along, and checked Nashville's property tax records instead. The Flannerys lived in a 1960s ranch on a street called Pennywell.

Pennywell turned out to be cut into a steep hillside, with the driveways in either direction roughly vertical. The lots were oversized, all the houses sat back from the road, and there were a lot of trees. In the summer I probably wouldn't have been able to see a thing. By now, most of the leaves had fallen, and in spite of the occasional fir tree, I got a pretty good look at the Flannery house. It was built of brick, long and low, and had charcoal gray trim with off-white accents. The driveway rose steeply before widening into a parking area. A basketball hoop was screwed to the wall above one of the garage doors.

There were no cars parked in the driveway, but I hadn't idled on the roadside more than a few minutes when a pearly white Chrysler came up Pennywell behind me and headed up the drive.

At that point I suppose I should have left, before they noticed me sitting there, but it was too tempting to linger, just in case I could catch a glimpse of David Flannery. I kept my eye on the Chrysler as it pulled to a stop in the driveway. After a moment, one of the garage doors rolled back remotely, and the car disappeared into the basement of the house. I put my own car in gear—they'd surely enter the house through the garage now—but I hesitated when the garage door didn't start rolling down again as soon as the car was inside. After a moment I was rewarded when three figures exited the garage into the driveway.

They were too far away for me to be able to see details, but Mr. Flannery—his name was Sam, or so the tax records said—was African-American, tall and bald. Mrs. Flannery, Virginia, was short, plump, and blonde. David was just about as tall as his mother, with caramel colored skin and short-cropped dark hair. All three of them were dressed in their Sunday best, and I guessed they'd been to church this morning, and had perhaps gone to lunch and then to a friend's house or to visit relatives or something.

They headed up what must be a walkway to the front door; Mr. Flannery and David in the lead, goofing around, and Mrs. Flannery bringing up the rear. She was looking around, and I shrank down in my seat. I couldn't see her clearly, so I knew there was no way she could see me, not through the windows of the car, but it was as though I could feel her eyes on me. When the front door closed behind the three of them, I took my foot off the brake and rolled down the hill.

"I need you to do me a favor," I told Dix later that evening, by phone. "I know you've got a lot on your mind right now, and I'm sorry, but we really should do this."

"What is it?" His voice was tired, without any of its usual humor.

"I found the boy in the photograph. His name is David Flannery. I know where he lives. I've even seen him, but only from a distance."

"OK," Dix said.

"I need you to call his parents and ask permission to come talk to them about Elspeth. That way I can go over there and meet him."

"You don't work for Martin and McCall," Dix said.

"They don't know that."

"You and I do." He drew breath and then blew it back out. "We can go together."

"I don't want you to have to come up to Nashville again. I'm sure you've got enough to do, with Abigail and Hannah and everything that's going on."

"It'll give me a change of location," Dix said. "And something else to think about. Catherine can take care of Abby and Hannah."

"If you're sure. I don't have the phone number—it's either unlisted or they don't have a landline—but I can find it if I have to." I could call Alexandra back, and have her ask Austin to ask David for his number.

"I can get it," Dix said. "I guess I'd better ask them to meet us in the evening sometime. After school's out. You do want to see the boy, right?"

"Please." I felt a little guilty holding back what Dr. Seaver had said about Elspeth's son being stillborn. But if Dix knew that, he might not think it necessary to talk to the Flannerys, and I needed his help with this. And besides, Dix really did need something else to think about. Although Sheila and what had happened to her was a sort of constant dull ache in the back of both of our minds—and probably sharper and much more immediate in his—he needed something to take his mind off it, even for just a little while. I remembered those horrible eight hours when I'd thought that Rafe was dead, and then I multiplied them by four—for the time since Dix learned that Sheila was dead—and multiplied them again—since Dix and Sheila had been married for eight years and had two children together while Rafe and I hadn't even been on speaking terms until four months ago—and considering all that, it was obvious that Dix's grief was so much more than mine had been, even though I'd felt like the world had suddenly come to a dead stop when I got the news.

"I'll take care of it," Dix said. "I'll call you tomorrow, OK?"

"Sure. Is everything all right?"

"No," Dix said, "it isn't. My wife is dead, and my children are crying, and something is going on that I don't understand, and I don't really have time to talk about it right now. I'll call you tomorrow. But I have to go take care of Abby and Hannah now. OK?"

"Sure," I said and hung up the phone, feeling even worse than I had when I'd called him in the first place.

Nine

At six o'clock the next evening, I was back in West Meade, this time heading up the steep driveway toward the house on Pennywell, watching the trees go by from the front seat of Dix's car.

He had called in the morning to tell me we were on for tonight. He must have been extremely persuasive to get them to agree to a meeting so soon. Or perhaps the mention of something to their advantage had tipped the scales for the Flannerys. The hint of an inheritance sometimes has that effect, at least in books.

"That was fast," I'd said when he called.

"Guess they want it over with," Dix had answered. "I'll see you tonight, sis."

"Wait a second. Is everything OK?"

"No," Dix said. "I'll see you later."

He picked me up at five thirty, looking bad. If I hadn't known it was impossible, I would have said he'd lost ten pounds since Saturday morning. His skin was gray, his eyes were dull, and his face was drawn. The black suit seemed to hang from his shoulders. When I asked him how his day had been, he merely shook his head, and we spent the drive from East Nashville to West Meade largely in silence, except for Dix asking directions and me providing them. It wasn't until we were two blocks away, heading up Pennywell toward the house, that he started talking.

"I did some research. There are no adoption records for David Flannery."

I turned to look at him. "Are you sure?"

"I'm not likely to make a mistake about something like that. He was born in St. Jerome's Hospital, and the mother and father listed on his birth certificate are Virginia and Samuel Flannery."

"I've never heard of St. Jerome's," I said. Nashville has plenty of hospitals—health care is a huge industry here—but St. Jerome's wasn't one I was familiar with.

"It's private," Dix said. "And small. With some sort of religious connection."

With a name like St. Jerome's, I'd assumed as much. "Apparently the family's religious. Austin said Virginia Flannery works for her church."

"Her husband's a financial advisor," Dix said. "He emphasizes a Christian approach to money. And he seems to be doing all right. Nice house." He ran an assessing eye over it as we pulled up into the parking area outside the double garage.

"It's a nice neighborhood. Expensive." I glanced at him, wondering if maybe now would be a good time to tell him that Dr. Seaver had told me Elspeth's baby had been stillborn. We were here, and he wasn't likely to leave again without going through with the appointment.

Then again, maybe Dr. Seaver was wrong? David looked so much like Rafe, at least in the picture, that it was hard to believe they weren't related.

"Ready?" Dix said.

"I guess." May as well get it over with. In a half hour we'd know something one way or the other.

VIRGINIA FLANNERY WAS GRACIOUSNESS ITSELF when she opened the door for us, but there was tension bleeding from every pore of her body, and her speech was rapid and jumpy. "Mr. Martin? I'm Virginia Flannery. Come in. Let me take your jackets. The dining room is through here. Can I get you something to drink?"

"That's not necessary," Dix said. "Savannah?"

I shook my head. "No thank you, Mrs. Flannery. We don't want to put you out."

"It's no bother," Virginia Flannery said, and I got the impression she wanted something to do with her hands. They were twisting together as she waited for us to come through the door from the front hall and into the dining room. "I'll just put on a pot of coffee while we wait for Sam to come downstairs. He just came home from work and he's changing." She glanced nervously up the stairs to the second story.

"That's fine, Mrs. Flannery," Dix said. "We're not in a hurry."

She sent him a look that said, rather clearly, that the sooner we said what we came for, the sooner we'd leave, and it couldn't be soon enough for her, but she bustled off toward the kitchen without uttering a word.

"Nervous," Dix muttered as he headed for the dining room table.

I nodded, following. Making sure my voice wouldn't carry to the kitchen I said, "Wouldn't you be?"

"At this point? Not sure. I didn't tell them what this was about on the phone."

"To some people, that's even more reason to worry." I pulled out the chair next to his and sat down, leaving the two chairs opposite for Virginia and Sam Flannery. There were faint voices from upstairs; Sam talking to his son, I assumed. Maybe David was doing his homework.

We were sitting at a mahogany table, on carved mahogany chairs with striped cushions. A big mirror above the matching buffet reflected the chandelier above the table, which sent prisms of light dancing across the walls. Under my feet was a faded but still beautiful Persian rug. It was all very tasteful, and quite expensive.

Virginia came bustling back after a minute or so, carrying cups and saucers. She put one of each in front of each of us and disappeared again. Next came spoons, real silver with a matching pattern, carefully placed onto real cloth napkins. Then the sugar bowl and pitcher of cream, porcelain with painted violets. Finally a prosaic thermal container of coffee, that she put on the table with another nervous glance through the door to the hallway and the stairs. "He should be down any... Oh! I think I hear him!"

She bustled back out of the room. Dix and I had time to exchange a look, but no more, before she came back, clutching her husband's arm, her hand pale against the brown of his skin.

Dix and I stood, and Dix extended a hand. "Mr. Flannery. I'm Dixon Calvert Martin, from Martin and McCall, attorneys, in Sweetwater. We spoke on the phone this morning."

Mr. Flannery nodded and shook. He looked less nervous than his wife, or maybe he just hid it better. He was tall and skinny, even taller than Rafe, but without any of Rafe's bulk, and comfortably dressed in wrinkled khakis and a T-shirt.

"This is my sister Savannah," Dix introduced me, and we shook.

"Have a seat," Sam Flannery rumbled. He had a deep voice for such a thin man. For a few seconds everything was quiet as we all got situated and assessed one another across the table.

I'd already had a chance to take stock of Virginia Flannery, who was plump, with short blonde hair touched with gray, and wary blue eyes, dressed in frumpy mom-jeans and an oversized blouse. Now I examined Sam for any resemblance to Rafe.

There wasn't any, other than the obvious one: they both had some African-American in their heritage. Sam probably more than Rafe: his skin was a few shades darker, and his features more classically black. His nose was a little flatter and broader and his lips fuller. He was bald, so I had to make a guess as to hair color, but I thought it would probably be black, or perhaps gray, and kinky. Rafe's is dark brown, like espresso. Sam's eyes, on the other hand, were lighter, almost golden brown. Rafe's are so dark they're almost black. And the eye shape was different: Sam's eyes were deep set and close together; Rafe's aren't.

While I was cataloguing differences, Dix was going through the motions, explaining that he was the executor for the estate of a woman who had died a few months ago in Sweetwater. Virginia turned to Sam.

"Do you know anyone in Sweetwater, honey?"

Sam shook his head. From the position of their arms, I thought they were holding hands under the table.

"Her name was Elspeth Caulfield," Dix said. I watched them both, but saw no flicker of recognition on either of their faces. "We found this in her house."

There was a pause.

"Savannah?" Dix said.

"Oh!" I opened my bag. "Sorry."

The picture of David hit the polished top of the table face up. For a second nobody reacted, and then I heard Virginia suck her breath in.

"This is your son David, isn't it?" Dix said, looking from one to the other of them. When neither answered, he added, "Can you tell me how it ended up in Elspeth Caulfield's house?"

Virginia shook her head. "I've never seen it before." Her voice was weak.

"But it's your son?"

She nodded.

"You didn't give it to Elspeth?"

"I don't even know who Elspeth is! I've never heard her name before, and I certainly wouldn't give her a picture of my son." She swallowed. "This is very disturbing to me."

It would be disturbing to me too, if David were my child and I learned that a stranger had a picture of him in her bedside drawer. A picture I hadn't given her.

"Is your son adopted?" Dix said.

There was a pause, then—

"Of course not!" Sam said.

"How dare you insinuate—!" Virginia said.

They both stopped to look at one another.

"Elspeth Caulfield left everything she owned to her son," I said into the silence. "This picture was in her house. She got pregnant when she was sixteen. More than twelve years ago. The boy she slept with looks a lot like your son."

"He's dead, too," Dix said into the silence that followed. I shot him a look, but couldn't really argue with the party line. Not when I myself had told him to keep the fact that Rafe was alive under his hat. But if there was a time I wanted to tell the truth, it was now. If David was Rafe's son, Rafe would want to know him. And David had a right to know Rafe.

Virginia and Sam exchanged a look. "David is our son," Sam said.

"Of course he is." Dix's voice was calm. "Nobody's arguing with that."

"You can check his birth certificate," Virginia said.

Dix turned to her. "I already have. Birth and death records are public."

"So you know we're his parents."

"Of course you're his parents," I said. "You've taken care of him probably from the day he was born. But—please forgive me—he doesn't look like either of you. He looks like Rafe."

"If you'll allow me..." Dix said, digging in his briefcase. He brought out—I blinked—a Columbia High School yearbook. A couple of yellow Post-It notes stuck out of the top of it.

Dix flipped it open and turned the book around so the Flannerys could see the page. It had rows of student portraits, one right next to the other. Dix put his finger on one. "This is Elspeth Caulfield. She's a sophomore in this picture. She didn't come back for her junior year. According to rumor, her parents took her out of school so they could hide that she was pregnant."

Virginia and Sam bent their heads together to take a look. I wondered whether that meant anything. If they had adopted David, would they refuse to look at his birth mother? Or would they want to?

"Is Rafe in that book too?" I asked Dix, *sotto voce*. He glanced at me. After a second he nodded and leaned across the table to flip to the second Post-It.

"This is Rafael Collier. It was his senior year. As you can see, he looks quite a lot like your son."

Neither of them answered. Sam leaned back, as if distancing himself from the yearbook, and folded his arms across his chest. I recognized the move from one of the many sales seminars I'd attended over the past few months, as a gesture of self protection. Of disassociating himself from what was happening.

Virginia looked up at Dix. "David is my son." There was a touch of desperation in her voice.

"Of course he is," Dix said. "Nobody is trying to take him away from you."

He leaned back too, casually, and crossed one leg over the other. "Let's talk hypothetically for a moment. Let's say that perhaps someone else gave birth to David and you adopted him. And let's say that the person who gave birth to him has now passed away. There are no other members of her family; she was the last."

I thought I noticed a slight lessening of tension in Virginia's face. Or perhaps it was just my imagination. I reached a hand across the table and slid the open yearbook toward me.

"Let's also say that the boy she had relations with when she was a teenager never knew about the baby, and in either case, he's dead now too. His only living relative is a grandmother who suffers from dementia and who has no idea that David exists."

This time it definitely wasn't my imagination. Sam's posture changed, became less guarded, more open. He exchanged a glance with his wife.

"There's no chance at all that anyone will be taking your son away from you," Dix said, abandoning the hypothetical. "All I'm trying to do is find my late client's heir. She left assets worth at least a hundred thousand dollars. The house is probably worth another hundred thousand. At least."

He glanced at me, the real estate authority. I nodded. From what I'd seen of the house, and from what I knew about real estate in Damascus, the tiny town where Elspeth had lived, probably more.

Sam and Virginia exchanged another long look. I glanced down at the yearbook, as Dix added, coaxingly, "It would help to pay for David's education."

"We can pay for our son's education on our own," Sam said.

"Of course you can. But it never hurts..." Dix's voice faded into the background as my eyes sought and found Rafe's face on the page in front of me.

While he'd been in his senior year at Columbia High, I had been a freshman. We'd never had much to do with one another, but I knew who he was. Everyone did. He was the biggest troublemaker in Maury county. And although I hadn't spared him a thought in the time between high school and meeting him again in August, I remembered quite well what he'd looked like back then. His face had been softer than it was now, more boyish, and his hair had been longer, braided into cornrows. He'd worn baggy clothes and what looked like the entire Fort Knox gold reserve in chains around his neck.

I smiled. Somehow, LaDonna must have convinced him to clean up for his yearbook photo. The cornrows were still there, but pulled back from his face, and instead of whichever oversized sports jersey he'd been planning to wear that day, he was dressed in a button down shirt and tie. I was willing to bet the tie would have been off and in his pocket the second he was out of the photographer's chair, but his mama had gotten a picture of her boy looking handsome, and that was all that mattered.

I reached out a finger to trace his face in the picture, and froze when Dix cleared his throat. When I looked up, I saw that Virginia was watching me.

"Sorry." I closed the yearbook and pushed it back into the middle of the table.

"Were you friends?" Virginia wanted to know.

I nodded. "Not in high school, but more recently. Back then, my mother would have locked me in my room if I'd had anything to do with someone like Rafe."

"My mother wasn't real thrilled when I told her was going to marry Sam, either." Virginia smiled at her husband. "Of course we were much older. But a mother never stops worrying about her child, does she?" She didn't wait for me to answer, just continued, "She got over it once she got used to him, even if it took a few years. And she adores David."

A shadow passed across her face, and the smile slipped off.

"Does he know?" I asked.

She must have decided to stop playing games, or maybe they'd reached an agreement while I'd been zoned out gazing at Rafe's face in the yearbook. At any rate, she shook her head without any prevarication. "Nobody knows. Not David, not my mother. Nobody. Mom's in Minnesota, and at the time when David was born, things were still strained between us. The fact that we had a baby made a difference. I was in my late thirties, and I think she'd given up hope she'd ever have any grandchildren. When she saw him, she said he had his father's smile. We were so thrilled she finally seemed to accept Sam that we didn't want to burst her bubble."

She smiled a little tearily, reaching for her husband's hand.

"Ginny hadn't told her that we were trying to adopt," Sam added. "We figured it'd be just another way we were failing. Couldn't get pregnant; had to get a baby from someone else. So we didn't tell her. And we haven't told David."

Virginia—Ginny—sniffed back tears. "From the first time I held him in my arms, he was mine."

"No one's going to take your son," Dix said again. He hesitated before asking, a little awkwardly, "Would you happen to know the name of his birthmother? Whether he is, in fact, my client's son?"

But Ginny and Sam both shook their heads. "We got no information about anything," Sam said. "Just a phone call that our son had been born, and we could come pick him up."

Ginny added, "The nurse who gave him to me said the hospital would take care of filing the birth certificate. When it arrived in the mail, it had our names on it."

"You didn't sign any papers? There's no official record that David was born to anyone else?"

Ginny shook her head.

"Would you be willing to have David undergo a DNA test?" Dix asked.

Sam and Ginny looked at one another. "I don't know..." Ginny murmured.

"He wouldn't have to know what it was for. You could come up with an excuse. Does he play sports?"

"Basketball," Sam said.

"Maybe you could tell him he needs another physical."

"We've always told him to tell the truth. I don't feel good about lying to him."

They'd been lying by omission for twelve years. I didn't see that this tiny additional white lie would make a difference.

"There might come a time when you'll wish you knew for sure," I said. "Or when David will."

They exchanged another glance. "We'll talk about it," Sam said. Ginny nodded.

There was a creak from out in the hallway, and I glanced that way. "Is David here?"

"He's upstairs doing his homework," Ginny said. "I don't want him to know about this. Not until Sam and I have had a chance to decide what to do. I'm sorry. I'm sure you'd like to meet him, but not tonight."

She sounded determined. I would probably be determined too, in her position. Nonetheless, I was disappointed. I'd been looking forward to meeting David. I wanted to see for myself just how much of Rafe was in him, whether he really looked as much like Rafe as it seemed from the photograph. But I also wanted to see him because—and I hadn't quite articulated this desire to myself, not in so many words—I wanted an idea of what the tiny life inside me might turn out to look like. If Rafe and Elspeth had created David, then Rafe and I would probably create something very similar.

When I didn't speak, Ginny added, with a look at my midriff, "Just imagine if it was your child."

My jaw dropped. I knew I'd put on a couple of pounds, but surely I didn't look pregnant?

"I spent ten years watching pregnant women," Ginny said. "I can pick them out long before they start to show. It isn't just in the stomach, you know. It's the hair and the skin and the look in their eyes. Although you *are* starting to show just a little. How far long are you? Two months? Three?"

"About that." I avoided looking at Dix.

"The father?" Ginny's eyes, pale blue, dropped for a second to the closed yearbook. I nodded. "And he's dead? I'm sorry."

"So am I," I said. Although not because Rafe was dead, because I knew better, but because I had to pretend he was and thus lie to everyone.

"Maybe you could let them adopt the baby," Dix said ten minutes later, when we had left the Flannerys and were in the car on our way back to East Nashville. Ginny and Sam had held firm to their need to discuss the situation before they agreed to anything, and Dix and I had had to be satisfied with that. They already had Dix's phone number, and I left them mine, and we took our leave. And when we were in the car, rolling down Davidson Road toward the interstate, Dix dropped his bombshell.

I found myself putting a protective hand on my stomach. "What do you mean?"

"They might be happy to have another child. Especially if it's their son's brother or sister."

"We don't know that David is Rafe's son," I said. "You know, I really wish they would have let us meet him."

"Would *you* have?" He continued without waiting for my answer. He probably figured he knew what it would be: a resounding no. "I think he must be. The photograph of him was in Elspeth's house, and he looks too much like Collier for it to be a coincidence."

I was quietly thrilled to see that there was a little bit of color in his cheeks and a touch of sparkle in his eyes. For the moment, he had something on his mind other than the death of his wife, and it was good to see that he still had the ability to care about other things, and to forget about his loss, even if it was just for a few minutes.

"You think they'll agree to do the DNA test?"

"It's several hundred thousand dollars," Dix said. "And no danger of losing their child. They'd have to be stupid not to."

When he put it like that, I guess I could see his point. "So we just wait?"

"Nothing else we can do," Dix said, and turned the car onto the ramp for I-40 in the direction of home.

Ten

"The autopsy confirmed cause of death," Detective Grimaldi told me by phone the following morning. "Drowning. Though the crack on the head probably didn't help. I'm pretty sure she was unconscious when she went in. It's just as well, really; drowning is a nasty way to go."

"Gah!" My own stomach protested at the thought. It was still early, and the conversation wasn't helping my morning sickness.

"Sorry," Grimaldi said, without sounding it. She was used to my squeamishness, and made no bones about that fact that she found it annoying and girly.

"No problem. You said she might have been in that parking lot to buy drugs. Was there any evidence that she'd been using?

"The M.E. found no evidence of drug use. If she had a habit, it seems to have been a recent one."

"I don't think she did," I said. "I just can't see my sister-in-law as a druggie, I'm sorry. She must have been there for something else. Maybe she was meeting someone. Any news on her phone calls?"

"The service provider got back to me with a list of her incoming and outgoing calls for the past week. There's nothing unusual there. Calls to her husband, her mother-in-law, her sister-in-law, a couple of friends, and her gynecologist."

"Dr. Seaver."

"I spoke to her. She confirmed what the autopsy had already told us."

My heart sank. I had a pretty good idea what was coming. "Sheila was pregnant. Wasn't she?"

Grimaldi sighed. "I'm afraid she was. About six weeks along. The M.E. confirmed it, and so did her doctor."

"So when I saw her at Dr. Seaver's office last week, it was about the pregnancy."

"Must have been," Grimaldi said. "We're trying to trace her movements on Friday. So far we're coming up empty. She was at home when your brother left for work in the morning. The alarm system was reset just after nine. I had your brother check with the monitoring company. She dropped her youngest child off at Mother's Day Out at her church just before ten. Thirty minutes later, she used her debit card to fill her gas tank at a station outside Sweetwater, near the interstate."

"If she drove straight through, she would have gotten to Nashville around noon," I said. I'd driven that distance plenty, in light and darkness, rain and shine, and I knew exactly how long it should take, door to door.

"Her debit card was used one last time, at a café in Brentwood at a quarter to one. A place called Sara Beth's. She must have had lunch there. After that, there's nothing. No purchases or charges on the card. Two phone calls. One to Dr. Seaver, one to a friend in Sweetwater. Both just after two o'clock."

"Have you asked them about it?"

"Dr. Seaver said it was a follow-up call after the appointment. No reason not to believe her. And the friend didn't speak to Sheila.

Sheila left a message. By the time her friend received and returned it, it was late and Sheila didn't pick up. I'm thinking she was already dead by then."

Probably so. "So now what?"

"We'll keep digging," Grimaldi said. "I'll let you know if anything new comes up."

"I'd appreciate that." I contemplated telling her about the Flannerys, but decided against it. It was none of her business, really. It had nothing to do with the case, and I didn't want to take any of her focus off the investigation into Sheila's murder. "I'll talk to you later."

"No doubt," Grimaldi said, and hung up. I did the same and got to my feet, wincing, and headed toward the kitchen for a refill of ginger ale.

It was still early, and I hadn't managed to get out of my jammies yet. The long skirt of the lacy nightgown swirled around my ankles as I padded barefoot across the floor, and when I looked down, the soft fabric curved over my stomach.

I've never been rail thin. There's always been a few extra pounds I'd like to lose. Although at the moment, my stomach looked bigger than usual. Good God, I really was starting to look pregnant!

I put a hand on it. It didn't feel any different. And it was much too soon to feel any kind of movement from inside.

Leaning against the counter, one hand on my stomach, I asked myself again what I was going to do. Did I have the courage to have the baby—Rafe's baby—and to bring it up on my own without any help from him, and with potentially very little help from my family? Would I be able to weather the stares from everyone I knew when I showed up with a baby whose complexion shouted to the world that I'd dallied outside my own gene pool?

Watching Virginia Flannery last night had been interesting. She'd said her mother hadn't approved when she wanted to marry Sam. There had probably been stares and comments. These days, people are a lot more used to interracial couples than they used to be, but in some circles, there's still stigma attached. Had people whispered about David, too? Had Ginny been made to feel people's prejudice when she took her son to the playground and the grocery school?

If she had, I doubted she'd cared. She clearly adored David, and loved Sam. Their sense of togetherness was beautiful. The way they communicated with just glances and movements, but no words. Bradley and I had never had that, not even in the beginning. Todd and I didn't either. Todd sometimes didn't seem to understand me even when I did use words.

Rafe knew instinctively how I felt. And he was never surprised by anything I told him.

But he didn't want anything permanent, I reminded myself. And I couldn't marry him even if he did. My mother would kill me.

On the counter next to my empty glass of ginger ale sat the abortion pill from Dr. Seaver's office, and I picked up the little cardboard sleeve and contemplated it, the way I did every morning on my trip to the kitchen for ginger ale and crackers. If I put it in my mouth and swallowed it, by tomorrow night, my situation would no longer be a problem. I wouldn't have to tell mother anything. I wouldn't have to tell Rafe anything. I could just go on as if nothing had happened.

If it was just that easy.

And like every other morning—so far—I put the pill back down and turned my back on it. I still wasn't ready to make a decision. Or at least not that decision. Not quite yet. I knew I'd probably end up having to terminate the pregnancy—preferably sooner rather than later, before doing so got any more difficult than it was already—but today, at least, wasn't the day I could bring myself do it. I told myself I still had some time to decide and left it at that.

Padding toward the bedroom, I pep-talked myself into another battle with nausea. It was time to brush my teeth.

Sara Beth's Café turned out to be a little hole in the wall in a strip mall in Brentwood. They served artisan sandwiches and quiches and other upscale, healthy-looking lunch foods at small round tables set close together in a space no bigger than my living room. There was an odor of incense in the air and only one waitress, dressed in a skimpy T-shirt in spite of the November temperatures, with a long apron over her super-skinny jeans. Her hair was halfway down her back, worn in dreadlocks, and she had silver studs in her ears, her nose, and through her bottom lip. The kohl outlining her eyes would have made Cleopatra weep with envy.

I ordered a drink and a salad and waited for her to come back with the fruit tea before I showed her the picture of Sheila I'd brought from home. "She was here on Friday. Do you recognize her?"

She contemplated it, head cocked. "Sure. Sat over there." She pointed to a table in the corner. "Had a roast turkey with field greens on ciabatta and a 7-Up."

"Was she alone?"

She squinted at me. "Why? Are you with the police, too?"

"She was my sister-in-law," I said. "That's my brother." I pointed to Dix's face in the picture. It was his, Sheila's and the girls' Christmas card. I'd just received it in the mail a week ago. And I realized, with a pang, that I wouldn't be getting one next year. Not one like this.

They were all dressed in red—Dix in a sweater, Sheila a silk blouse, and Abby and Hannah in matching corduroy dresses—and all four were grinning like mad at the camera. It was especially poignant to see Sheila's beautiful smile, knowing she was lying cold and dead on a slab at the morgue. And Dix's relaxed face looked nothing like it had the last time I saw him, just last night.

The waitress examined Dix and nodded. I guess she'd noted the family resemblance and decided I was who I said I was.

"Sheila was his wife," I added. "She died Friday night. We're trying to figure out what she was doing in Nashville that day. She didn't live here."

"She didn't really talk to me." The waitress shrugged. "Sat down and looked at the menu. Ordered her food. Ate it."

"Was she alone?"

She nodded. "Oh, sure. Came in alone, left alone, didn't speak to nobody."

"Did she do anything? Read a book? Make a call? Text message?"

"She looked at her watch," the waitress said. "A couple times. I asked her if she was waiting for someone, and she said no, she had an appointment she didn't want to be late for."

"Did she say where?"

But of course she hadn't. "Just that it was at one o'clock."

Sheila's appointment had to have been somewhere fairly close, then. Detective Grimaldi had said she'd used her debit card at Sara Beth's at a quarter to one. If her appointment was at one and she didn't want to be late, she couldn't have driven far after she finished lunch.

"Thanks," I said, and the waitress nodded and bustled off toward the kitchen, while I busied myself with gnawing the lipstick off my bottom lip and thinking about where Sheila might have been headed.

The area where Sara Beth's was located, was full of businesses. There were several office parks a half mile to the west, and business buildings lined both Franklin Road and Old Hickory Boulevard for a mile or so in both directions. I'd passed insurance agencies, retail spaces, tailors, dentists, lawyers, other restaurants and coffee shops, a bookstore, a couple of banks... Sheila could have been on her way practically anywhere.

"I don't suppose she said anything about what kind of appointment it was?" I asked hopefully when the waitress arrived with my chicken salad. "Dentist? Doctor? Lawyer?"

The waitress pondered for a second, her gaze faraway. "I don't think so. I'm not sure, though. I'm sorry. It's a couple of days ago, and I didn't know I'd have to remember."

"That's OK," I said. It wasn't like I could remember the exact exchange I'd had with the waitress at the Café on the Square in Sweetwater on Thursday, either. "If you remember anything, would you give me a call?" I dug a card out of my bag and gave it to her.

She told me she'd be happy to, and flounced off. I devoted myself to eating. For two.

My cell phone rang halfway through the meal, and when I checked the screen, I saw it was Denise Seaver's number. "Dr. Seaver? What can I do for you?"

"I'm calling to remind you," Dr. Seaver said, "that if you plan to use that pill I gave you—" the abortion pill that was sitting on my kitchen counter, "—you'll have to do it today or tomorrow. After that, you'll have to have an in-clinic procedure if you choose to terminate the pregnancy."

"Oh." I hadn't realized I'd left it so long. "Thank you."

"No problem." She hesitated, then added, "Any news about Sheila?"

None I felt good about sharing. "I haven't heard."

"Do you know what she was doing in Nashville?"

"I'm... I think they're close to figuring that out. She had an appointment in Brentwood."

"Brentwood," Denise Seaver said. "Really?"

"Do you know someone in Brentwood she might have been going to see?"

She was quick to deny it. "Oh, no. Not at all."

"OK," I said. And opened my mouth to continue. She got in before me.

"I should go. I just called to remind you about the pill."

"I appreciate that."

There was a moment of silence before she said, "Can I assume... have you made a decision to terminate the pregnancy?"

"Not yet." I was quick off the mark myself, I realized. "I'm not sure what I'm going to do yet. I need more time. I don't want to make the wrong choice." Once I made it, it would be irrevocable, after all. I couldn't change my mind once I'd popped the pill.

"Of course not." Her voice was back to its professional and comforting cadence. "You need to make the choice that's right for you.

There's still plenty of time to have an in-clinic procedure. And you know, Savannah, even if you decide to have the baby, and then change your mind, there are options. There are plenty of couples who can't conceive, who would be happy to adopt a newborn. If it comes to that, I can put you in touch with someone who'll—"

"Speaking of that," I interrupted, "remember when I asked you about Elspeth Caulfield's baby? You said he was stillborn."

Dr. Seaver made a noise of agreement.

"Someone must have misinformed you. He's alive and well and almost twelve years old."

"Excuse me?"

I didn't even think twice before I blurted out my exciting news. Doctor-patient privilege, right? "His name is David Flannery. He was adopted by a family in Nashville just after he was born. At least we think he's Elspeth's son. We won't know for sure until we do a DNA test, and the parents haven't agreed yet. But I don't see why they won't. And he looks just like—" I caught myself a second before I said a name I shouldn't be saying. "Elspeth," I finished lamely, when in truth, David Flannery looked nothing at all like Elspeth. At least not in the photo I'd seen.

"That's wonderful," Dr. Seaver said warmly. "Your brother must be happy. But you won't know for certain until the boy's DNA has been tested? When will that be?"

"I'm hoping they'll call soon, to let me know they agree to do it. We spoke to them last night, so they should have had enough time by now to make a decision."

"Good luck," Dr. Seaver said lightly. "I really should be going."

"Of course." Her lunch break was probably over and she'd have to start seeing patients again. Nice of her to have checked up on me. "I'm sorry to have kept you."

"Just keep me updated on what you decide to do," Denise Seaver said, and rang off. I went back to eating salad.

I spent the rest of the afternoon trying to figure out where Sheila might have gone after Sara Beth's on Friday. When I left the café, I actually spent an hour just driving around Brentwood in every direction, turning back after I'd gone fifteen minutes and making note of any interesting businesses along the way. It didn't help. I didn't even know that Sheila's appointment had been for. For all I knew, she could have gotten off the interstate here just so she could eat at Sara Beth's, perhaps because someone had recommended it, or because, being pregnant, she couldn't wait any longer. I could certainly relate. And then after lunch she'd gone back onto the interstate and continued north until she was close to downtown. She could have been headed to Music Row. Or one of the universities. Or the hospital district. She might have made it to that part of town in fifteen minutes if she'd known exactly where she was going.

It was a futile errand. So I gave up, and turned into the parking lot of a Target superstore instead, and amused myself for a while by looking at the clothes. While I'd been married to Bradley, I'd been able to afford to shop for designer clothes in rather more upscale establishments than this, but now that I was on my own, and I was down to scraping the bottom of the savings account whenever I needed something new to wear, I'd lowered my standards considerably. And Target really has a lot of very cute clothes. In fact, I fell into temptation and bought a lovely cardigan with the little bit of money that was left on my credit card. It was soft and gray and draped beautifully, and it had a row of rosettes down the front that drew attention away from my stomach. I did talk myself out of getting the pair of maternity jeans, but I did note the price and size for future reference, should I have need for them.

Driving back to East Nashville, I faced facts, not for the first time.

There was a big part of me that wanted this baby. I'd wanted a baby once before, and had lost it. And although I'd realized, in retrospect, that it might be better this way—a child would have tied me to Bradley for all eternity, even after our marriage dissolved, which it would have eventually—I did occasionally lament the loss.

Now I had a second chance. I could have a baby. I'd have to raise it on my own, and I'd probably have to deal with a fair amount of unpleasantness and prejudice and difficulty. Plus, I'd be irrevocably tied to Rafe until the day I died. But somehow that thought failed to fill me with the same sense of vexation as the thought of being unable to get away from Bradley.

And it wasn't just that I was a little bit in love with Rafe. Maybe even more than a little bit. Or maybe it would be more accurate to say I was infatuated with him. Or in good old lust.

Whatever the correct term, I found him fascinating. He was different from anyone else I'd ever associated with. He was certainly different from anyone else I'd ever slept with. But since that list began and ended with Bradley, that wasn't big news.

Rafe was nothing like Bradley, in bed or out of it. Where Bradley had been cool reason and thorough professionalism, a Southern gentleman to the bone, Rafe was heat and passion and laughter and exasperation and joy. I didn't have to pretend with him. I could be me, with all my flaws and insecurities and occasional inappropriate questions. He didn't expect me to be anything but who I was. And he made me happy. Being around him was sometimes difficult, sometimes frightening, usually fun. Occasionally it was peaceful. But it always made me feel alive, like I wasn't just watching life go by, from up on the pedestal where Todd put me, but I was taking part in it.

Having Rafe's baby would be tough. Financially, I had no idea how I would manage. I could barely feed myself at the moment. My mother would certainly have conniptions. Todd would be horrified. So would a lot of other people. And Rafe might not be precisely happy, either. He hadn't signed on for fatherhood. He hadn't signed on for any kind of relationship at all. What if he wished he'd never slept with me and had no plans of ever talking to me again?

Or worse, what if I told him I was pregnant and he felt compelled to be a part of the baby's life? Not because he wanted to, but because he felt he had to. What if he asked me to marry him, to make the baby legitimate?

Silly to worry about that in our day and age, I suppose, when babies are born out of wedlock all the time, but I was brought up the old-fashioned way, and he knew it, so maybe he'd think he had to offer...

The phone rang, just as I reached East Nashville and this depressing point in my cogitations. I fumbled it out of my bag and glanced at the display. The number wasn't familiar. A potential real estate client, maybe? That'd be nice. If I ended up with another mouth to feed, I'd need all the clients I could get. Child care isn't cheap. Maybe I could move back to Sweetwater and dump the baby on Catherine whenever I needed to work...

"This is Savannah," I chirped.

"This is Aislynn," a voice answered. "I work at Sara Beth's. We spoke a couple hours ago?"

"Of course." The waitress with the piercings. "What can I do for you?"

"I've realized something," Aislynn said. "Your sister-in-law said she was going to see the doctor."

"Really?"

"Yeah." She lowered her voice. "See, when her sandwich was ready, Jerry, the guy behind the counter, took it out to her himself. He probably tried to flirt with her, and she told him she was going to see the OB."

"Really?"

"Sure. Probably telling him—without telling him, you know—that she already had a boyfriend. Or a husband."

"Right," I said. That made sense, actually. "So Jerry told you this?"

"Uh-huh. I told him about your sister-in-law, and that she'd died, and that you were trying to figure out what she'd been doing on

Friday, and he said she'd been on her way to the doctor. Because she was pregnant."

Aislynn pondered for a moment before she added, "Cause, she could just have been lying. I'd lie, if Jerry tried to pick *me* up."

"She didn't," I said.

"'Scuse me?"

"It wasn't a lie. She really was pregnant. And married."

"That'll make Jerry feel better, anyway," Aislynn said. "So does that help?"

"It helps a lot. Thank you."

"Great," Aislynn said. "Listen, I gotta go. I'm gonna keep your card, OK? My girlfriend and I have been talking about getting a place together."

She hung up before I had the chance to gush about how much I wanted to help her and her girlfriend—girlfriend?—buy a new place.

I spent the time before dinner looking up obstetricians and gynecologists. Not unexpectedly, there were hundreds. The majority was located in and around the hospital district in midtown, where several of the teaching hospitals are. Vanderbilt University Hospital had a fair few OBs on staff, and so did Meharry Medical College. Add in Metro General Hospital (across the street from Meharry) and Baptist Hospital, Centennial Hospital, and St. Thomas Hospital, all within a stone's throw of midtown, and a pregnant woman could have her pick.

When I focused on obstetricians just in Brentwood, the number became more manageable. There were still a couple dozen, but that's easier to consider dealing with than a couple hundred. The problem was, I had no idea how to deal with them at all. It wasn't like I could call and ask whether Sheila Martin had had an appointment there at one o'clock on Friday. They wouldn't tell me if I did. And where on the list would I start? Should I call them all alphabetically? Or organize them geographically and spend a couple of days dropping by?

At least a half dozen of the obstetricians seemed to be grouped together with the same address—

And that's when I realized that that address happened to be another hospital. A small private one located in Brentwood, just a few miles from Sara Beth's Café.

St. Jerome's Hospital.

Where David Flannery supposedly had been born.

Eleven

I was watching HGTV when the phone rang. It was almost eight o'clock and I was ready to crawl into bed. I considered not answering, but thought better of it. Just in case it was another potential client. Or someone with information about Sheila.

"This is Savannah."

"Miss Martin?" The voice was vaguely familiar, and it took me a second to place it.

"Mrs. Flannery?" I admit it, my heart skipped a beat.

"Yes," Virginia Flannery said, "it's me. Have you seen David?"

I blinked. "He was upstairs doing his homework last night. So no, I didn't get a chance to meet him."

"That's not what I meant." Her voice was shaking so much I had a hard time understanding what she was saying.

"OK." I did my best to keep my own voice calm and even. "No, I've never seen David. Except in that photograph I showed you. Why?"

"He's gone," Ginny said.

"Gone?" It was a stupid thing to say. I mean, it wasn't as if I thought I'd misheard.

"I dropped him off at school this morning. He went to classes until the end of the day. He was supposed to have basketball practice afterwards, but it's extracurricular, so when he didn't show up, the coach didn't call to let me know. I went to pick him up at five, and he wasn't there."

"Maybe he went home with a friend," I said.

"I've called everyone. I thought maybe..." She trailed off.

That I'd grabbed her son to forcibly test his DNA? Surely I hadn't come across as that much of a nutcase. Had I?

"Did you call the police? Ask them to put out an Amber Alert?"

"They can't," Ginny said. "There's no evidence he's been abducted."

"They think he ran away? Why would he...?"

I stopped when I realized what she was thinking. I'd heard a noise out in the hallway when we'd all sat around the table in the Flannerys' dining room last night. What if David had been curious about the people who were visiting, and curious why his parents had told him to stay out of sight? What if he had crept down the stairs for a peek at Dix and me? He could have gotten an earful. He would have heard that he was adopted. That his biological mother was dead. That his biological father was, too.

Suddenly it made perfect sense that Ginny Flannery asked if I had seen David. I was the logical place for him to start his search if he was trying to learn more about where he came from. Dix was in Sweetwater, but I was in Nashville; much more accessible for a curious eleven-year-old. And I'd left my card with the Flannerys yesterday. All he'd had to do was call the office, and Brittany would have told him where I lived.

"I haven't seen him," I said again. "And he hasn't called."

Virginia sniffed wetly. "He's just eleven! Anything could have happened to him."

I could certainly understand how she felt. I already felt a touch of the same panic myself.

"I have a friend with the police," I said. "She works homicide, so she wouldn't normally have anything to do with a missing person case. But if I call and tell her what's going on, I'm sure she'll do everything she can. I don't know how much that is, but I'm sure it's better than nothing."

"OK," Ginny sniffled.

"I'm going to hang up and call her, all right? You just stay home and by the phone. Maybe he just needed some time to think and he'll be home soon."

"Maybe," Ginny said. "Thanks, Savannah."

"Don't thank me. I'm sorry we created problems by showing up. Tell me exactly what he looks like."

I jotted down notes while she spoke, and then I told her to call me if David came home or called, before I disconnected and immediately dialed Tamara Grimaldi's number. "Detective."

"Ms. Martin." She sounded tired.

"I need a favor," I said.

"Oh, sure. The Metropolitan Nashville Police Department exists to do your bidding."

I ignored the sarcasm. "This is important. It's about a missing child."

That eliminated both tiredness and snark. I imagined her sitting up straight, coming to attention. "Whose child? Not one of your brother's?"

"God, no." After Sheila, Dix would fall apart if something happened to Abigail or Hannah. What a horrible suggestion. "Not Dix's child. Rafe's."

There was a beat. Then—

"How can it be missing?" Tamara Grimaldi asked, her voice somewhere between reasonable and a second away from calling in the men in the white coats. "Isn't it in your stomach?"

"Not that child." Sheesh. And yes, it was still in my stomach. "His son. Almost twelve years old. David Flannery."

"He has a son?"

"It's a long story. Rafe knocked up a girl named Elspeth Caulfield when he was in high school. You remember Elspeth; she died two months ago."

"Of course," Grimaldi said. We'd both been there when Elspeth died—Grimaldi outside the trailer and me hiding in the closet—and I figured neither of us were likely to forget it. At least not so soon.

"Elspeth had a will. She left everything to her son. Dix is her executor. He has spent the past couple of months looking for the boy. We finally found him, and talked to his parents last night. He must have overheard, and realized he was adopted. They hadn't told him. Now he's gone. He left school early instead of going to basketball practice, and nobody knows where he is."

"If he wasn't abducted, we can't issue an Amber Alert," Tamara Grimaldi said. "I'm sorry, but those are the rules."

"They already know that. I thought maybe you could do something. Unofficially. Tell the patrol cars to look out for him, or something."

"I can do that," Grimaldi said. "Tell me about him."

"I have a picture on my phone. I'll send it to you when we're finished talking. But he's eleven and ten months. Five six. A hundred and five pounds. Dark hair, brown eyes, medium skin. He looks like Rafe. When he left home this morning, he was dressed for school, so he must have had on khakis, a white shirt, and maybe a blue blazer." Unless he kept that in his locker at school and put it on when he got there.

"Hopefully he's wearing more than a blazer now," Tamara Grimaldi said. "I'll put out an APB to the patrol cars and let you know if anything happens. Anything else I can do for you?"

I hesitated. "I know Rafe isn't supposed to have any contact with anyone in Nashville while he's pretending to be Jorge Pena. But do you think you could get a message to him? It's his son. And he doesn't even know we've found him."

"Does he know the boy exists?"

"I showed him the picture before he left," I said. "Remember when I said I needed to talk to him before he left town?"

"I remember," Detective Grimaldi said, "although I must admit I thought the big emergency was something else."

I blushed. OK, yes. I'd wanted to touch him just to make sure he really was alive and breathing and I'd been misinformed when I was told he was dead. I'd also wanted to kiss him again. But in addition to that, I hadn't thought it fair to let him leave town without telling him that he might have a son. "Please. Just ask Wendell if it would be OK to have him call me. Just this once. I wouldn't ask if it wasn't important."

Tamara Grimaldi said she'd contact Wendell Craig and ask, and meanwhile, she'd do what she could to let every patrol car in Nashville know to keep an eye out for David. I gave her the Flannerys' number and settled in to wait for the phone to ring.

It never did. Eventually I fell asleep on the sofa with the TV still on and the sound muted, and the phone on the coffee table two feet from my ear, but by the time I woke up, it hadn't made a sound.

It was, as they say, déjà vu all over again, except this time it was barely four thirty in the morning, and still dark outside. The only reason I knew the time at all, was because of the digital display on the bottom of the TV. Someone was at the door, but unlike last time, when Detective Grimaldi had been knocking, quietly but persistently, this time whoever was out there really was hammering.

I scrambled off the sofa and fought back a wave of nausea as I staggered to my feet. Maybe it was David. Maybe he'd finally made his way across town and had found me.

I didn't look out the peephole before I unhooked the chain and pulled the door open. Maybe I should have. If I had, I would have been better prepared for what I saw outside.

For a second I didn't believe my eyes. Then the nausea won out, and I turned on my heel and scurried into the bathroom, where I spent the next few minutes hanging over the commode. By the time I got back out into the living room, Rafe had walked inside, locked the door, and made himself comfortable in a chair.

"That ain't quite the welcome I was hoping for, darlin'," he said when I walked through the door.

"Sorry." Since there was no chance he'd want to kiss me now, I curled up on the sofa again, at a safe distance, and tucked my bare feet up under myself.

"You sick or something?"

"Something. But don't worry, it isn't contagious."

He grinned, white teeth against golden skin, and my stomach did an appreciative swoop. Or maybe it was just morning sickness. "Remind me to make it up to you when you're feeling better."

"I'll do that." I managed a smile back, but it was pretty wan. We sat in silence for a moment, just looking at one another.

I knew what I looked like—pale, with my hair lank, no makeup, and dressed in yoga pants and an oversized T-shirt that hung past my hips and covered the tiny baby bump I'd started to develop.

Rafe must have driven—or more likely ridden his Harley— through the night to get here, but he looked none the worse for wear. Although he resembled Jorge Pena rather more closely than I liked. I'd only met Jorge once, but he'd scared the bejeebers out of me. Rafe's hair was longer than usual, nicely cut and gelled, and the match to Jorge's little goatee that he'd started the last time I saw him, had grown in completely now. I liked him better without the facial hair. In deference to the colder weather, he was wearing a Henley instead of his usual T-shirt, with the sleeves pushed up to bare muscular forearms. A black leather jacket was tossed carelessly over the back of one of my dining room chairs, and at the moment he was leaning back, long legs stretched out, arms folded across his stomach, smiling.

"That my shirt, darlin'?"

I looked down at it. "Um... yes."

He quirked a brow. Just one, the other didn't even twitch. "Miss me?"

"I guess maybe a little."

"Looks like maybe more than a little."

This conversation was familiar to me. We'd had the same one, practically verbatim, two months ago, when he'd come back from another trip to Memphis to find me sleeping in his bed. Just the thought of what had happened next had me blushing, and from the curve of his lips, I thought he probably remembered too.

"I didn't expect to see you," I said.

He shifted on the chair, and tamped down the heat in his eyes. "Tammy called."

Rafe is the only person in the world who calls Tamara Grimaldi Tammy and gets away with it. Not even her mother calls her Tammy, or so she says. I've told him she doesn't like it, and I don't doubt that she's told him the same thing herself, but Rafe is nothing if not persistent.

"I figured as much," I said. "But I didn't expect you to drop everything and come running."

If I had, I would have made sure to wear something more attractive. Although it was entirely possible that no lacy nightgown in the world could compete with the knowledge that I slept in his shirt because I missed him.

"Jorge got called away on a job," Rafe explained. And added, "Did you think I'd sit on my hands in Atlanta while my kid's running loose in Nashville?"

"I didn't really think about it at all," I admitted. "I just thought you should know what was going on."

"You wanna tell me?"

"I'll tell you what I know. It isn't much." I ran through the past couple of months: Dix's failed efforts to track down Elspeth's heir and my eventually finding him through the logo on his shirt coupled with the lucky coincidence that I happened to know Austin Puckett, who happened to go to the same school as David. "Dix and I went to talk to the Flannerys two days ago. David's birth certificate says that he's

Virginia and Sam's son, but they admitted that they'd adopted him soon after birth. There are no adoption records anywhere, so the only way to prove that he's Elspeth's son—and yours—is through DNA. But they haven't told David he's adopted, so they weren't sure they wanted to do it. They asked for time to think about it."

Rafe nodded. His jaw was tight, and he looked a little pale, but it could have been just the flickering light from the TV playing across his skin.

"When she called this evening, I thought she was going to tell me they'd decided to go ahead. Instead she said that David is missing. He went to school, skipped basketball practice, and apparently hit the road. Either that or someone snatched him."

"Who'd snatch him?" Rafe asked, with the sort of calm that isn't reassuring at all.

"No idea. But when a kid goes missing, there's always that possibility. Even if he left on his own, someone could have grabbed him along the way."

Rafe nodded, his lips tight. "So where do you think he is?"

"I have no idea," I said. "I'm hoping he's just upset and needs some time alone to think. That he's holed up somewhere. At church, maybe. It can't be easy, at almost twelve, to realize your parents aren't your parents after all."

"I know what I woulda done," Rafe said.

"What's that?"

"Gone to Sweetwater. Elspeth's dead, but he knows where she was from, right?"

I nodded. If David had heard the conversation, he would have heard that Elspeth died in Sweetwater.

"If this kid's anything like I was at twelve, he's there by now." He got to his feet.

"Wait!" I scrambled to my feet. "I have to change." And my stomach was rebelling again.

"Make it quick," Rafe said. "I wanna get there before he moves on."

FIFTEEN MINUTES LATER WE WERE in the Volvo heading down Interstate 65. Rafe was driving. I'd had to talk him out of getting back on the Harley. He thought it would be faster, but if we found David down there—and Rafe seemed pretty certain we would—how would we get him back to Nashville? Three of us wouldn't fit on the bike, and I had no intention of being left behind. So I gave him my keys and told him he could get us there faster than I could.

For the first few minutes of the drive, neither of us said anything. I was too busy fighting back nausea while absorbing the fact that he was back, even if it probably wasn't for long. There were so many things I wanted to talk to him about—Sheila's death, my pregnancy, the fact that the Flannerys, including David, thought he was dead—that I had no idea where to start. So I fell back on something else instead; something he'd said earlier. At the time, it seemed less fraught with difficulty than any of the other subjects I could bring up. I suppose that says rather a lot about where my mind was at that moment.

"You said something earlier, about maybe David being like you when you were twelve."

"Yeah?"

"Old Jim died that year, didn't he?"

He shot me a look out of the corner of his eye. "So?"

"The sheriff told me once that he thought you might have had something to do with it."

"Sheriff Satterfield?"

I nodded.

"Thinks I killed my grandfather?" From his voice it was impossible to tell whether he was offended, horrified, or amused. Maybe a little of all three. Or maybe he was just curious.

"I think it's more that he thinks your mother might have," I said apologetically. "And that you helped." Apparently they'd been one another's alibi at a time when Old Jim had wandered outside dead drunk and drowned in the Duck. The river, that is. A small branch of it runs through the Bog, the sad and sorry little trailer park where Rafe spent his formative years.

"That what you think, darlin'? That I helped my mama kill her daddy?"

"I don't know what to think," I said. "I know if you did, he probably deserved it. Everyone says he wasn't a very nice man."

Although that didn't make it all right to kill him.

"He was a mean son of a bitch," Rafe corrected, "and he deserved to die slowly and painfully with lots of time to think about all the shit he put everyone in his family through. Drowning was too good for him."

Yikes.

"But I had nothing to do with it. I was inside, watching TV. So was my mama. And we didn't hear nothing, and we didn't see nothing, and we didn't know nothing. Not until the next morning, when one of the neighbors found him."

"You didn't go looking for him?"

"Why'd I go looking for him?" Rafe said. "We were just happy he was gone."

I had no answer to that, and after a few seconds he took his eyes off the dark road in front of us to glance over at me. "Listen, Savannah."

If he called me by name, I knew I'd better pay attention. He only did that when he was dead serious about something. The rest of the time he called me by that old Southern catch-all phrase, *darlin'.*

"Yes?"

"I ain't a murderer. I may have killed some people—" Like Perry Fortunato and Jorge Pena, "—but that was cause I didn't have no choice. It was them or me, or them or you. Did you want me to let Perry do what he wanted to do to you?"

"Of course not," I said with a shudder. I was glad Perry was dead. He was a double murderer—would have been a triple if Rafe hadn't saved me—and although seeing him rot in jail for the rest of his life should have been sufficient, and might have been sufficient had things turned out differently, I'd been relieved when he died.

"Then don't ask me things like that, darlin'. I'm liable to take it personal." He flashed a grin, but it didn't reach his eyes.

"I'm sorry," I said.

He shrugged. We drove another few minutes in silence.

"My sister-in-law is dead."

At first I got no reaction, then—"Your brother's wife? Cute little blonde?"

I nodded.

"You gonna ask me if I killed her too?"

"Of course not," I said, piqued. "I'm sorry I hurt your feelings, but that was uncalled for."

"Sorry."

"I forgive you. She died on Friday. Drowned in the Cumberland River. After getting robbed and hit over the head. Tamara Grimaldi thinks she was there to buy drugs."

"Your sister-in-law?"

"I don't think she used drugs," I said.

"No kidding," Rafe answered. After a second, he added, "What's that gotta do with any of this?"

"As far as I know, nothing. Sheila was in Nashville for a doctor's appointment. With an obstetrician."

"She pregnant?" I tried to read something—anything—into his tone of voice, but if he had feelings about pregnancy, or about pregnant women, one way or the other, I couldn't tell.

"So it seems," I said. "She hadn't told Dix yet."

"You sure he was the father?"

I blinked. "Of course I'm sure." The only reason she hadn't told him anything was because she was afraid of another miscarriage. Sheila would never cheat on Dix. Would she?

"Whatever you say," Rafe said with a shrug. "But if he wasn't, and he found out that she'd been screwing around on him..."

"My brother is not a murderer!" And besides, he'd been in Sweetwater that afternoon. Hadn't he?

"Fine," Rafe said. "So maybe she'd gotten involved with someone else. Someone she shouldn't have been. And when she got pregnant, that guy killed her."

"Where would she meet someone else? She spent all her time in Sweetwater."

"Maybe she was doing the nasty with Satterfield," Rafe said with a grin. "That'd be interesting."

I snorted. "You'd love that, wouldn't you? Seeing Todd go to jail for murdering Sheila?"

He shot me a glance. "No chance of that happening, darlin'. Not with Sheriff Satterfield working the case."

"He isn't. It happened in Nashville. It's Tamara Grimaldi's case."

"Tammy'll find whoever did it," Rafe said.

"I hope so."

He must have heard something in my voice, because he sent me a sharp look. "You ain't getting mixed up in it, are you, darlin'?"

"Of course not," I said. Having lunch at Sara Beth's wasn't getting mixed up in anything. And I had a perfect excuse for calling obstetricians. Not that I was about to tell him that. Not yet. Right now, Rafe's and Elspeth's child was more important than Rafe's and mine; he had enough on his mind and I didn't need to add anything more.

So I returned to the real issue, the important one. "When we get there, where are we going to go?"

"I can think of three places," Rafe said, "Elspeth's house, my mama's house, and the graveyard."

I nodded.

"If he's trying to figure out who he is, he's gonna wanna see where his folks came from. And he's probably gonna wanna see where they are now."

"You're not there," I said. When he 'died,' Tamara Grimaldi had told Sheriff Satterfield that Rafe's grandmother wanted the body brought to Nashville for burial. The sheriff hadn't quibbled. Probably happy to get rid of him, even dead.

Rafe shook his head. "Nope."

"What'll he do when he realizes it?"

"No idea. We'll figure it out as we go."

I nodded. "Damascus is closer than Sweetwater. Do you want to start there?"

"May as well," Rafe said.

Twelve

We got to Elspeth's house a few minutes after six o'clock. Damascus was just starting to wake up; there were lights in a few windows along the way, and we met a car or two on the road, but it was still dark and mostly quiet. The big Victorian behind its picket fence showed no signs of life.

"Stay here," Rafe said when he opened the car door.

"Don't be silly." I did the same on my own side. "This is an eleven year old boy. And I'm sorry, but you're scary."

He turned to look at me as I swung my legs out. "Scary?"

"To someone who doesn't know you. At least he knows who I am." I stood and slammed the door. Rafe did the same, and came around the car.

"At least stay close," he said.

"No problem." I hooked a hand into the back pocket of his jeans, and tagged along behind him as he opened the gate—it squeaked—and moved up the walk toward the house.

I thought he'd go up on the porch and knock on the door, but he didn't. He took a sharp right instead, through the dead grass and scattered leaves. We walked slowly, with Rafe's eyes scanning the yard and house. I did my best to look around too, but my night vision isn't fantastic, and I had no idea what to look for.

About halfway around, he stopped. I stopped to, per force, when I bumped into his back. The leather jacket was soft against my cheek, and I could smell it, mixed with a spicy, citrusy scent I recognized from the shirt I'd been sleeping in. The smell of Rafe.

"What?" I whispered.

I thought I'd been pretty quiet, but he still put a finger to his lips to warn me to pipe down. Then he used the same finger to indicate a broken cellar window.

I nodded. There was no way to know, of course, but the window might mean that David had been here. And that he might still be here. Inside, sleeping.

We made our way back around the house and onto the porch, where Rafe stopped in front of the door. I let go of his jeans to let him work unhampered.

It wasn't the first time I'd seen him pick a lock, but he must have practiced since last time. Or perhaps the equipment he carried in his pocket made it easier than the bobby pins he'd removed from my hair then. Either way, it was just a few seconds before the front door was unlocked. Rafe pushed it open carefully, while I held my breath hoping the hinges wouldn't squeal.

We moved into the foyer, with its soaring ceilings and hardwoods floors. Rafe pushed the door shut behind us—the lock caught with a soft click—and looked around.

"Holy shit," he breathed. I followed his gaze and smothered a giggle.

"I forgot about that."

'That' was a giant reproduction of a romance novel cover, blown up to thirty times its paperback size, and displayed in an ornate gold frame above the fireplace mantel. The name *Barbara Botticelli* was emblazoned across the top in crimson letters, while over the bottom, the words "Slave of Passion" curled.

The cover was the usual sexual confection: the swooning heroine, her long blonde hair undone and the bodice of her hoop-skirted gown gaping, was clasped in the hero's brawny arms, her soft white hands clutching his muscular shoulders and her head thrown back, the better to allow him access to the pounding pulse at the bottom of her throat. He was naked to the waist, of course, and bore an uncanny resemblance to Rafe. All of Barbara Botticelli's heroes did. It wasn't until I realized that Barbara was Elspeth, or vice versa, that I understood why. Until then, I'd just thought it was my own fixation that saw him in every book by my favorite author. I hadn't picked up a Barbara Botticelli romance since Elspeth died, and I didn't think I'd ever want to read one again. Now that I knew that Elspeth had pictured Rafe every time she'd written a love scene, having to read them set my teeth on edge.

He glanced at me, a curious combination of shock and fascination on his face. "Is that...?"

"Elspeth. And the closest approximation the artist could make of you, without a picture." Or, alternatively, Elizabeth and Benjamin, the hero and heroine of "Slave of Passion."

He looked at it again, wincing slightly. "Why?"

"You know why. She was hung up on you. Enough that she shot Marquita and tried to kill both Yvonne and me for being too close to you."

"She was crazy," Rafe said. "I slept with her once, more than twelve years ago. We were kids. It didn't mean shit."

"Obviously it meant more to her than to you. You told me she'd been pursuing you for months. And in justice to her, if she wanted to keep the baby—David—and someone took him away from her, she had the right to be upset."

"Upset, maybe," Rafe conceded. "But she didn't have the right to try to kill you. Or anyone else."

"Of course not. I'm not saying she did. Or that you did anything wrong. She was old enough to know what she was doing when she threw herself at you. But she probably didn't think about the fact that she might get pregnant." I know I hadn't. "And I guess she couldn't help feeling the way she did about you afterwards." Any more than I could help the way I felt about him now.

"I never promised her anything—" Rafe began, and I shushed him.

"I know you didn't. And we should talk about this later. If David's here, we have to try to find him."

He looked like he might want to keep talking about it, but he nodded. "Where?"

"Bedrooms upstairs, living room through there." I pointed to a door down the hallway to the right.

"I'll go up. You take the living room." He started up the stairs, his heavy boots somehow not making the slightest noise as he ascended. I headed for the hallway, doing my best to be equally quiet.

In the end it didn't matter. The house was empty. We searched it from top to bottom, and no one was there. Not David, nor anyone else.

Someone had been there, though. There was an empty can of Diet Coke and a container that had once held a microwaveable macaroni and cheese meal in the trash can. Rafe's lips curved in appreciation when he saw it.

"Looks like he can take care of himself."

"Are you sure it was him?"

He glanced at me. "Who else could it be? It's recent. The drops of Coke are still tacky, and the cheese hasn't hardened. Someone did this last night. If it was somebody homeless, they'd still be here. No reason to think anyone'd come by and find them at six in the morning."

"Do you think he slept here?"

"Doesn't look that way," Rafe said, looking around. "He probably got here pretty early. Ate something and figured he'd have time to get to the next place he was going before dark."

"Which was?"

"Sweetwater. Either the cemetery or the Bog."

"I vote for the Bog," I said as we made our way toward the front door. "He's just a kid. I don't think he would have chosen to visit the graveyard at night. The Bog is scary enough."

Rafe nodded. He glanced at the picture above the mantel one last time. "I don't really look like that, do I?"

I looked up, too, cocking my head. The male model they'd gotten to pose for Benjamin was stunning. Tall and dark, with skin the color of caramel and muscles in all the right places. His face was beautiful, with perfectly chiseled lips, a narrow blade of a nose, elegantly arched eyebrows, and big, dark eyes.

No, Rafe didn't look like that.

"Not really. At first glance, maybe a bit. The coloring, the height, the..." I waved my hand. Muscles. "But he looks a little too soft."

"Soft?" He looked again.

"Pretty. You're not pretty. And he doesn't look dangerous at all."

"And I do?"

I turned to examine him. Six three, with muscles that put Benjamin's to shame. Long legs, broad shoulders, slim hips. Dark eyes that could switch from liquid heat to stone in an instant. Straight brows, straight nose, and lips that looked like they were made for kissing... when they didn't look like they were carved from stone. And those weren't even the things that warned people off. It was the way he moved, the way he always seemed aware of what was going on around him, of who else was nearby and what they were doing. That edge, that told everyone around him that this was a man who was used to taking care of business, and who wouldn't scruple to use any means necessary to achieve his ends.

Funny how that part of him made me feel safe rather than threatened.

"What?" he said now.

I did my best to wipe the smile off my face, not quite succeeding. "There's nothing soft about you."

"Hell, no." He smiled back.

"That's not what I meant." I blushed.

"Sure," Rafe said and winked. "If you're good, I'll show you later. Let's go, darlin'. I don't wanna miss him."

I nodded, and preceded him out the door.

THE BOG IS ON THE south side of Sweetwater, off the road to Pulaski. Damascus is on the northwest, halfway to Columbia. It took us twenty minutes to drive the distance between the two. By the time we reached Beulah's Meat'n Three, the sun was on its way up over the trees, and Beulah's was open for business.

"Hungry?" Rafe asked as the Volvo approached.

I averted my eyes from the cinderblock building as my stomach objected to the thought of grease-laden eggs and grits and biscuits. "No."

He gave me a closer look. "You all right, darlin'?"

"Fine," I said. "Just a temporary thing."

"Sure." He didn't say any more. We continued toward the Bog in silence.

For years and years, the Bog housed the undesirables of Sweetwater. The Colliers, white trash if ever there were, lived there, in a singlewide trailer, among others of their ilk. Big Jim, according to the sheriff, had drunk and fornicated his way through life, knocking his wife and his kids around the whole time. Rafe's Uncle Bubba died in prison. LaDonna got herself in the family way at fourteen, and Rafe himself was in trouble practically from the day he was born.

A year ago or so, someone had bought the land and slowly evicted everyone who lived there, with the idea of building a new subdivision of affordable homes. LaDonna had been the last to leave, in a body bag last summer. No connection to anything; she had a drinking and drug

146 | Jenna Bennett

problem, and the official verdict was that she'd accidentally overdosed. Sheriff Satterfield, spurred on by Todd, had done his best to prove that Rafe had had something to do with it, but there was no evidence, and Rafe said he didn't, so there was nothing the sheriff could do. He seemed fine with it; it was Todd who'd been more upset.

Anyway, when the real estate market took a further dip, the subdivision plans had been put on hold. These days, the Bog was a ghost town. No one lived there, and Sweetwater doesn't have a big problem with homeless people wandering around looking for a place to crash, so when we pulled up next to the Colliers' old single-wide mobile home, there wasn't a living soul to be seen.

"It looks deserted," I said as I got out of the car.

Rafe nodded, glancing around. He appeared relaxed, hands in his pocket and a pair of dark glasses shading his eyes from the sun that was now peeking over the cypress trees, but there was tension in his shoulders and in the set of his mouth. "I'll have a look around."

He started to walk away.

"Rafe?"

He turned around. "Yeah?"

"Something wrong?" He had well-honed instincts from his life of crime, and if he thought there was reason to worry, I'd like to know.

He looked at me for a second before he grinned. "No. Just a lot of bad times I'd rather forget about."

"So there's nobody lying in wait for us with a gun, or anything?" Like the last time I'd been here.

"Not unless David brought a water pistol," Rafe said and sauntered off to investigate the nearest abandoned clapboard shack.

I turned my attention to the Collier trailer.

The last time I'd been here, two months ago, was the night Elspeth and Jorge Pena had died. Everything looked about the same as it had then, with the exception of the sparse tufts of grass and other vegetation. Back in early October, it had still been green. Now the grass was yellow and the trees were bare. The ground was dusty and hard, and dry leaves rustled across the toes of my shoes. There were no footprints or tire tracks worth mentioning.

"How do you suppose he's getting around?" I asked Rafe over my shoulder, but he was gone. Inside one of the buildings, probably. I hoped David wasn't doing anything stupid, like hitch-hiking, but at eleven, it was hard to imagine any other way he'd be able to travel. He might have caught a Greyhound bus from Nashville to Columbia, but from there, it was either walking or hitching a ride.

Or bicycling. A red bike, girl type, was leaned up against the back wall of the trailer. It hadn't been here last time I was.

The kitchen door into the Colliers' old trailer still hung wide open. I climbed through into the decrepit kitchen, and glanced around. It looked just as it had the last time I was here: chintzy pressed-wood cabinets with shiny brass handles topped by a faded laminate countertop. An almond colored scratch-and-dent refrigerator and a dirty stove, still encrusted with old food stains, completed the look. Dead cockroaches with their legs in the air lay here and there on the chipped vinyl floor. I wrapped my arms across my chest as a shudder of revulsion brought on another wave of morning sickness. I needed to eat something soon, or I'd pass out.

A sound from the back of the trailer brought my head up again. It was a sort of scramble, quickly suppressed, as if someone had heard me and had thought of making a run for it, but then reconsidered.

"David?"

There was no answer. And no more sounds. I exited the kitchen and headed down the hallway, my boots sliding across the dirty shag carpets. The black mold growing on the baseboards seemed to have taken over another few inches of wall since the last time I was here, and the low ceilings felt like they were pushing down on me. My heart was beating fast; it was impossible not to remember the last time I'd walked down this hallway, and what had happened then.

The big pool of dried blood just outside the door to Rafe's room brought on another almost-dash to the bathroom. Bile rose in my throat and I had to push it back down. When I stepped over the blood and into the doorway, I saw David. He was standing under the centerfold from a long ago dirty magazine that the teenaged Rafe had kept tacked to his wall: a well-endowed blonde with a few scraps of white lace covering her considerable assets gazed limpidly out of china blue eyes. David wasn't looking at her. He was staring at another big blood stain in the middle of the room, and didn't look up until I said his name again.

He really did look a lot like Rafe. Tall for his age, and already starting to develop a more masculine shape. He had Rafe's dark eyes, those same straight eyebrows, and the same shape to his face, although David's cheeks and jaw still had the softness that Rafe's had lost. A dusting of dark fuzz adorned his upper lip. I already knew he had Rafe's smile, although it wasn't in evidence at the moment.

I assumed he recognized me from the other night, but he didn't greet me. On the other hand, he didn't ask me who I was, either. Instead he glanced back down at the dried blood on the floor. "Is this where my mom died?"

There was a quaver in his voice that reminded me that no matter how mature he looked, and how cool he played it, he was just a child.

I looked at the floor too, and for a second I could see Elspeth's small body splayed there in the aftermath of the shooting, a crimson stain spreading across her chest. I swallowed. "Yes."

"What about over there?" He glanced at the blood in the doorway. "My dad?"

His voice caught on the last word. In the span of thirty minutes two nights ago, his whole world had come tumbling down. He had learned that the two people he'd trusted above all others, his parents, weren't really his parents at all, and had been lying to him for almost twelve years. And on top of that, he'd heard that his real parents, his biological parents, were both dead, both in the last few months. Now he was standing in his father's old room, looking at his mother's blood, with a mixture of eagerness and fear in his eyes, and I found I couldn't lie to him anymore. Party line be damned; after everything he'd been through in the past two days, he deserved the truth.

I shook my head. "The man whose blood is over there was named Jorge Pena. He shot your mother. Your biological mother, Elspeth. Ginny is still your real mother, just as Sam is your real father. Jorge came here to shoot Rafe, and Elspeth wouldn't get out of the way. She died trying to protect him."

And yes, she'd been a homicidal nutcase. But this was a scrap of comfort I could give the boy. His mother had died heroically, trying to protect Rafe, and I owed her for that. David didn't need to hear that she was a murderess herself, and that she would almost certainly have spent the rest of her life in prison, or a mental institution, had she not been killed.

"Where was he?" David looked around.

I pointed to Rafe's bedroll, still lying against the wall. He'd been sitting there in the dark waiting for Jorge, naked to the waist so Jorge could see just how vulnerable he was, how easy it'd be to shoot and kill him, and he'd taken my breath away when I walked in on him. I'd begged him to leave, to let Tamara Grimaldi take care of Jorge, and he had refused. Then he'd stuck me in the closet while he took care of Jorge himself. I'd stood there listening to what was going on outside, to the threats and the shots, and when the bullets stopped flying and I stepped out of the closet and into the room, it had been with no idea what I'd find. For the first few seconds I'd been sure Rafe was dead, and the relief when I realized he wasn't had been stronger than any I'd felt before in my life. Until the next day, when I'd spent eight hours thinking he'd died after all, only to learn he hadn't. The relief from that had blown anything else out of my head and out of existence for a while.

There were a few drops of blood on the bedroll, from Rafe's shoulder wound, but nothing like the pools of dried blood on the carpet. From the crumpled state of the blankets, I assumed the bedroll was where David had slept until I woke him. He was a brave boy; you couldn't have paid me to spend the night here.

"So this guy Jorge shot my mom," David said. "Who shot Jorge?"

"Rafe did." With the gun hidden in the bedclothes. He hadn't been quite as vulnerable as he'd looked.

"So they were both here together, and both of them had guns, and Jorge shot my mom and my dad shot Jorge?"

In a nutshell, yes. David didn't need to know that his biological parents hadn't actually been working together, and hadn't even seen each other for more than twelve years before that night. It would serve no purpose to tell him that Elspeth had been there looking for me, so she could kill me. Much better to let him believe, as he obviously did, that his biological parents were some sort of crime-fighting superhero team.

"That's right."

"Wow," David breathed, looking around, eyes shining. I was glad to see that he seemed to feel a little better. The blood and the deaths had been replaced, at least in his mind, with heroism and sacrifice.

"Your parents are pretty worried about you," I said gently. "Your mom and dad. Ginny and Sam."

David glanced at me, opened his mouth, and seemed to think better of speaking.

"Your mom called me yesterday to ask if I'd seen you. I don't think she realized you were actually trying to get down here."

"I wanted to see it," David said, looking around. "Where my real parents were from."

"Sam and Ginny are your real parents. They've been there for you every day of your life. And I'm sure if you'd asked, they would have driven you here. Elspeth was only seventeen when you were born.

That's just a few years older than you are now. And she didn't tell Rafe about you, but trust me, even if he'd known, he wasn't in a position to take care of a baby back then."

David blinked. "Why not?"

I hesitated. How much did I tell the kid? Who did I owe loyalty to here? And what would I have wanted if he was my child? Biological or adopted?

In the end I went with the truth. "He was eighteen. And when you were born, he was in prison."

David's eyes, so much like Rafe's, widened. "Why?"

"That's something you're going to have to ask him yourself."

"He's dead," David said. "Isn't that what you told my parents? I mean, Ginny and Sam?"

He looked miserably torn, poor kid. It couldn't be an easy situation to be in. And it was just about to become more complicated.

"He's outside," I said.

David shot a startled look at the cloudy window. "Outside *here?*"

"Right outside the window. If you want to meet him, this is your chance. He'll probably have to go back to Atlanta tomorrow." If not sooner. I wondered whether he'd told anyone he was leaving, or whether Jorge Pena had just dropped off the face of the earth. What was it Rafe had told me earlier? That Jorge had taken a job?

"He's outside *here?*" David repeated, as if he couldn't quite believe what he was hearing. I smiled.

"Come on. It's time to go, anyway. Your parents are worried sick about you. Your mom thought you'd been kidnapped; I bet she hasn't slept all night. And I have to call Detective Grimaldi and tell her that we've got you so she can call off her APB. There's been a lot of people looking for you."

I kept up a chatter of conversation while I steered him down the hallway toward the kitchen and the door to the outside. He listened and didn't speak, but he kept twisting his neck from side to side, taking in the inside of the trailer. It might have been dark by the time he arrived last night, so this might be the first chance he'd had to look at everything. Or maybe he was like me, astonished by the way some people live. From what little I'd seen of David's home, it was nicely maintained, in good repair, in good taste—everything Rafe's childhood home hadn't been. I wondered if David regretted his eagerness to meet his biological father now that he could see for himself where Rafe came from.

But no, when we got to the kitchen door and pushed it open, David was first through, looking eagerly around him. "Where is he?"

"The car is parked on the other side. He's probably there."

He loped off, without even looking back at me. I scurried after.

Thirteen

Rafe was leaning on the hood of my car: legs crossed at the ankles, arms crossed over his chest, and eyes hidden behind dark glasses. Except for the leather jacket, which he hadn't needed the first weekend in August, he looked very much like he had that morning outside Mrs. Jenkins's house four months ago, when I saw him for the first time after twelve years. Just like then, that aura of danger, of him being someone you wouldn't want to tangle with, was very much in evidence, and David's steps faltered for a second as he rounded the corner. Mine had done the same back in August, I remembered.

"Is that him?" His voice was hushed.

I nodded. "That's Rafe."

David swallowed audibly before squaring his shoulders and starting forward. I watched Rafe unconsciously do the same: straighten up and take a steadying breath before removing the sunglasses.

David stopped a few feet in front of him. "I'm David Flannery. Are you my dad?"

Rafe shot me a look over David's head. I nodded. "Yeah," Rafe said, his voice husky and a little unsure, like I'd never heard it before, "I guess I am."

I turned away, and if I had to sniff back tears while I reached for my cell phone, I don't think that's anyone's business but my own.

"Mr. Craig is fit to be tied," was Tamara Grimaldi's greeting to me when she answered the call.

"Really?" I answered. "Why is that?"

"Turns out your boyfriend walked off the job yesterday. Just up and left. Said he'd be back, but he had something he had to do first."

"He's not my boyfriend," I said.

"You're having his baby, aren't you?"

"Don't talk about that!" I shot a nervous glance over my shoulder. It wasn't as if Rafe had any way of being able to hear me, let alone hear Grimaldi—he was twenty feet away, talking to David—but just the fact that it was said out loud when he was anywhere in the vicinity was enough to throw me into a tizzy.

"Ah," Grimaldi said, sounding satisfied, "so he *is* with you."

"Of course he is. You called him, didn't you? You must have known he'd drop everything and head for Nashville."

She made a noise of assent. "So he's there, but you haven't talked about it yet?"

"We've had other things to do."

"I can just imagine."

I flushed. "Not that. How can you even joke about that, at a time like this?"

Her voice changed, turned serious. "You two looking for David Flannery?"

"We've already found him."

"Where are you?"

I told her we were in Sweetwater.

"He made it all the way there?" She sounded impressed.

"He made it to Damascus first, to Elspeth's house. He ate dinner there. Then he made it here, to the Bog. I think he may have borrowed Elspeth's bicycle for the last bit of the trip."

"Resourceful kid," Grimaldi said, and then seemed to think better of it. "Wait a second. He's there? Where three people were shot two months ago?"

"I found him standing in Rafe's room looking at the blood," I said. "And I know it's supposed to be a secret that Rafe's still alive, but I couldn't lie to him. Not then. He had to know that at least his biological father survived. It looks like a small massacre took place in there."

Grimaldi took the news in stride. "I doubt the Flannerys move in circles where Mr. Collier's survival will be big news."

I wouldn't be too sure about that, but obviously not for the reason she thought.

"We'll drive David home," I said. "We'll probably leave here in a couple of minutes, and it'll take us the best part of an hour and a half to get back to Nashville, with morning rush hour coming on. Would you call and tell his parents he's OK? I'd rather not do it myself."

"Gonna spring Mr. Collier on them without warning?" Tamara Grimaldi asked.

"I think it's better than telling them I lied before. If they knew their son was bonding with his biological father right now, it'd only make them worry."

"That's true. Sure, I'll call them."

I thanked her. "By the way, I forgot about it in the excitement of David disappearing, but I spoke to the waitress at Sara Beth's Café yesterday, and she said Sheila was on her way to a doctor's appointment when she was there on Friday. With an obstetrician. Someone who delivers babies."

"I know what an obstetrician is, Ms. Martin," Detective Grimaldi said. "Did your new best friend happen to catch the name of the obstetrician, as well?"

"She didn't. But there are only a handful of them within ten or fifteen minutes of Sara Beth's. Almost half are together at St. Jerome's Hospital. Which also happens to be where David Flannery was born." I explained the situation with the lack of adoption papers and the fact that Sam and Virginia Flannery were listed on his birth certificate as David's parents when they had admitted to adopting him.

"That's interesting," Grimaldi said. "I'll look into that."

"I'd appreciate it. Thank you."

"So you're pretty sure he's Mr. Collier's son, I take it?"

"It'll take DNA to prove it," I said, "but yes. You should see them. They look so much alike it's uncanny."

"Maybe I'll drive out to the Flannerys myself, just to have a look. And to make sure everything's all right. There might be some fireworks when the parents realize their son's father isn't dead after all."

"We'll see you there," I said, and hung up.

I ENDED UP IN THE BACKSEAT on the way back to Nashville. Rafe drove and David took the passenger seat, while I curled up in the back. I missed most of their conversation, just caught bits and pieces every once in a while as I drifted in and out of sleep. Rafe had woken me up at an ungodly early hour, and with what was going on inside me, I needed lots of extra sleep anyway. It's not easy, creating a newborn from scratch.

When we pulled up outside the house on Pennywell, both Ginny and Sam were in the driveway waiting for us. So was Tamara Grimaldi, next to her unmarked SUV. And when the Volvo stopped and David opened his door and got out, his parents both converged on him. Or rather, they started forward and then stopped, perhaps fearful of overwhelming him. For a moment, all three of them stood there, just staring at one another, before David took a step forward. It broke the ice, and Virginia and Sam both fell on him, laughing and crying, touching and patting and making sure he was all right.

I opened the door on my side and climbed out. Rafe did the same, and Tamara Grimaldi wandered over to join us. All three of us stood in silence and watched the reunion. After a minute, the Flannerys moved, as one intertwined, three-headed, six-legged creature, toward their front door.

They were halfway there when Sam broke away and turned back. Ginny and David hesitated, and David stopped to look over his shoulder. His gaze locked with Rafe's for a second, and I could feel the connection between them crackle. Then Ginny tugged on David, and he turned back to his mother.

Sam stopped in front of us. "Thank you." His voice and face were sincere. The remark may have been addressed to both of us, but he looked at Rafe, and when he stuck his hand out, it was Rafe he intended it for. It was obvious he'd figured out who Rafe was; the expression in his eyes when he looked at Rafe—this grown-up version of his son—was half awed, half nervous.

Rafe hesitated for a second before taking the proffered hand. "Thank *you*," he said, and I'm sure Sam caught the implication, just as Rafe had obviously caught Sam's. There were a lot of layers to this conversation. Sam nodded once before he turned to follow his wife and child inside the house.

After two steps, he turned back to me. "Thank you for your help, Savannah. We'll call you, OK?"

"OK," I said.

The door closed with a firm click, a sort of final statement, shutting us out of their lives, at least for the time being. I snuck a peek at Rafe. He was watching the closed door, his face impassive, but his eyes simmering with a mixture of emotions I wasn't sure I could name. Anger? Regret? Sadness? Loss?

"Thanks for bringing him back," Tamara Grimaldi broke the silence.

I turned to her. Rafe did too, and after a second his lips curved in amusement. "Afraid I'd take him and run?"

Grimaldi shrugged, a little sheepishly. "The thought crossed my mind."

The smile turned into a grin. "Mine too. But I ain't that stupid. I wouldn't get far before some cop pulled me over and hauled my ass back to jail."

"They wouldn't," I said. "He's your son."

"Parents get convicted of kidnapping their own children all the time," Tamara Grimaldi informed me, and Rafe added, "You don't know that, darlin'."

He was right, I didn't. Not officially. It would take DNA to prove it. But I knew. We all did. Including Ginny and Sam. With the resemblance between them, Rafe couldn't have denied David if he'd wanted to. Hopefully, after this, the Flannerys wouldn't refuse them the opportunity to get to know one another. The relationship would probably end up being more big brother/little brother than father and son, but at least Rafe would learn to know the child he never knew he had.

"So where are you two off to now?" Grimaldi asked, sharing a look between us.

I glanced at Rafe. When he didn't immediately say he had to hit the road to get back to Atlanta, I said, "I need food soon, or I'm going to pass out."

"Breakfast at the Pancake Pantry? My treat." Grimaldi smiled.

I waited for Rafe to object. When he didn't, I said, "Sounds great."

"I'll meet you there." She headed for her car. I walked around mine to the passenger seat, leaving Rafe to get back behind the wheel.

He was quiet on the drive to the restaurant in Hillsboro Village, and mostly quiet during the meal itself. If he noticed me eating like I hadn't seen food for days, he didn't comment. Grimaldi didn't either, although she arched her brows at me. I shrugged. There was nothing I could do about it. The tiny life inside me was insistent on being fed, a lot.

We couldn't talk about what Rafe was up to in Atlanta—TBI undercover investigations need to be kept undercover until they're completed—and I didn't want to talk about David Flannery or—God forbid—my pregnancy, so we ended up talking about Sheila and what was going on in Detective Grimaldi's investigation instead. It was perhaps strange conversation for a meal—at least the waitress seemed to think so; when the words 'the last murder I was hired to do' passed Rafe's lips, she even stopped making eyes at him—but my life had become about a lot of strange things, I reflected. A year ago, you wouldn't have found me sharing breakfast with a homicide detective and a convicted criminal, discussing a current murder case. All in all, I thought I liked my life better now, even if it wasn't the sort of life I'd ever thought I'd have.

"You haven't done any murders," I said in response to Rafe's statement.

He shot me a look. "How d'you know? Ain't more than a couple hours since you asked me if I'd helped my mama kill her daddy."

Tamara Grimaldi arched her brows.

"You said you hadn't. And if you didn't kill Old Jim, and you didn't kill Billy Scruggs," the man he'd gone to jail for beating up, "I don't think you'd kill anyone else."

"You think those two are the biggest bastards I've come up against in my life, darlin'?" His smile was amused.

"No," I said; he had, after all, come up against Perry Fortunato and Jorge Pena, both of them bigger bastards. Or in Perry's case, at least crazier. Jorge was just your average, run-of-the-mill hired killer. "But I think you can control yourself better now. You're not twelve anymore. Or even eighteen. And besides, you told me you've never killed anyone other than in self defense." Or defense of me.

Rafe shrugged. "To get back to what I was saying: the last murder I was hired to do was killing a pregnant woman. She'd slept with the wrong guy, one who had a wife, and the wife wanted to get rid of the girlfriend before the husband got any ideas of leaving. Seemed there was a bit of money at stake."

"Oh my God," I said, putting my fork down with a clatter, "what did you do?"

He glanced over. "I didn't kill her."

"Of course not. I didn't think you had."

"The TBI told her what was going on. I went to the apartment and fired a shot into the wall. Then I left again. The ambulance showed up and took her away, with a sheet covering her face. They drove her to the hospital, where she was declared DOA—"

"Dead on arrival," Grimaldi translated. She had put down her fork too, and was listening with her chin in her hand and an interested look on her face.

"—she was moved to the hospital morgue, where they put a toe tag with her name on the toe of a Jane Doe, and our girl left through the back door to a safe-house in another part of town. The TBI is putting together evidence to charge the wife with murder for hire."

"Sounds like you're having fun," Grimaldi said with a grin, one Rafe returned.

"It has its moments."

"I told you earlier," I said, "Sheila wasn't cheating on Dix."

Grimaldi looked taken aback, and I turned to her. "Rafe suggested it. That she slept with the wrong guy and he killed her when she got pregnant. He suggested it might be Todd Satterfield. Or maybe you think Dix did it?"

Rafe shrugged. "It happens."

"I know it does," I said, "but not in my family. My brother didn't kill anyone. Nor did Todd. Much as you might wish him to."

"A man can hope," Rafe said.

"So what are you two planning to do next?" Grimaldi wanted to know, sharing a look between us. She was sitting on one side of the booth, Rafe and I side by side on the other. Every once in a while his thigh would touch mine under the table, and heat would curl through my stomach, even though I wasn't sure he was even aware of doing it.

I'd always been hyper-aware of Rafe physically, long before I admitted to anyone, even myself, that I was attracted to him, and now I felt like the entire side of my body was prickling.

I said, "I'm sure we'll come up with something."

Rafe's mouth curved in amusement, but he didn't speak.

"No doubt," Grimaldi said dryly and went to pay the bill.

"When do you have to go back?" I asked when we were in the car, with him behind the wheel once more, and me in the passenger seat. I'd waited long enough for him to volunteer the information, and he hadn't, so I thought I might as well ask. At this point, I was beyond worrying about his figuring out that I liked him. I was pretty sure he already knew that.

His mouth curved. "Something you wanted to do, darlin'?"

I nodded. "There's a hospital in Brentwood I'd like to visit."

This obviously wasn't the answer he'd been expecting. "Hospital?"

"It's where David was born. It's listed on his birth certificate. And I think it may have been where Sheila went the day she died."

"You think it has something to do with what happened to her?"

"I have no idea," I said, "but it's interesting."

"Did Sheila know anything about David?"

"Not that I know. Dix might have mentioned something to her, although it's not like she'd be particularly interested if he did. She didn't know you or Elspeth."

He nodded. "What're you gonna tell 'em when we get there?"

"I'll come up with a story," I said.

"No offense, darlin', but you're not a good liar."

"Maybe I'll surprise you. I've been practicing."

"Yeah? What's it you been lying about?"

"You," I said. "Mostly."

He glanced at me. "Me?"

"Everyone thinks you're dead. My family, my friends. And I can't tell them you're not."

"Been talking about me a lot, have you?"

You have no idea, I thought, but I didn't say it. "It was hard to avoid. For a while, everyone in Sweetwater was talking about what happened."

He nodded. "Satterfield propose again?"

"Only a few times." Four or five. Maybe six.

"You say yes yet?"

I shook my head.

"Why not?"

It would have been the perfect time to say, "Because I'm pregnant, and it's your baby."

I didn't. "Not ready," I said instead.

He grinned. "Having too much fun playing the field?"

Hardly. "I just don't know if I want to marry Todd. I know I should, but..."

"But?"

"But I can't. At least not yet."

He nodded.

"So what about you? Have you been playing the field in Atlanta?"

"I've been working," Rafe said. "Ain't many opportunities to meet women when you're dealing with the dregs of humanity."

"No hookers with hearts of gold?"

"Plenty of hookers. No hearts of gold. These people'd kill their grandmother for the gold in her teeth." He shook his head. "No, darlin'. No hookers. Nobody else, neither. I've been good."

"Right," I said. I'd believe that when I saw it, and not a moment before.

St. Jerome's Hospital turned out to be just a few miles from Sara Beth's Café, tucked away amongst two or three upscale motels on the quiet back side of a little hill. It looked like a friendly enough place: a big brick building, three stories, that reminded me a little of St. Bernard Academy. Perhaps a lot of these religious buildings had the same architect way back when.

The lobby was sunny and bright, and the freckled redhead behind the information desk greeted us with a friendly smile when we walked in. "Can I help you folks?"

"Please." I put a hand on my stomach. "I'm looking for a doctor. A certain doctor. My sister-in-law recommended him—" three quarters of the staff at St. Jerome's were male, so chances were good that whoever Sheila had come to see, if she'd come to see anyone at all, was a man, "—but I can't remember the name. Someone who specializes in difficult pregnancies?"

The nurse, whose nametag identified her as Molly Murphy, looked sympathetic. "How far along are you, sweetie?"

"Just over two months," I said, truthfully. "I lost a baby around two months once before, and I'm a little worried."

"Any pain?"

"Oh, no. No, everything's perfectly normal. And I'd like to keep it that way. I just wanted to see if I could set up an appointment. For later. In a few days or a week, maybe. Whenever the doctor has time in his schedule."

Molly nodded. "But you can't remember the doctor's name? Can you ask your sister-in-law again?"

"I thought maybe you could look it up. You know, if you have a log. Or an automated system. Here." I dug in my purse and pulled out the photograph of Dix and his family. "This is her. Sheila Martin."

I handed it over the counter. Molly took it and turned it over—the inscription read, *To Savannah, Merry Christmas and Happy New Year, Sheila, Dix, Abigail and Hannah.*

"You're Savannah?" she asked.

I nodded. "Savannah Martin. That's my brother." I pointed. Just like last time, my resemblance to Dix seemed to do the job.

"I remember her," Molly said. "She was here just a few days ago, wasn't she?"

"She might have been."

"She had an appointment with Dr. Rushing. I think it was Friday. And you're right; Dr. Rushing does specialize in difficult pregnancies. In fact—" she looked up as the doors from the outside opened again, with a hiss, "here he is now."

I swung on my heel. Next to me, Rafe did the same. So far he hadn't said a word; I guess maybe my suddenly amazing facility for lying had completely bowled him over. Little did he know I hadn't said anything yet that wasn't a hundred percent true.

Through the door came a scrawny scarecrow of a man: as tall as Rafe, about fifty pounds lighter, and thirty years older. He had a ring of white hair around the back of his head and none at all on top, where the bright lights reflected off his pate like sunlight off a pond. A shiny suit hung from his shoulders as if suspended from a hanger, and a pair of scuffed shoes, perforated brown, stuck out below.

"That's Dr. Rushing?"

Molly Murphy beamed. "That's him. Dr. Rushing!"

The doctor blinked myopically in our direction. "Good morning. Need help?"

"New patient for you, Dr. Rushing!" Molly sang. "This is Savannah Martin and her husband...?" She turned to Rafe, expectantly.

He shook his head. "We ain't married."

Molly looked disapproving. There was a fat gold band on her left hand, as well as a pretty little crucifix on a chain around her neck. "But you *are* the father of the baby?"

Rafe glanced at me. "Of course," I said.

"A pleasure to meet you, Miss Martin." Dr. Rushing clasped my hand in his. "Come along, dear. Back to my office. We'll have a chat." He towed me past the counter and through the lobby, down a hallway toward the back of the building. I glanced over my shoulder at Rafe, who arched his brows at me from where he followed along behind, hands in his pockets.

Dr. Rushing's office was on the right, a friendly little room with yellow walls and light pine furniture. A big cork-board on one wall was covered with photographs of happy parents with beautiful children, inscribed with thanks and good wishes from people Dr. Rushing had helped. Rafe wandered over to it.

I had something more immediate on my mind. I looked around for an examining table, and I was happy to see there wasn't one in the room. It would have been awkward if the doctor had insisted on examining me, and had announced that I was pregnant. It would have cemented my bona fides in his eyes, certainly, but it might have shocked Rafe, and this definitely wasn't the way I wanted him to hear the news.

"Have a seat." Dr. Rushing gestured to two chairs in front of the desk. "You too, young man." He waved Rafe over.

It was like being back in school, and being brought to the principal's office. Not that that had ever happened to me. It had happened to Rafe plenty, which may be why he looked so comfortable with ignoring the request.

"So you're pregnant," Dr. Rushing said as he seated himself behind the desk. I nodded. "How far along?"

I told him weeks and days. "I had a miscarriage once before. When I was married to my ex-husband."

"You're divorced?"

I nodded.

"And this is not your husband?" He glanced at Rafe.

"No," I said.

"In that case I'm afraid we won't be able to help you, young lady. I'm sorry, but this facility has very strict rules about morality."

Rafe opened his mouth, and I made sure to get in before him. "Always?"

"Excuse me?" Dr. Rushing said.

"I had a girlfriend who got pregnant while she was still in high school. Obviously she wasn't married. And I think she had her baby here. Elspeth Caulfield?"

Dr. Rushing blinked. "I'm sorry," he said, "I'm afraid I don't know your friend."

"I understand. It's a long time ago, after all. Almost twelve years." I smiled sweetly. "How about the Flannerys? Virginia and Sam? Their son David was born here."

Dr. Rushing shook his head. "I'm afraid not. And now, if you don't mind, I'm afraid I'll have to ask you to leave. My next appointment will be arriving in a few minutes."

"Of course." I got to my feet. "I'm sorry to have wasted your time, Doctor. I'm sure I can find someone who specializes in difficult pregnancies somewhere else. I'll just have to tell Dr. Seaver it didn't work out."

"Who?"

"Dr. Denise Seaver. In Columbia? She recommends you highly. In fact, I'm pretty sure she was the one who sent Elspeth here twelve years ago. Although if you don't remember her, she probably saw someone else." I flashed another sweet smile. "Have a nice day, Doctor. Thank you for you time."

I headed for the door. Rafe followed, with a polite nod. We closed the office door gently behind us and headed for the outside.

Fourteen

"Not bad," Rafe said appreciatively when we were back in the car and on our way to East Nashville.

"Excuse me?"

He grinned. "I woulda believed every word of that."

"Oh." It was another perfect opportunity to say, "That's because I wasn't lying." I thought about saying it. I even got as far as to open my mouth. But I didn't want to give him the news in the car, I wanted him somewhere where I could actually see his face when I told him I was expecting his baby, and anyway, before I could speak, he'd continued.

"He had a picture of David on his wall."

"He did?"

"From a couple years ago," Rafe confirmed. "With his folks. Looked like he was seven or eight, maybe."

The doctor must be on the Flannerys' Christmas card list. And he'd definitely lied about knowing them. Or if he hadn't precisely lied, he'd been evasive.

I pulled out my phone.

"Who're you calling?" Rafe asked with a sideways glance.

"A woman in Sweetwater. Dr. Denise Seaver. She was Elspeth's gynecologist back when Elspeth was pregnant. Mine too, for that matter." I waited for her voice. "Dr. Seaver? It's Savannah Martin."

"Hello, Savannah," the doctor said. "What can I do for you? Have you made a decision?"

"Actually, I have. But that's not what I'm calling about." Not with Rafe next to me in the car.

"No?"

"I just visited Dr. Rushing. At St. Jerome's?"

"I see," Dr. Seaver said, her voice wary.

"That's where Sheila was on Friday afternoon. Before she died."

"Are you sure?"

"The desk nurse confirmed it. Did your recommend she go there?"

"I might have mentioned the option," Dr. Seaver said. "Emil Rushing is the best doctor in Nashville for difficult pregnancies."

"Did Elspeth Caulfield have a difficult pregnancy, too? You sent Elspeth there to have her baby, didn't you? Her parents were religious, and they didn't want anyone to know she was pregnant, that's why they took her out of school when she started showing. They probably home-schooled her for a year. And they took her to St. Jerome's to have the baby..."

Dr. Seaver didn't confirm it. But she didn't deny it either, which gave me impetus to go on.

"Dr. Rushing has a picture of David Flannery on his wall. David's birth certificate says he was born at St. Jerome's. But Ginny Flannery didn't give birth to him. I think Elspeth did, and then Dr. Rushing must have given him to the Flannerys. The hospital took care of the birth certificate. Ginny said so. The records probably show that Elspeth's baby was stillborn, just as they told you. And then they made it look like Ginny gave birth to David herself."

"This is all very interesting," Dr. Seaver said politely, "but if you're going to accuse a great man like Dr. Rushing of unbusinesslike conduct, I think you'll need a little more than this, Savannah. Elspeth was underage when she gave birth. Her parents must have signed the adoption papers. There is nothing illegal about it."

"Rafe was eighteen," I said. "And he didn't sign anything."

"Rafe Collier is dead, Savannah," Dr. Seaver reminded me. I shot a glance to my left, where Rafe, very much alive, was maneuvering the car up along I-65 toward home. "There's no one left who cares what happened twelve years ago. If you think about it, telling Elspeth that her baby was stillborn was a kindness. And David is better off now than he would have been with either of his biological parents."

She hung up without saying goodbye.

It galled me to know that she was right. Rafe hadn't been in a position to take care of David, and where Elspeth might have been slightly less kooky had she been able to keep her baby, she had already been weirdly obsessed with Rafe by the time David was born. She probably wouldn't have been the most nurturing mother in the world, either. But Ginny and Sam loved David to pieces, and had given him the kind of life he wouldn't have had with either of his natural parents.

"I think I upset her," I said, looking at the phone.

"She hang up on you?"

I nodded. "She told me that because you and Elspeth are both dead—supposedly—there's no one left who cares what happened twelve years ago. And I still don't really understand why Sheila would. She's never seen David, so it isn't like she'd recognize his picture, and she didn't know you or Elspeth, right?"

Rafe didn't answer, and for a second, an unworthy, slightly crazy thought invaded my mind. I nudged him. "Rafe. Right?"

"What?"

"She didn't know you, right? You're not saying that she slept with someone other than Dix because she slept with you, and the job you took was to come to Nashville and kill her?"

"You've lost your mind," Rafe said.

"It makes perfect sense." In fact, it explained everything.

"Only to someone who ain't thinking straight," Rafe said. "No, darlin'. I've never even spoken to your sister-in-law, much less touched her. Why'd I want her when I can have you?"

I had no idea, but it was obviously the right thing to say, because I could feel myself melt down to a puddle of goo.

"You didn't answer my question earlier," I said.

"What question's that?"

"When you have to go back. You left in the middle of an investigation, right? How long before Wendell comes beating down my door to drag you back to Atlanta to finish the job?"

"Something you wanna do, darlin'?"

"Earlier, you said when I was feeling better, you'd make it up to me."

"You feeling better now?"

"Much better," I said demurely.

"Then I've got all the time you want." He shot me a hot grin that made my toes curl, and stepped on the gas. "No sense in wasting any of it, though."

No sense at all, I thought.

WE MANAGED TO PARK THE CAR and get up the stairs and through the door to my apartment without scandalizing the neighbors, but no sooner had the door shut behind us, than I had my back against the wall and Rafe against my front, with his lips on mine and my hands buried in his hair holding him in place. He locked the door with one hand while the other was already busy working its way under my jacket and sweater.

"Kitchen?" he murmured against my throat a little later.

"What?"

"I promised you next time we'd do it on the kitchen counter."

I puffed out a breath of laughter. He had, too. Two months ago, in Mrs. Jenkins's house. The first time we made love it had almost happened on the kitchen table, and then it had almost happened in the hallway on our way upstairs. We'd made it up to bed, but he'd warned me that next time we'd just use the kitchen counter to avoid the wait.

The kitchen counter where my abortion pill lay.

"The bed's more comfortable. And not far away." I tugged him in the direction of the bedroom.

"You sure?" He glanced into the small kitchen alcove on our way past.

"Positive. There's not much room in there. Come on."

We were into the living room now, and I pushed the leather jacket off his shoulders and tossed it on the sofa on our way past. The green Henley was soft and warm under my hands, but neither as soft nor as warm as the skin underneath. When I skimmed my hands up over the muscles in his stomach and chest, I could feel him tense under my hands. For a few seconds, it sounded like he stopped breathing.

The Henley ended up on the floor of the bedroom, before the backs of my knees hit the foot of the bed. I fell over backwards, and Rafe leaned over me, hands braced on either side of my ribs. "You sure about this, darlin'?"

I looked up at him, into those dark eyes, hot with passion and promises.

Oh yes, I was sure. All the worry of the past two months melted as if it had never been. When I was with him, there was nowhere else I wanted to be. When he was here, he was all that mattered. The rest of the world disappeared. I'd brave any amount of disapproval and anger from my mother and Todd, any number of stares and whispers from strangers, for this. And because I was afraid he'd see it all in my eyes— see just how desperately I loved him at that moment—I looked away, down to his shoulder, where a small, puckered scar was still faintly pink. A chilling reminder of a bullet from Jorge Pena's gun.

I reached out and smoothed a hand over it.

"I thought you died," fell out of my mouth. A statement that said a whole lot more than I'd intended to admit, had he been listening.

"You ain't getting rid of me that easy, darlin'." He grinned.

I smiled back, and skimmed both hands up to his shoulders and around his neck to pull him down on top of me.

"I'M HUNGRY," I SAID FOUR hours later.

After we exhausted ourselves the first time, I'd fallen asleep. So had he, worn out from no sleep last night and quite a lot of strenuous activity this morning. I'd woken up a couple hours later to the feeling of a hand on my skin, moving steadily south, and soon we were busy again. After two months of missing him, I found I'd lost rather a lot of my inhibitions, and it was quite a while before we came up for air.

Now we were in bed, still tangled together under the comforter, and it was way past lunchtime. My stomach felt hollow and achy.

Rafe grinned lecherously. "I can fix that."

"You're horrible." But I couldn't keep back a smile, even as I blushed. "After all that, you think I still want more?"

"I always want more," Rafe said simply. "If I didn't have to go back to Atlanta, I could spend a couple days right here in this bed." He stretched, his leg sliding against mine, and the crisp hairs on his calves rubbed against my skin.

"Do you have to leave right now?"

"Soon. I wanna be back there by tonight." He tossed off the blankets and got out of bed. I watched as he padded toward the door: naked, gorgeous, and totally comfortable with himself, all smooth golden skin and hard muscles. "But first, I'm gonna see what I can find to eat. Gotta keep my strength up." He winked at me over his shoulder before slipping through the door into the living room. I snuggled back down under the blankets, smiling.

It was just a minute or two before he came back. I opened my eyes when something hit the bed a few inches from my face.

"Better take that as soon as possible," Rafe said.

There was something wrong with his voice, and when I opened my eyes, I saw that there was something wrong with the rest of him, too. He was getting dressed, for one thing. He'd already pulled the Henley over his head, and was in the process of fastening his jeans. And his eyes were hard, and his mouth tight, and when he looked at me, it was without any of the heat or desire from earlier.

"What's wrong?" I asked, my heart starting to beat faster.

"What makes you think something's wrong, darlin'?" He finished zipping up the jeans and started pulling on his boots.

"I thought you didn't have to go yet."

I sat up, clutching the blankets to myself. The expression in his eyes made me feel like I was something slimy that had crawled out from under a rock, and all I wanted to do was to cover myself. That judgment in his eyes hurt, especially after the way he'd been looking at me earlier, like I was beautiful and precious and worthy of being worshiped.

As I snugged the blankets closer to my body, something rustled, and I looked down at the thing he'd tossed on the bed earlier. I felt all the blood leave my face when I recognized the wrapping on the abortion pill from the kitchen counter.

"You don't wanna wait too long before you take that," Rafe said. "We don't want no little accidents."

We didn't?

"Nice girl like you can't be having babies with somebody like me."

"I told you before," I said, "I'm not that nice."

He nodded. "Yeah, I got that. Loud and clear."

"No..." That wasn't what I'd meant.

But how could I blame him, really? He must think I'd bought the pill to take after sleeping with him, to make sure I wouldn't get pregnant. The morning-after pill. Have your cake and eat it too. All the fun and none of the consequences.

And from where he was standing, it made perfect sense. In his position, I'd probably believe the same thing.

"It's not what you think..." I tried.

"Sure." He nodded. "No worries, darlin'. I get it. Fun and games. Last fling before you marry Satterfield and become that woman you told me about, who spent two years faking orgasms for her ex-husband."

Both boots were on now, and he was facing me, hands curled at his sides and his eyes simmering with something other than desire. Right now, I could see what other people saw in him: that edge of danger, of violence, lurking just underneath the surface. He looked like he was ready to put his fist through the nearest wall.

"I'm sure glad I was able to help you get over that little hang-up, darlin'. Wouldn't want another husband of yours to be unsatisfied in bed because his wife was frigid."

"You don't understand," I said.

"I understand just fine, darlin'. You said it from the start. That night you came to me after Satterfield proposed? I asked if I could look forward to you thinking about me every time you needed to fake another orgasm."

And I hadn't answered because the idea had been so shocking. And, I suspected, true.

He added, "Don't worry about it. Ain't like I'm all that eager to get fitted for a ball and chain myself, you know."

"I'm sure." He'd certainly never led me to believe that he was interested in anything more than just the occasional roll in the hay. I was frankly surprised he was back for more. I'd thought I might not see him again after the first time.

"I'm just gonna head out now. Maybe I'll stop by next time I'm in town, see if your legs are still open. If you ain't married by then."

He turned on his heel and walked away.

"Rafe," I called after him. "Wait a second. Rafe!"

The only answer was the sound of the front door slamming shut.

It took me a second to get over the shock. Had he really just walked out on me?

And then it took another few seconds to get out of bed and throw a dress over my head. I ran out in the hallway and down the stairs, half hoping he'd already come to his senses and was on his way back, but by the time I got downstairs, there was no sign of him. From down the street I could hear the sound of an engine, a deep angry growl, catching and then fading into the distance.

I cried myself to sleep. By the time I woke up again, it was turning dark outside, and the lighted display on the alarm clock on top of the bureau told me it was going on for seven.

The first thing I noticed was that I was in pain.

Not the pain from earlier, like a dull ache in my chest and my head from too many tears. This was physical pain. Sharp pain, stabbing through my body, causing me to curl up on my side and moan. The bed was wet, warm and sort of sticky.

It had been warm and sticky before too, but those stains had dried while I slept. I could feel them, sort of hard and a little scratchy. This was different.

Another stronger wave of pain knifed through me, along with a ripple of panic, and I scrambled out of bed, waiting for the expected surge of nausea that always came with getting up, and instead found myself bent double, supporting myself on the night table until the pain passed. Something wet trickled down the inside of my leg. When I raised a shaking hand to turn on the light on the bedside table, it took three tries to find the switch. In the soft amber glow of the lamp, the splotches of bright blood glistened wetly against the white cotton sheets.

"No!"

I knew what was happening. It had happened before, and I recognized the symptoms. But this time it wouldn't happen without a fight. Losing Bradley's baby had been one thing. Losing Rafe's was something totally different. After all the agonizing I'd done over this pregnancy, after all the back and forth and the anguish I'd felt before finally making a decision, there was no way I'd allow fate to take my baby without fighting tooth and nail to keep it.

I staggered over to where I'd dropped my dress earlier, and pulled it over my head. It covered the worst of the bloodstains, and it was the best I could do. I had made it into the bathroom and was on my hands and knees with my head under the sink looking for a pad I could use to contain some of the bleeding when there was a knock on the door.

"Savannah!"

Abandoning the bathroom and the pad, I headed for the door, supporting myself on walls and furniture as I went, staggering through the living room and down the hallway to the front door.

It took another few tries to get the lock turned and the chain unhooked. When I pulled the door toward me, I had to hold on to the knob to keep on my feet. Rafe opened his mouth, took one look at me, and turned pale, or as pale as I'd ever seen him. "What happened?"

I didn't have enough breath to spare to answer, so I hiked my skirt up high enough for him to see the blood. He turned a shade paler. "Fuck!"

"Doctor," I managed.

"Right. Sure." He swung me up in his arms. I was no feather to begin with, and I'd gained another five pounds since I'd gotten pregnant, but he had no problems carrying me down the hallway to the stairs and down the stairs and across the courtyard outside. When we reached the Volvo, he put me down for a second to open the door. I clung to him for support, and crawled into the seat as soon as the door was open. He closed it behind me and slid across the hood of the car to get to the driver's side door faster.

The nearest hospital to my apartment is Skyline Medical Center. On a good day, with normal traffic, it's possible to get from one to the other in about thirteen minutes. Rafe made it in eight. We wove in and out of traffic on Ellington Parkway like it was the Indy 500, back and forth between the three lanes, laying on the horn whenever someone didn't get out of the way fast enough. Rafe didn't slow down for exit ramps, other cars, or anything else. We were lucky there were no accidents in our wake. When we pulled up behind the hospital, outside the entrance to the emergency room, he came to a dead stop with a squeal of brakes, and was out of the car and around to my side before I'd gotten myself together from being flung forward against the seatbelt.

"C'mon." He scooped me up again and carried me through the automatic doors into the lobby. "I need a doctor!"

The next little bit was a blur, between the pain and the hustle of nurses and doctors. Rafe was left behind in the lobby, and the last thing I saw before they wheeled me into the ER itself, was him falling into a seat and leaning forward, burying his face in his hands. They were streaked with blood from lifting and carrying me, and I wanted to tell him to go wash, but I didn't have enough breath.

"Who's your next of kin?" a young black nurse with braided hair asked me. "Him?" She tossed her head in the direction of the lobby, and the beads on the bottom of the braids jangled together.

I shook my head. "My mother."

"You want I should call her?"

God, no. Having my mother show up for this was the last thing I wanted.

"We have to call someone," the nurse said.

I thought about asking her to call Dix, but then I realized that Dix had his hands full with Abigail and Hannah. "Fine. Call my mother." I managed to recite the number.

Things went a little blurry again after that. I ended up in a bed in a room with heavy shades on the windows. Someone did an ultrasound and someone else drew blood. The verdict of both tests was that my tiny blueberry had died, and now my body was in the process of getting rid of it. What they had to do now, the nurse explained to me, was give me medicine to reduce the bleeding since there was too much of it, as well as something for the pain, since I thought there was too much of that as well.

"There's nothing you can do to save my baby?"

She looked sympathetic. "It's already too late, hon. The baby died a day or two ago. By the time the bleeding starts, it's much too late to change anything."

She patted my hand and bustled off. I buried my head in the pillow and had another good cry. Until the pain medicine made me woozy and I nodded off again.

At some point they sent Rafe in to see me, because I opened my eyes and there he was, sitting in a chair next to the bed, with his head bent and two fingers pinching the bridge of his nose as if his head hurt.

I didn't know how much time had elapsed, but it was a good bet it was at least an hour or two since we got to the hospital, and a couple of hours before that, that he walked out of my apartment. For all I knew, it might be the middle of the night. When I saw him, my eyes filled up again with tears. "You're still here," I managed.

He looked up. "D'you think I'd leave you? Alone?"

I swallowed. "I wasn't sure what to think." He'd walked out once, and it wasn't that hard to imagine him doing it again. And besides, he'd told me he wanted to get back to Atlanta tonight.

"They wouldn't tell me nothing. Just that the danger was over and you'd be OK." He drove a hand through his hair in frustration. "I asked if this was normal after taking one of those pills, and they said no."

"I didn't take the pill," I whispered. "I wanted this baby."

I could see the question in his eyes, but he didn't ask. "If you didn't take the pill, what was all that bleeding from?" He sounded like it was the first time he'd been faced with blood, when I knew very well it wasn't.

I smiled weakly. "Surely you've seen blood before. After Brenda Puckett, and Perry Fortunato, and Elspeth, and Jorge…"

"That was someone else's blood. This was yours." His voice was flat. I felt a shiver of something frightening in the pit of my stomach. Although, with everything else that was going on down there, it might just have been the medication. Or the miscarriage. "What happened? Was it something I did?"

I could see fear in his eyes. It was the first time I'd ever seen him show even a hint of fear. I'd seen him face death, people with guns, people sent to kill him, but I'd never seen him look afraid. Not until now.

"Nothing happened," I said. "Nobody did anything. It wasn't the sex. It just happened. I'm prone to it, I guess."

It was a horrifying thought. I hadn't realized, until I lost it, just how much I wanted this baby. My eyes filled again.

"Prone to what? Stomach ulcers? Gallstones? PMS?"

I drew a breath, willing the tears away. "I had a miscarriage."

He stared at me, blankly, and I added, "I was pregnant, but now I'm not. I lost the baby."

Rafe's eyes widened, and he stared down at his hands. They were perfectly clean, although they'd been streaked with blood earlier, and I guess maybe the thought was enough. I reached out, with some effort, and covered one of his hands with mine, but before either of us could speak, the door opened.

"Savannah, darling!" My mother came rushing in, and then was brought up short when she saw Rafe. "Oh!"

I took my hand back as calmly as I could, although my first inclination had been to snatch it away in hopes that she wouldn't notice.

Rafe, to his credit, got to his feet before greeting her. "Evening, Miz Martin."

Mother nodded, her nostrils pinched as if she had smelled something unpleasant.

Rafe turned to me, "Think I'll go get a beer. Or something stronger. See you later, darlin'."

He sauntered toward the door. Mother jumped out of the way as he got closer, and he nodded politely. "Ma'am."

"Call me," I said to his back.

Mother frowned. Rafe glanced at me over his shoulder, but didn't answer.

"What was that man doing here?" mother demanded, before 'that man' had even closed the door behind him. I had to take a breath before I answered, just so I wouldn't scream at her.

"He brought me to the hospital. He knocked on the door just after I started bleeding."

"I thought he was dead," mother said, and sounded disappointed that he wasn't.

"You thought wrong. And I don't want you to talk about him that way. He has every right to be here."

Mother looked nonplussed. "What right could he possibly…?" she began, and then lightning seemed to strike. She flushed a painful scarlet, from the silk scarf around her shoulders to her expensively tinted hair. "You mean… you and he…?"

"Whose baby did you think it was?"

Mother fluttered her hands daintily. "I assumed you and Todd had taken the honeymoon early…?"

I shook my head. "The only man I've slept with since I divorced Bradley, is Rafe."

Mother looked stricken. "But darling… I called Todd! He's outside in the lobby!"

Where Rafe was also going. I struggled to sit up. "Oh, God! They're going to kill each other." Todd knew it wasn't his baby, and seeing Rafe would only reinforce that fact. Rafe probably thought the baby was Todd's, or if he didn't think so now, he'd start thinking it when he saw Todd. "I have to get out there!"

"Dixon is there," mother said, pushing me back against the pillows. "He'll take care of it."

Had mother brought the whole family with her? Surely Dix had more important things on his mind at the moment than his sister's messed-up love life. And God only knew what would happen if he got in the middle of a confrontation between Rafe and Todd. Todd had been looking for an opportunity to have at Rafe for a while now, and this was just the excuse he'd been looking for. Dix would certainly not be able to stop him. Either of them. "They'll kill him too! Get me out of here; I have to find them!"

I managed, somehow, to push mother out of my way and stagger into the hallway.

Things were already heating up. Rafe and Todd were squaring off. Todd looked every inch the lawyer, in his charcoal gray suit and with his cold eyes and clipped diction, while Rafe was clearly hot under the collar and spoiling for a chance to hit someone. Anyone. He'd probably prefer to hit Todd, but if Todd didn't oblige, he'd settle for hitting someone else. His hands were curled into fists, and tension radiated from every line in his body. Dix was hovering on the sidelines, seemingly not sure what to do, or whom to interfere with.

Before I could get any closer, the manure hit the fan. Todd said something that must have pushed Rafe over the edge, because the next thing that happened, was that Todd bent double from a jab in the solar plexus, and then crumpled to the floor from an uppercut to the jaw. Rafe snarled something I didn't catch, and brushed past Dix and toward the door.

"Rafe!"

I wasn't able to put much power behind the word, but it was enough. He heard me. And stopped; turned.

If I live to be a hundred, I don't think I'll ever forget the look on his face. Usually, he's almost too adept at hiding his feelings, but this time, for whatever reason, he wasn't so successful.

The anger was obvious, in the tightness of his jaw and the flat blackness of his eyes. But it didn't quite mask the other emotions. There was pain lurking at the back of his eyes, and vulnerability in the curve of his mouth. And bleakness overlaying everything else. Like he felt the same staggering sense of loss that I did.

He looked at me for a moment, but when I didn't say anything else—when I couldn't, because the look on his face had blown every coherent thought out of my head—he turned away. I tried to get my voice to cooperate, but it wouldn't. I tried to reach for him, but it was too late; his back was already turned. I wobbled.

Catherine moved to catch me. I shook her off. Managed a whisper. "Go. Talk to him…"

She looked at me for a second. Glanced at mother. Went.

The others surged around me, cutting Catherine off from view. I tried to crane my neck, to see her—them—but it didn't work. Mother hustled me back into the hospital room again, and back into bed, while Dix and Bob Satterfield set Todd upright and followed. I let them all bustle around trying to make me feel comfortable, because I really was feeling horrible. Doubly horrible now that Rafe had walked out on me a second time. And this time I wasn't sure I could trust him to come back.

Fifteen

I left the hospital the next morning. There was no need to stay and nothing more anyone could do for me. The excessive bleeding had stopped, and horse sized pills were keeping the pain at bay. I had enough for only a few days; after that I guess I was expected to be OK. Physically I thought I probably would be; emotionally I wasn't so sure.

Rafe never came back, and it took all my powers of persuasion to convince Todd not to press charges. In the end I think I succeeded only because Dix told Todd that if he had said to him, Dix, what he'd said to Rafe, Dix would have hit him too.

"What?" I'd asked, looking from one to the other of them. Neither had obliged me. Todd blushed, while Dix simply shook his head, his lips tight. Whatever it was, it must have been bad if he didn't feel he could repeat it in front of mother.

"I thought he was dead," Todd said, bending an accusatory eye on his father. "You said he'd been shot."

"So I was told," the sheriff answered, fixing me with a beady eye. "Young lady?"

Mother's lips tightened, as if she wasn't quite sure I merited the honorific after what she'd just found out about me.

"He did get shot," I said. "And that first day I thought he was dead, too. Dix can tell you. He was the one who gave me the news, and he knows I really believed it."

Dix nodded.

"It wasn't until later that I found out it was something the TBI and the police cooked up to send him back undercover for a while."

"Back?" the sheriff said.

"He's been feeding the TBI information for ten years. Since they arranged for him to be released from prison early."

"I always thought that was suspect," Todd sniffed. "Hard to imagine Rafe Collier getting time off for good behavior."

I ignored him. It seemed safer. Instead I turned to Catherine, who walked back into the room at that point. "Did you catch him?"

She nodded.

"Did you ask him to come back inside?"

She nodded again.

"Well, where is he?"

"He said he'd take your car back to your place and pick up his bike. Then he had to get on the road."

"He's not coming back?"

Catherine shook her head.

"I think," Dix said, with rather admirable restraint, "that he might have preferred to have heard the news from you and not Catherine, sis."

Probably so. "There just hasn't been time. He showed up at the crack of dawn," earlier, actually, "and then we had to rush right out and look for David. You didn't hear about that, did you?" I explained about the phone call from Virginia Flannery I'd received a day ago. "We found him in Sweetwater. He'd already been to Elspeth's house, and when we found him he was asleep in the trailer in the Bog."

"What was he doing in Sweetwater?" Dix wanted to know.

"He wanted to see where he came from. He and Rafe talked for a while, and then we had to take him back to his parents, and Detective Grimaldi was there, so we went to breakfast with her, and then I talked Rafe into coming with me to St. Jerome's Hospital in Brentwood. It's where David was born, and it's also where..."

I stopped before I could blurt out that it was where Sheila had been on Friday afternoon. I wasn't sure Dix had heard about the pregnancy, and I didn't want to be the one to tell him. I thought I'd leave that dubious chore to Grimaldi, who was used to giving people bad news. And besides, thoughts of pregnancies made me cry right now.

"Who's David?" Todd wanted to know.

Dix turned to him. "The boy in the picture we found in Elspeth Caulfield's house. Savannah tracked him down. We're trying to prove that he's Elspeth's son. That way I have someone to give her estate to."

"Is he Collier's son too?" Todd wanted to know, through what sounded like gritted teeth. Dix's voice didn't change its calm cadence.

"We assume so. We won't know anything for sure until the parents agree to let the kid take a DNA test." He turned to me. "Any word on that?"

"They saw Rafe," I said, "and I told David the truth. If they refuse now, it'll be because they won't want to admit it. There's no question that they already know."

"I thought you said you didn't know for sure," Todd objected.

I glanced at him. "You didn't see them together. Dix will need the DNA to prove that David is Elspeth's son, but there's no doubt whatsoever that he's Rafe's. Everyone could see it."

Todd subsided. I turned my attention back to Dix. "Anyway, after the hospital we went back to my apartment, and then we got into an argument, and Rafe walked out and left me there, and by the time he got back I had started bleeding, so we came here. There just wasn't time to tell him."

Although that wasn't quite true and I knew it, even if Dix didn't. I could have told Rafe the truth when his arrival caused me to run to the bathroom. Or after the trip to St. Jerome's, when he complimented me on my dishonesty. I could have stopped the proceedings in my apartment to tell him. A quick warning—"Be gentle; you don't want to hurt the baby,"—would have done the trick. And maybe if I had, this wouldn't have happened. I had asked both the doctors and the nurses, and they'd all told me the sex, no matter how enthusiastic, had had nothing to do with the miscarriage, that the baby had already been dead, but I couldn't shake the guilt. I wondered if maybe Rafe couldn't either.

"He had to go back to Atlanta," I told the nurse when she asked about him the next morning. "I'll be staying with my mother for a couple of days."

It wasn't my choice. I'd rather have gone back to my apartment to lick my wounds in private. If I stayed with mother, she would lecture me on safe sex and prevention and not giving the milk away for free—not that I thought she'd entertain the notion of Rafe actually paying for the proverbial milk. Not the usual way, by marrying me. But the hospital staff had been adamant about my having someone with me. Maybe they were worried that the temptation to end it all would be too much if I didn't have supervision.

They needn't worry. I was distraught, short-tempered, and prone to tears, but I wasn't suicidal. No, I was channeling that other famous Southern Belle, Scarlett O'Hara, and trying to convince myself that tomorrow was another day, and another chance to set things right with Rafe.

Todd and his father had left the previous night. The realization that Rafe was alive, and more, that I had been pregnant with his child, seemed to have brought home the point once and for all that I wasn't likely to marry Todd anytime soon. I guess he probably felt he had no business being there, and I was honestly glad to see him go. I liked him, and I thought it might be nice if we could end up being friends someday, but until he was ready for that, it was easier for both of us if he'd just stay away.

Dix spent the night in my apartment. Abigail and Hannah were settled with Catherine and Jonathan for the night, so he had nothing to get back to, and I could imagine he might prefer to stay at my place rather than face the empty bed at home. When I told him he'd have to change the sheets on my bed, he didn't bat an eye, although mother winced.

Bob Satterfield had offered to drive her back to Sweetwater, and Dix offered to bring me to her in the morning, but she insisted on staying in the hospital with me. I don't know why, because it wasn't as if she attempted a heart to heart or anything. Maybe she just felt maternal because I was upset and in pain.

I was in a wheelchair on my way toward the exit the next morning when my cell phone rang. Of course my first though was that it might be Rafe, so I scrambled to dig the phone out of the depths of my handbag. When I finally had it in my hand, I saw that it wasn't Rafe calling at all, it was Tamara Grimaldi. That, then, gave me something else to worry about.

"Detective?"

"Ms. Martin."

"Is he OK?"

"That depends on which he you're talking about," the detective said grimly.

Cold fear clutched at my heart and made it difficult to talk. "I was talking about Rafe. He rode out of here last night not in a good frame of mind, and he drives like a bat out of hell even under the best of circumstances, which these weren't."

"What happened?" Grimaldi asked.

"He found out about the baby. In the worst possible way."

"What's the worst possible way?"

I swallowed. "I had a miscarriage."

She was silent for a moment. "I'm sorry. You still hadn't told him you were pregnant?"

"It's worse. Remember that pill you saw at my place?"

"Mifepristone," the detective said. "Used for abortions up to nine weeks."

"Also used for the morning after as an emergency contraceptive. He thought I'd bought it to avoid getting pregnant. So he told me to be sure I took it, because we didn't want any little accidents. He tore out of my apartment in a hurry, and by the time he came back I was bleeding. So he brought me to the hospital thinking I'd taken the damn pill and had a bad reaction to it. And instead he found out that I've been pregnant for two months without telling him. By now I'm sure he's figured out what the pill was really doing there—that I was considering getting rid of the baby; *his* baby—and he went back to Atlanta. He didn't even say goodbye. Catherine spoke to him before he left, but he didn't come back inside to talk to me."

By now I had tears running down my face, and the nurse, who had started out looking embarrassed, like she was trying not to listen, looked deeply sympathetic, while mother gazed at me like she had never seen me before.

"I'm sorry," Grimaldi said. "When I have a free minute, I'll contact Mr. Craig and make sure everything's OK and Mr. Collier got safely back to Atlanta."

"I'd appreciate that." I sniffed.

"Meanwhile, something else has happened. You didn't tell me you were planning to visit St. Jerome's Hospital yesterday."

"It was a spur of the moment thing," I said, just as we reached the car. I got out of the wheelchair with my best attempt at a smile and a thank you for the nurse, and crawled into the front of Dix's SUV. The passenger seat had already been reclined. Dix closed the door behind me, and opened the back door to hand mother into the back seat.

"Learn anything interesting?" Grimaldi asked.

"Dr. Rushing had a picture of David Flannery on his cork board. And my sister-in-law was there on Friday afternoon."

Dix shot me a look as he got behind the wheel and turned the key in the ignition.

"What did you talk to the doctor about?" Detective Grimaldi asked.

I thought back. "Nothing, really. Nothing specific. Why?"

"He's dead," Grimaldi said bluntly.

"Dr. Rushing? You're kidding. He was fine yesterday."

"I'm sure he was. This wasn't natural causes."

I should have known. MNPD Homicide doesn't get called in for just any death.

"Seems he did it himself," Grimaldi added. "Single gunshot to the head."

Ouch.

"When I started investigating, I happened upon your name in the visitor's log. Were you there alone?"

"Rafe was with me," I said. Both mother and Dix glanced at me. We had left the hospital now, and were headed toward the entrance to Interstate 65.

"You said you and he were together most of yesterday afternoon," Grimaldi said; I nodded, although I knew she couldn't see me. "When did he leave and come back? Between which times?"

"Oh, come on! You thought he'd killed Brenda Puckett, and then you thought he'd killed Lila Vaughn. You even told me you thought he might have killed Marquita. Now you're trying to pin this on him?"

"I don't think he killed Dr. Rushing," Grimaldi said calmly. "Any more than I thought he'd killed Lila Vaughn or Marquita Johnson. Brenda Puckett, yes. But that was before I knew who he was."

"So what are you suggesting, then?"

"I'm suggesting," Grimaldi said, "that although you may not have talked to Dr. Rushing about anything upsetting, your boyfriend might have gone back there to ask a few more questions about David. He might have put the wind up the good doctor. I'm sure we can agree that Mr. Collier can be persuasive when he wants to be?"

He can. Both when it comes to sweet-talking women and when it comes to convincing people to admit things they'd rather keep to themselves. I had seen him in action once before, and poor truculent nineteen-year-old Maurice Washington, Alexandra Puckett's unsuitable boyfriend, had sung like a canary. If Rafe had decided to lean on poor old Dr. Rushing, the old man would have folded like a bad hand of cards.

"If he did, he didn't say anything about it." But then he'd had other things on his mind both coming and going, so maybe that wasn't surprising. And I could certainly imagine that, coming out of my apartment after that argument, he might have wanted to take his frustrations out on someone. He couldn't take them out on me— nothing anyone could say would make me believe that I'd ever be in any kind of danger from Rafe—but if he'd remembered Dr. Rushing's refusal to admit anything about David, he might have thought that a second trip to St. Jerome's made sense.

"Guess I'll have to ask him," Detective Grimaldi said. "Thanks, Ms. Martin. I'll be in touch." She made to hang up.

"Wait!"

"What?"

"When did Dr. Rushing die? Did he leave a note? Did he say anything about..." I hesitated, shooting a glance at Dix out of the corner of my eye, "...anything?"

"If there's a note, we haven't found it yet. I won't know about time of death until the M.E. has finished the autopsy. It seems Dr. Rushing stayed after business hours last night. The desk nurse left at five, and he was still in his office then. She thought he must be doing paperwork, because his appointments were over for the day."

"Who found him?" I asked.

"She did. When she came to work this morning she noticed that his car was still parked in the same spot. Apparently it wasn't his usual spot. When he came back from lunch yesterday, someone had taken it and he had to park somewhere else. This morning his car was still there, while the usual spot was empty. Ms. Murphy thought it was strange, so she went to check on him. She found him slumped over his desk."

I winced at the image my mind supplied. I'd been in that office less than twenty four hours ago; I could picture the space and Dr. Rushing's head only too well.

"Is there anything we can do? Dix and I and mother are on our way down I-65 toward Sweetwater. We'll be passing Brentwood in a few minutes. We could stop by."

Grimaldi hesitated. "Are you sure you feel up for it?"

"Honestly? I'm hopped up on so much morphine I don't feel a thing." I felt detached, like I was watching the world through glass, but I was pain free. And something like this might take my mind off my own misery for a while.

"I'm not sure what you can do," Tamara Grimaldi said, "but if you were here yesterday, you might notice something. Sure, if you don't mind, feel free to stop by."

"We'll be there in a few minutes." I put the phone away and instructed Dix to exit the interstate in Brentwood.

"A crime scene?" mother asked from the back seat. "Really, darling, don't you think you should just go home and rest and not get involved in such unpleasantness?"

"This might have to do with Sheila. She was there Friday afternoon. Now the man she had an appointment with is dead. I'm sorry if you think it's unladylike of me, but if there's anything I can do to help, I'm going to do it."

"If it has to do with Sheila, we're going," Dix said, in a voice that brooked no argument, and aimed the car toward St. Jerome.

Sixteen

Tamara Grimaldi met us in the lobby of St. Jerome's Hospital, and it was interesting to see mother's and Dix's reactions to her.

Dix had met her before, of course, last week at the morgue. But he'd probably been too focused on other things then to really notice what she looked like. At least I got the impression, until she greeted him, that he didn't recognize her.

As for mother, she reacted much the same way I did the first time I met Tamara Grimaldi. Uncomfortable, intimidated, and struck by my own shortcomings. At first I'd wondered if the detective might be gay, because I was used to women making more out of themselves than she did. Not that she's unattractive. Not pretty, by most people's opinion, but striking, in an athletic, very competent sort of way. The sort of way that can give a woman like me—women who don't hold down important, world changing jobs; women whose concerns revolve around men and babies—serious feelings of inferiority.

She's about my height, give or take an inch, and ethnic-looking. Olive complexion, dark eyes, dark curly hair cut short, aquiline nose, always dressed in low heels and a pantsuit or jeans. Today she was working, so it was a suit. Charcoal gray with thin stripes. Crisp blue shirt underneath. Very business-like. Very no nonsense. Very unlike the pink dress and gray cardigan I was wearing. It was the same gray cardigan with rosettes I'd bought at Target two days ago, thinking it would hide my growing belly well, and I must admit that wearing it now, when there was no more belly to hide, was hard.

"Mr. Martin." Grimaldi greeted Dix first. "I'm sorry to drag you out here."

"Savannah's right," Dix answered, and shook the hand she offered. "If it can help you figure out what happened to my wife, we want to help."

Grimaldi nodded and turned to me. Dix had made the trip to my apartment this morning to pick up the dress and cardigan, since the dress I'd worn to the hospital last night had been ruined. I'd even put on makeup, since mother has me trained to believe that a lady doesn't set foot outside the house without her face on. I didn't think I looked all that bad, considering everything I'd been through, but Grimaldi's dark eyes registered worry. "You look like hell," she said bluntly.

Mother looked scandalized. I managed a weak smile. "You've seen me look bad before." Most recently two months ago, when I'd arrived in her office fresh off an hour long crying jag, blotchy, wild-eyed, and beside myself, accusing her of having lied when she told me that Rafe would be fine, because I had it from a reliable source that he was dead.

She smiled, although it didn't reach her eyes. "He's all right. I spoke to Mr. Craig. Mr. Collier made it to Atlanta without incident and is back to work this morning."

"Thank you." I couldn't help the catch in my voice.

"Any time. I'm sorry things worked out this way." She put her hand on my arm for a second. The detective is usually so undemonstrative that it was like getting a great big warm hug. Then she turned to mother. "Mrs. Martin. I'm Detective Tamara Grimaldi with the Metro

Nashville PD. I'm in charge of the investigation into your daughter-in-law's death."

"A pleasure," mother said politely and shook the detective's hand. I got the distinct impression she didn't mean what she said. I think mother would have been much happier just going home to her safe little insular world where bad things only happened to other people. She'd had quite a few shocks in the past few days, between Sheila's death and the suspicion of drug abuse, and my pregnancy and miscarriage and the fact that I was involved with Rafael Collier, who—oh, yes—wasn't quite as dead as everyone had hoped.

"Not quite suite what you can do here," Grimaldi said when the formalities were over, "but I appreciate your willingness to help. Ms. Martin," she turned to me, "you've been here before. Did you go into Dr. Rushing's office yesterday?"

I nodded. "He came in from outside while we were talking to the desk nurse. When she told him we were there to see him, he asked us to come back to his office."

Grimaldi led the way down the hall with a wave of her hand. "Just out of curiosity, what did you give as the reason you were here?"

"I told the truth," I answered. "I said I was pregnant—" my throat tightened at the realization that this was no longer true, "—and that I'd miscarried before. That's true, too. The nurse looked up Sheila's name and told me that Sheila had been here to see Dr. Rushing. Then the doctor came in and took us back to his office for a quick consultation before his first appointment. I mentioned Sheila, but he didn't react to her name at all. He did react to Elspeth's, but he refused to tell us anything about David."

I thought for a second before I added, "You know, it might have been Rafe who put the wind up Dr. Rushing. You saw them together."

Tamara Grimaldi looked confused for a moment before she caught on. "Mr. Collier and David? Yes, I did."

"They look enough alike to be father and son, wouldn't you say?"

"No doubt at all," Grimaldi nodded. "So what you're suggesting is that Dr. Rushing got worried when you and Mr. Collier started asking questions about David?"

She pushed open the door to Dr. Rushing's office and waved us through. "Look at anything you want, but don't touch anything. We haven't finished processing the scene yet."

I looked around, even as I continued the conversation. The body had been removed, thankfully, and if I squinted, the blood spatter wasn't too noticeable. "There's something strange about David's adoption. And it has to have originated here."

I told her about the Caulfields and their religious background, how Elspeth had come to St. Jerome's to have her baby, and how Dr. Rushing told her—and her gynecologist—that the baby was stillborn. "The hospital took care of the birth certificate, and when it arrived in the mail, it said that David was Ginny and Sam Flannery's biological son. They weren't about to make a fuss over it, and for almost twelve years things have been fine. But then Rafe shows up, and he looks just like David—or David like him—and Dr. Rushing gets nervous because he knows that everything wasn't on the up and up with the adoption. Elspeth's parents probably had the right to approve it on her behalf since she was a minor, but Rafe was over eighteen, and he didn't agree to anything, and Dr. Rushing wouldn't have known how much he knew. Elspeth could have told Rafe twelve years ago that David was stillborn, and if so, I bet Rafe would have a hell of a legal case."

I glanced at Dix, who nodded. "He could sue for custody and a whole lot of money, and he'd probably win."

Mother looked scandalized again. "Surely he won't try."

"I doubt it," I said. "He knows he couldn't have provided any kind of home for David back then, and I doubt he would have wanted the poor kid to grow up the way he did, in the Bog with LaDonna." Rafe had loved his mother, as evidenced by the fact that he'd spent two years in jail for beating up the man who had hurt her, but I didn't think he would have wished his own childhood on anyone, let alone his own son. "He knows that Ginny and Sam have taken care of David better than he'd ever have been able to."

"You don't think he'll try to get custody?" Detective Grimaldi asked.

I shook my head. "David is happy. Taking him away from Ginny and Sam after twelve years would be cruel. It certainly wouldn't be in David's best interest, and I think any judge would probably agree."

Dix nodded agreement.

"And Rafe isn't really in a position to provide a home for David now either. Not with the work he does. He goes away for weeks and months at a time, and it's not like he can take a kid into the criminal underworld with him. Or that he'd want to." I sighed. "I just hope the Flannerys see their way clear to let David and Rafe get to know one another—surely he has at least that right! —and now that they've met and know about each other, it would be just as cruel to deny them that."

Dix nodded again. I was happy to see that he agreed with me. Mother didn't seem so sure.

"What do you think?" Detective Grimaldi said, abandoning the issue of Rafe and David for the moment. She looked around Dr. Rushing's office. "Anything look different to you?"

I looked around too. It seemed the same. Desk, chair, filing cabinet, cork-board full of pictures of happy families. Rafe had mentioned seeing a photo of David from a few years ago pinned up. I wandered over to the wall where the cork-board hung to see for myself. Tamara Grimaldi, meanwhile, addressed Dix. "Did your wife know Elspeth Caulfield? Or Mr. Collier?"

Mother sniffed, probably at the idea that Sheila would know Rafe. I looked at her—*I* knew Rafe—and mother blushed. Dix shook his head. "Not that I know of. Savannah's the only one of us who's had any kind of contact with him, and that's only been in the past few months, since he came back to this part of Tennessee. I've only seen him once—

until yesterday—and that was at Marquita Johnson's funeral. I didn't talk to him, just saw him and Savannah together. We've discussed him, but Sheila's never said anything about having met him. And if she knew Elspeth, she's never mentioned that, either. I doubt it."

"Elspeth seemed to be a bit of a loner," I added over my shoulder. "Author, you know. She probably spent most of her time alone, interfacing with the computer." And making up stories in which she and her most recent incarnation of Rafe got the happily ever after she'd been denied in life. I couldn't help but feel sorry for her, in spite of the fact that she'd done her best to kill me.

Grimaldi said, "So Sheila wouldn't have recognized David Flannery?"

Dix had to think for a second. "I've had a picture of him at the office for a few months. She might have seen that. I don't remember showing it to her, though, and it was kept in a file, not out in the open."

"Where is it now? The picture?"

"Savannah took it," Dix said, with a glance at me.

I nodded. "Last Thursday. I have it at home." I put my finger on an empty space on the cork-board. "There's a picture missing here."

I hadn't taken the time to inspect the board when we were in Dr. Rushing's office yesterday. I'd been too busy talking. But I had noticed that it was filled, every square inch of cork covered. There hadn't been any gaps.

"The photograph of David Flannery?" Detective Grimaldi suggested.

I shook my head. "That's up there." I pointed towards the top of the board, where a younger David was grinning at the camera from between his beaming parents.

Everyone moved closer to have a look. Mother was the only one who'd never seen neither David nor a photograph of him, and when she did, and saw the resemblance to Rafe, whom she *had* seen recently, I could see the shock in her eyes. She turned to look at me. I have no idea why, or what the expression in her eyes meant, but personally the sight of David brought tears to my eyes. He looked so much like Rafe that it hurt, but more than that, he looked so much like my own child might have looked, had I been able to keep it.

"Any idea what's missing?" Grimaldi asked, her expression sympathetic, as if she knew what was going through my mind. I swallowed and shook my head.

"I didn't spend any time looking at the board. I left that to Rafe, while I talked to Dr. Rushing. Rafe might remember."

"I don't think Mr. Craig would be best pleased if I asked Mr. Collier to drive back to Nashville so soon," Grimaldi said dryly. "It seems they're at an important point in the investigation. When Mr. Collier up and left night before last, it came close to blowing the whole thing sky-high."

I felt myself turn pale. "He's not in danger, is he?"

Tamara Grimaldi shrugged. "No more than he always is, I think. Or no more than he was before he dropped out of sight for twenty four hours."

"That doesn't sound good," I said.

Dix glanced at me, and so did mother. Both their expressions were hard to read. At a guess, I'd say mother was surprised bordering on shocked, not to mention dismayed, about my obvious concern for a man she had never thought I'd show the least little bit of interest in. Dix, meanwhile, was under no illusions about my feelings for Rafe. If he was surprised at all, I suspect it was because I was no longer trying to deny them. But after everything that had happened, there just didn't seem to be any point. Maybe that was the shocker. That I didn't bother to pretend not to care.

"He'll be all right," Grimaldi said. "He knows how to take care of himself. And if you don't mind my saying so, he seems to have the devil's own luck."

She had a point.

"Take a picture of it," I said, indicating the cork-board, "and send it to Wendell. He'll show it to Rafe, and Rafe can tell you whether he remembers what was there."

"I could do that." Grimaldi pulled out her phone to snap a shot of the cork-board. While she was busy, Dix turned to me.

"What was Sheila doing here, Savannah?"

"Dr. Rushing was a specialist in difficult pregnancies," I said.

"Sheila wasn't pregnant. Was she?"

"I'm sorry, Mr. Martin," Detective Grimaldi said. "Yes, she was."

She jumped to grab his arm when Dix turned as white as a sheet. "Here. Sit down." She lowered him into the chair I had occupied the previous day. "Put your head between your knees. Concentrate on breathing."

Dix took a breath, but his head popped up again almost immediately. And though his face was pale, his eyes blazed with anger. "Are you telling me this bastard killed not just my wife, but my baby as well?"

Mother clicked her tongue. It was probably Dix's language that offended her. If she was outraged at the idea that someone had killed her grandchild, or even shocked at the news that Sheila had been pregnant, I hope her reaction would have been stronger than just a tsk.

"I'm afraid so," Tamara Grimaldi said. She kept her hand on Dix's shoulder for a moment. I hoped he derived some sort of comfort from it, although he probably didn't realize what an outpouring of sympathy it was.

Dix took another breath. "If he hadn't been dead, I would have wanted to kill him."

Mother tsked again, and Dix turned on her. "You knew about this, didn't you? For how long?"

"She told me after her first appointment with Dr. Seaver," mother said, in her well-modulated, ladylike voice. "Last Thursday."

"What about you?" Dix turned to me.

"The detective told me a couple of days ago. After—" I swallowed, "the autopsy."

"And neither of you thought I had a right to know?" His angry question included the detective. She was the one who answered, her voice gentle.

"It was just a few days since I'd had to tell you that your wife was dead. There seemed to be no need to call back two days later to let you know that she'd been pregnant. You were already grieving, and I didn't want to add to it."

"I had a right to know!"

"Of course you did. And I would have told you. I just judged that it was better not to tell you right then." Her tone was soothing but not at all placating; there was an undertone of steel, of absolute certainty that she'd done the right thing. Dix must have heard it too, because he didn't argue. Instead he turned to me.

"What's your excuse?"

"I don't have one," I said, "other than that I'm a chicken. Like the detective said, you were already grieving, and there didn't seem to be any point in adding to it. Especially not over the phone. And I was busy."

"Sleeping with your boyfriend," Dix said bitterly. I flushed and bit my lip. I'd done more than that, including figuring out where Sheila had been on Friday afternoon and tracking down David Flannery, but yes, there'd been a little bit of self indulgent sex in there too.

Before I could say anything in my defense—before I could decide whether I should in fact say anything, or whether it would be better just to let him vent his anger and grief without interference—he'd closed his eyes. "I'm sorry, sis."

"That's OK. I love you. I didn't want to hurt you." I put an arm around his shoulders and looked up at the detective. "I think maybe it would be best if we went home. Too difficult all around being here right now."

She nodded. "I'll walk you out."

When we got out to the car, she added, "Thanks for stopping by. I'll let you know if anything comes of the empty space on the cork-board."

"I'd appreciate that."

I'd appreciate it even more if she'd toss any little tidbit of information she had about Rafe my way. I knew I probably didn't deserve his forgiveness after not telling him about the baby, *his* baby, the first chance I got, but the idea that I might never see him again, that he might not want to see me again after this, was more devastating than I could have imagined.

Seventeen

We got to Sweetwater just before noon. Jonathan had dropped Abigail at school with his own two eldest on his way to the office, while Hannah was at home with Catherine and little Cole. With nothing else he needed to do, Dix headed to work. Mother and I ended up in the parlor. In spite of the early hour, she poured herself a sherry. I guess maybe she felt she'd earned it. Or maybe she needed the Dutch courage for the job ahead. When she sat down across from me, on great aunt Marie's antique velvet love seat, I braced myself automatically.

"I'm worried about your behavior, Savannah."

No doubt. Grabbing the proverbial bull by the horns, I said, "I know he's not someone you would have chosen for me to get involved with."

"No," mother admitted readily, "but—"

"I never intended to fall for him. It just happened. He's..." I hesitated, trying to put into words what it was that Rafe was, that was so appealing to me. The best I could come up with was, "...different. Being with him is..." I hesitated again, before settling for, "—easy."

"Yes," mother said, "but..."

"I only slept with him once. Well, until yesterday, anyway. Twice now."

"Darling," mother protested, wincing delicately.

Right. Too much information. "Sorry. But I want you to understand that I haven't been carrying on an affair for months and lying about it. It was just the one time, that night when Todd proposed two months ago."

Mother looked taken aback. "You went to that man after Todd proposed? Savannah..."

"I love him," I said, no doubt shocking mother almost as much as I shocked myself. We were both silent for a while. I don't know what thoughts were running through my mother's head, but for myself, I was reeling. I'd fought feeling anything at all for Rafe for months. I had told myself and anyone else who'd listen that we were just friends. Acquaintances, really, since I really didn't know him well enough for us to be anything more. But then the incident with Perry Fortunato happened, and it's hard not to develop an attachment to a man who saves your life and gets hurt in the process. I had just about gotten used to the fact that I'd developed a sort of crush on him. I knew I had fallen for him a little; in fact, I thought I might almost be a little bit in love with him.

Almost and just a little.

All that was out the window now. I had suspected as much when I thought he was dead and I'd come close to going out of my mind with grief and loss. But I hadn't been willing to put what I felt into words. Now that I had blurted out the truth without thinking, I had stunned not only my mother, but myself.

I faced her again. "I'm sorry you don't care for my behavior. And I'm sorry the man I've fallen in love with isn't good enough for you. I'm sorry I can't just marry Todd and give you the son-in-law you want. But I'd be miserable married to Todd, and contrary to what he thinks, he wouldn't be happy, either."

Mother opened her mouth, probably to argue, and I shook my head. "I know my own heart, mother. Even when we were dating in high school, it was more to make you and Pauline happy than because I was in love with him."

"But Rafael Collier...!" mother moaned, and followed it up with the expected, "what will people say?"

"I don't care what anyone says. Not anymore. I cared so much about what people might say that I was afraid to tell him I was pregnant. I thought about having an abortion because I was too afraid of what people would say. He saved my life three months ago, and I was too afraid of what people would say to admit that I was in love with him!"

Tears were running down my cheeks, probably ruining my makeup, and mother looked acutely uncomfortable. A Southern Belle isn't supposed to make a spectacle of herself, not even in the privacy of her mother's front parlor. I was taught to always be proper, controlled, pleasant. Not this sobbing mess.

"He left knowing I'd been pregnant and hadn't told him. He probably thinks I didn't want the baby. He'll never be able to forgive me. He probably won't even want to."

"Maybe he's relieved," mother said, sipping from her sherry. Unlike me, she looked proper and controlled, if not precisely pleasant.

I blinked away the tears hanging in my eyelashes. "Excuse me?"

"Maybe he's relieved that things worked out this way. I'm sure he enjoyed your attention, darling, but he probably knew nothing would come of it in the end."

I dried my cheeks. "What do you mean?"

"Well," mother said apologetically, "you're not really from the same social strata, are you?"

"So?"

"So are you sure he wasn't just having some fun? Men do, you know."

"Yes," I said, "I know."

"Well, have you ever discussed anything permanent, darling? Or was it all just..." She paused delicately, "physical?"

I bit my tongue, hard. This was something else I knew I'd have to deal with if I could talk Rafe into forgiving me: the many idiots who'd think that the only thing a woman like me could see in a man like him was the sex. The excitement. The forbidden fruit.

Rafe was used to that. Every time we went somewhere together, some woman or other made eyes at him. And if it wasn't a woman, it was Timothy Briggs. It had been like that since high school. Yvonne McCoy hadn't made any secret of having been curious about what he'd be like in bed, and although poor Elspeth probably thought she was in love with him, the truth was that she hadn't known him well enough for that.

Was it possible that he thought that's all it had been for me too?

And could I blame him, when I'd done everything I could to hide how I felt? Could I blame him when I hadn't vehemently denied his facetious statement that I'd marry Todd but think about him every time I had to fake another orgasm?

Dammit, I'd done everything except tell him straight out that I was only interested in, as mother would say, one thing. So no, I couldn't blame him at all for thinking I'd bought that damn morning-after pill to avoid getting pregnant. From his point of view, if all I'd wanted was a quick and dirty affair before tying the knot with Todd and settling down to being a proper Southern wife, the last thing I'd want was to risk getting pregnant.

I pushed it all back down. I'd take it out later and look at it, but not until I was alone. Now I faced mother and did my best to come across calm. "No, we never discussed the future. I didn't think we had one, and I'm sure neither did he. I have no idea how he feels about me. He told me he wasn't in a hurry to be fitted with a ball and chain, but..."

But that had been while we were arguing, and while he thought I'd taken steps to short-circuit any little 'accidents' we may have inadvertently caused. He hadn't meant it.

Had he?

"If you say so, darling," mother said doubtfully. "As it happens, I didn't intend this conversation to be about Mr. Collier."

"Then why did you bring him up?"

"I didn't," mother said. "You did."

"No..." But when I looked back on it, I realized she was right. She'd told me she was worried about my behavior, and I'd jumped to the conclusion that the biggest behavioral problem from my mother's point of view had to be my choice of bed-partner. Apparently I'd been wrong.

"You're a grown woman, Savannah," mother said.

Nice of her to notice. I'm too well brought-up to actually say that, of course. I just smiled pleasantly.

"And you'll do as you want, of course."

I fully intended to. I'd already lost too much by not listening to my own heart instead of worrying about what everyone else thought. I didn't say that, either.

"But do you really think it's wise to engage yourself in police matters?"

I blinked. "You mean, Sheila's death?"

Mother nodded.

"It's not that I'm engaged, really. Tamara Grimaldi is more than capable of handling the investigation without any help from me. She's good at what she does. But when I learned that Sheila had been to see Dr. Rushing, at the same hospital where David Flannery was born, and I had a perfect excuse because I was pregnant myself," I swallowed, "I didn't think it could hurt to pay a visit. I did it just as much for Rafe and for David as for Sheila."

Mother didn't look convinced.

"I've never looked for trouble, mother. When Walker pulled a gun on me, I was just sitting an open house. He wanted Mrs. Jenkins, and I happened to be in the way. Same thing when Perry Fortunato tried to kill me. It was an open house then too, and I had no idea he'd come home early and find me in his goody closet. It could have happened to anyone. And I can't help it that Elspeth Caulfield lost her mind. She hadn't even seen Rafe for twelve years; it's not like I could foresee that she'd be so possessive of him that she'd try to murder anyone she thought was a threat to her happy ending."

"We just don't want anything to happen to you, darling," mother murmured. "You're all the way up there in Nashville, all alone with no one around you..."

"I have plenty of people around me. If I'm in danger, Detective Grimaldi will assign me some protection. She has before. And I can usually trust Rafe to protect me from anyone trying to hurt me." Like Perry Fortunato and Elspeth Caulfield.

"He's in Atlanta," mother said.

"He'll be back. He can't pretend to be Jorge Pena forever. Sooner or later he'll run into someone who knows who he really is, or someone who knows Jorge. And then he'll be back."

I had to believe that. Had to believe that he'd survive whatever crazy situation they'd put him in, and that he'd return to Nashville at least long enough for me to clear the air and tell him the truth. I had no control over what he did after that, whether he'd want anything to do with me after what happened—whether I'd ever meant more than a feather in his cap or another notch on his bedpost—but for now, at least, I had to hold onto the belief that he'd be back and I'd see him again.

I got to my feet. "I think I'd like to lie down for a little bit. I still don't feel very well."

"Of course, darling," mother said and put the sherry glass on the table, a faint wrinkle between her elegant brows. "I'll help you make the bed."

I waved her back down. "I spent eighteen years here; I know where everything is. And the hospital didn't say I couldn't do normal chores."

They'd told me not to lift anything over ten pounds, and not to have sex again until the bleeding had stopped and I'd been examined by my own gynecologist and given a clean bill of health. I doubted the bedclothes were covered by the ten pound rule, and the only man I'd be interested in having sex with was at least five hours away and probably not interested in having sex with me, so everything was under control. I made up the bed in my old room and crawled in. And lay there in the cool quiet, staring up at the ceiling. My body was insistent about needing rest, but my mind was awhirl with too many thoughts for me to be able to sleep. The medicine made me feel sort of floaty and maybe a little high. I've never used illegal drugs, so it's not like I'd recognize the feeling from anywhere, but whatever the drugs did, they didn't make me sleepy. There were just too many things on my mind for sleep.

Was mother right and Rafe really only wanted me in bed? Sure, yes, that was probably all he thought he could have, since I'd never given him any indication that I wanted more. But if he knew that I cared about him, that I—my mind hiccupped—loved him, would he want more? Or had I just been an amusing pastime and now he was done with me? I wasn't the type of woman he'd normally get involved with.

Then again, I had no real idea what kind of woman he usually got involved with. The only two women I'd met, who had had any kind of intimate relationship with Rafe, were Elspeth Caulfield and Yvonne McCoy. Both more than twelve years ago, both blonde—all right, Yvonne was more of a redhead—blue-eyed, Caucasian girls. Sure, there was precedent for someone like me. But all they'd been, both of them, were one night stands. I'd hardly been more than that myself.

Clearly he'd had a lot of practice since high school. Or so I assumed. I didn't honestly have enough experience to know. But he certainly knew what he was doing, and I doubted he'd been celibate for twelve years. I knew nothing at all about those other women. The one thing I did know, was that whoever they were, they hadn't lasted. He wouldn't sleep with me while he had a girlfriend waiting somewhere else.

Would he?

I turned and buried my face in the pillow. This kind of thinking was driving me crazy. Yes, he might have a girlfriend in Memphis. He'd spent a lot of time there. Years. My certainty that he wouldn't sleep with me if he had a girlfriend elsewhere was based on nothing but what I wanted to believe. If he thought our relationship was just about sex, there was no reason why he wouldn't sleep with me and someone else at the same time.

He could be with her right now. No doubt leaving her as breathless as he'd left me yesterday afternoon.

I rolled over, gritting my teeth.

But he was working, I reminded myself. There might not be another woman. Surely he wouldn't indulge in gratuitous sex while he was on the job?

And did it matter?

Even if there wasn't anyone else, and even if I could somehow convince him to give me, give *us*, another chance, was I the kind of woman who could keep his attention for very long?

Not likely, I figured. We had so little in common apart from enjoying rolling around on a flat surface together. At least I enjoyed rolling around with him. He seemed to have a good time too, but he might have felt the same way after sleeping with Yvonne and Elspeth and all the others. I might be nothing special to him.

I forced my mind off the subject before I started chewing the hundred-year-old wallpaper. And then promptly went back to thinking about him again.

Would he be able to remember anything about the missing photograph from Dr. Rushing's cork-board? He'd been looking for pictures of David, so he might not have noticed much else.

The photograph of David and the Flannerys was still on the board. Unless there had been two, and both Dr. Rushing and Rafe had missed it, it seemed the missing picture must have been of someone else. But why remove it? We hadn't asked about anyone else.

Had someone other than us stopped by later in the day and asked about another child? It seemed fantastically coincidental, but maybe not impossible. If there was something fishy about David's adoption, Dr. Rushing might have cut a few corners in other cases, as well.

Or—I remembered Detective Grimaldi's question—had Rafe headed back to Brentwood after leaving my apartment yesterday afternoon, to take some of his frustrations out on Dr. Rushing? Having an angry Rafe Collier banging on the door would be enough to put the wind up many a man.

I twisted on the bed and faced the ceiling again.

Would Detective Grimaldi tell me what Rafe said? Would she tell me if she talked to him? Would she tell me how he was? Whether he said anything about me?

My cell phone rang, and I lunged for it. "Yeah?"

"Savannah?" a voice said. Female, somewhat familiar. It took me a second to place it, and by then she had introduced herself. "This is Denise Seaver."

"Of course." Not who I wanted, but better than going another round with my own thoughts. "What can I do for you, doctor?"

"I just received your file from Skyline Medical Center."

She paused to give me time to respond. When I didn't, she continued, "I'm not quite sure whether what happened came as a relief or not. The file said the miscarriage wasn't self-induced...?"

I firmed my voice. "I wanted this baby. I know it didn't sound like I did, but it was never about want, just about being afraid."

"Then you have my condolences. We should set up an appointment for you to come in to my office in a few days. How do you feel right now?"

I said I felt fine, and was lying down. "My mother insisted on bringing me to Sweetwater. I guess I'll probably be here a few days."

"Any pain?"

"None at the moment," I said. "I have pills."

"So I see." She mentioned the name of the medication I was taking; it must be in the file. Would be in the file, I guess. "Be careful not to drink alcohol while you're taking it. It doesn't mix well."

"I understand." One thought lead to another, and I added, "Did you hear about Dr. Rushing?"

Her voice changed, became wary. "What about Dr. Rushing?"

"He's dead. Last night."

"Dear me," Dr. Seaver said. "How do you know?"

"I was there yesterday. My name showed up in the visitor log. There's a photograph missing from the cork-board."

"Excuse me?"

"When we were there yesterday, the whole board was filled. Now there's a gap. The doctor must have taken something down."

"Interesting," Dr. Seaver said politely. "Why?"

"I assume because he didn't want anyone to see it. If there was something wrong with David's adoption, maybe there was something wrong with someone else's, too."

"There wasn't anything wrong with David's adoption. Mr. and Mrs. Caulfield agreed to it on behalf of their daughter. She was a minor." Dr. Seaver's voice held a hint of impatience.

"Rafe wasn't. And he didn't sign anything."

"Rafe Collier is dead, Savannah."

"No, he's not," I said. Now that my entire family, plus Todd and Sheriff Satterfield, knew the truth, I didn't care who else found out. "He was with me at St. Jerome's yesterday. He's probably telling the police about that missing photograph right now."

There was a pause. "I don't understand," Dr. Seaver said. "I heard that he'd died. A few months ago."

"You heard wrong. He's very much alive. And upset about David."

"Dear me," Dr. Seaver said again. "Perhaps that's the reason Emil decided to end it all. If Mr. Collier threatened to sue..." She trailed off.

"Perhaps. " Although in my opinion, it would be more likely that Rafe had threatened Dr. Rushing with grave bodily harm. Probably without saying a word, because I didn't think he'd actually lay a finger on the old man. I was still stuck on that missing photograph, though. What would be Dr. Rushing's point in getting rid of it if he was planning to kill himself anyway? And where was the photograph now? Hidden? Shredded? In an envelope in the mailroom? Dr. Rushing hadn't left work, so the photograph had to be around. It couldn't have walked out of St. Jerome's on its own.

"Any word on Sheila's funeral?" Dr. Seaver interrupted my thoughts. "I'd like to attend. Unless you would prefer for it to be just the family?"

I pulled my thoughts together before they strayed too far afield. "I think that would be fine. It's tomorrow at eleven."

We exchanged particulars, and the doctor hung up. I lay back down on the bed and closed my eyes, willing my mind to go blank so I could get some sleep.

Eighteen

The funeral was well-attended. The whole family was there, of course, with Abigail and Hannah looking lost enough to break my heart in their little black velvet dresses and with black ribbons in their blonde curls. Dix had tears running down his cheeks throughout most of the service. The girls didn't, but were big-eyed and solemn. I wasn't sure they really understood what had happened, and that was probably best, but they did seem to know that something was wrong. Hannah had taken to sucking her thumb again, a habit Sheila had spent several months trying to break last year.

"I've tried to tell her that her mama wouldn't want her to suck her thumb," my mother confided in me, "but she just looks at me with those big eyes, and I don't have the heart to say anything else."

I shook my head. "She'll stop on her own when she's ready. If it gives her comfort right now, just let her do it. No girl ever graduated from finishing school sucking her thumb."

Mother looked at me in silence for a moment before she said, "You'll make a good mother, Savannah."

I had to swallow back tears at that, wondering if I'd ever get the chance. Two miscarriages with two different men must mean there was something wrong with me, I figured, and if so, I might never be able to have children.

Physically I was feeling pretty much back to normal, without a lot of pain or fatigue. I had taken a pill before the funeral, because I knew I'd be doing more standing and walking than I'd been used to. Of course, emotional health was a different issue altogether. I still cried easily, without much provocation, I had bursts of anger if anything rubbed me the wrong way—usually followed by more tears— and I went into deep pits of despair and doubt. I still felt guilty, too: although everyone said the enthusiastic sex hadn't contributed to the miscarriage, I couldn't help thinking that if we hadn't indulged, maybe none of this would have happened.

Rafe hadn't called. Not that I'd expected him to. He hadn't called me in the two months prior to knocking on my door in the early hours of Wednesday morning, either. Tamara Grimaldi assured me he was all right, that she'd spoken to Wendell and Rafe both, and that they were just focused on wrapping up the investigation in Atlanta. Apparently things were once again hairy, coming to a head, and Rafe was in the not unfamiliar position of walking around with a target on his back. I was too exhausted to worry as much about it as perhaps I should. But, "He can take care of himself," Tamara Grimaldi told me, "he'll be fine," and I lacked the energy to fret.

She drove down for the funeral, dressed in her usual boxy, black suit. I'd seen it in a few funerals already, as the detective had a habit of attending 'her' victims' services. She'd been at both Brenda's and Lila's, and here she was at Sheila's.

"Thanks for coming," I said when she walked through the door to chapel. "Any news?"

"Not much since I spoke to you yesterday. The autopsy confirmed Emil Rushing's TOD around seven PM Wednesday night."

A couple of hours after business ended. "Took him long enough to decide to do away with himself. It isn't likely he'd have any appointments that late."

The detective shook her head. "The last legitimate appointment was at four thirty, and the doctor was alive and well when the patient left. The desk nurse saw him afterwards."

"Did you talk to Rafe? Did he go back to St. Jerome's after the first time?"

"He says not," Grimaldi said.

"Well, what did he do during those couple of hours? He had to go somewhere."

"He won't say. Says it isn't any of my business."

"Can't you make him tell you?"

"No," Grimaldi said, with heavy patience, "I can't. He isn't a suspect, and he knows I can't arrest him. I don't have a whole lot of leverage, Ms. Martin."

In her frustration she'd raised her voice, and mother sent us a look from the other side of the entrance, where she was greeting guests. I smiled apologetically and drew the detective a few steps back. Lowering my voice, I asked, "Did he remember the photograph, at least? The one that's missing?"

"He did." She sounded slightly more pleased about that. "A boy, maybe two. Blond hair, brown eyes, dressed in a Halloween costume, complete with pony. That's the only reason he remembered. That pony."

"Some people spare no expense," I said.

"I had tech support do a search of photo studios that offered Halloween pictures with horses this year, and lucked out. There was a place in Mt. Juliet that did."

"That isn't too far from here." Or from Nashville, more specifically. At least an hour and a half from Sweetwater, but no more than thirty or forty minutes from anywhere in Nashville. "So you know who the child is?"

Grimaldi nodded. "It took a lot of cross checking—there were a lot of people who had their kids photographed on top of that pony—but I have an appointment with the parents this afternoon, when I'm finished here. We'll see how it goes."

"Bet you anything the boy is adopted," I said. "But you'll find no records of it."

She shook her head. "Here's what we're thinking right now. You and Mr. Collier put the wind up Dr. Rushing by questioning him about David. Dr. Rushing stayed late at the office to warn the other families whose adoptions he'd facilitated that something ugly might be coming down. This particular family decided to take matters into their own hands, and one of the parents took a drive to St. Jerome's. Let's assume, for the sake of ease, that it was the father. That way I can call him 'he.'"

I grinned, quite possibly my first since Wednesday night.

"He went to Dr. Rushing's office, removed the photograph from the wall and the file from the filing cabinet, and maybe he even killed Dr. Rushing, or maybe Dr. Rushing did that himself. Then our guy went back home and destroyed the paperwork. Or tossed it in a dumpster on the way. Husband and wife alibi each other, of course, but that doesn't mean anything."

"I like it."

"I do too. But it's just a theory. I'll know more this afternoon after I've spoken to them."

She looked around. "Guess I should find a seat."

"I appreciate your coming down. I know you're busy. I'm sure Dix will appreciate it, too. He's over there." I pointed to where Dix was talking to Aunt Regina. The next time I looked in that direction, Grimaldi was squatting on the floor in front of Abigail and Hannah, engaged in what seemed to be a serious conversation, while Dix was watching all three of them from a few yards away.

She left after the service, rather than following the procession to the cemetery. "She had an appointment this afternoon," I told Dix when he asked after her. "With someone who might have a connection to the case."

He nodded distractedly. "She talked to Hannah and Abby."

"I noticed."

"I think whatever she said made them feel better."

"That's great." Now, if she'd only solve the murder so Dix could feel better, too. Or so he might at least achieve a sense of closure from the knowledge that whoever had killed his wife would pay for it. Actually feeling better would probably take longer than just six days.

Apart from the detective, most everyone else who had been in the chapel came along to the graveside, and from there to the mansion, for the catered funeral food that mother had laid on. Dr. Seaver was there, as promised. So were a lot of women who must be friends of Sheila's. And—surprisingly—Yvonne McCoy.

Or maybe her presence wasn't so surprising. She'd told me once that she used to have a crush on Dix in high school. Not that she had the bad taste to flirt with him at his wife's funeral, of course. In fact, Yvonne looked quite decorous, in black slacks and a striped shirt, under a dark coat. A far cry from the last funeral where we'd crossed paths: Marquita's. Yvonne had come straight from work in a skimpy skirt and a stretchy top that dipped dangerously low over her Double D breasts, and she had kissed Rafe and made me want to hurt her.

Now she came over and expressed her condolences to Dix before dragging me into a bone-crushing hug, squashing my face against her wool coat and heavily sprayed hair. "Thank you!"

"What for?" I asked, fighting my way free.

There were tears in her eyes. "The sheriff said it was you who found me the morning after Elspeth tried to kill me. If you hadn't, I would have died before anyone else came by the house."

"Oh," I said. "It was... I mean, you're welcome."

She stepped a little closer and lowered her voice, squeezing my hand. "I'm so sorry about Rafe."

This time it was my eyes filling with tears. Not, as she thought, because he was dead, but because of everything that had happened. And because she was squeezing too hard. "Me too."

Dix glanced at me, but didn't comment. "How are you feeling, Yvonne?" he asked instead.

Yvonne smiled and let go of me. "Better. Almost back to normal. Other than that I have to give up low cut shirts and navel rings because of the scars. But it's a small price to pay compared to being dead."

She wandered off without realizing what she'd said. "She didn't mean it," I told Dix as soon as she was out of ear shot.

He managed a smile. "I know, sis. And I'm happy for her. I'm sorry to have lost Sheila, but I don't want anyone else to suffer instead. Except maybe whoever did it to her."

"You don't think it was Doctor Rushing?"

"I hope not," Dix said. "I want whoever it is to suffer."

I couldn't blame him.

"Detective Grimaldi will figure it out. She's solved a lot of other murders; she'll solve this one too."

Dix put an arm around me and pulled me in so he could kiss the top of my head. "I love you, sis."

"I love you too," I said.

The moment was interrupted when another woman came up to give Dix her condolences. She was a once-pretty brunette with thin cheeks and shadowed eyes, whose well-made clothes fit poorly, like they'd been made for someone fifteen pounds heavier, or someone else altogether. She spoke softly, too softly for me to hear. And she looked vaguely familiar, but I couldn't place her. Some other old friend from high school I hadn't seen in more than twelve years, maybe?

When she walked off, I leaned closer to Dix and spoke out of the corner of my mouth. "Who was that?"

He glanced at me. "Marley Cartwright."

"The woman who murdered her baby?" In my surprise, I neglected to keep my voice low, and my cheeks were hot as I craned my neck for another look.

"That's her."

She'd already been swallowed up by the crowd. I turned back to Dix. "She didn't look like a murderer."

Then again, who was I to judge? Elspeth hadn't looked like a murderer either, yet she'd killed Marquita and stabbed Yvonne and tried to shoot me. Looks can be deceiving.

"Did you see her?" Dix asked Todd when the latter walked up to do his duty a little later.

"Who?" Todd glanced around the room.

"Marley Cartwright."

"No! She was here?" He gave the room another, more thorough look. There was still no sign of Marley.

"She must have left," I said. "It can't be fun, being here with everyone staring at her."

Todd, who hadn't met my eyes yet, avoided them yet again. He looked at me, but not *at* me; his gray-blue eyes hit somewhere around my hairline. "I imagine not."

"How is the trial going? Has it started yet?"

"Monday," Todd said and turned back to Dix. It was a clear dismissal. I met my brother's eyes for a second. He shrugged. I smiled politely and took myself off so the two of them could talk in peace. The last thing I wanted was to come between my brother and his best friend. If there was ever a time when Dix needed his friends, it was now.

So I wandered off, and left them alone. Truth be told, I was less concerned with Todd's attitude toward me than I was about his attitude toward Dix. As long as Dix's and my relationship survived unscathed, and Dix's and Todd's relationship didn't suffer because of Todd's and my relationship, I was satisfied.

I found Denise Seaver, my mother, and Audrey sharing canapés on great aunt Marie's velvet love seat in the front parlor. And they must have noticed Marley too, because when I walked up to them, Audrey was saying, "Can't believe she'd have the nerve to show her face here!"

Mother lifted a stuffed mushroom to her mouth, but before popping it in, she shook her head sadly. "Bless her heart, she looked awful."

"Well, wouldn't you?" I asked. "If someone thought you had killed your child?"

Mother looked like she thought strangling me at birth might not have been a bad idea. "Darling...!" she protested.

"I'm sorry. I know it isn't pleasant. But imagine what it must be like for her. What if she didn't do it?"

"I'm afraid she did, Savannah," Dr. Seaver said seriously.

"How do you know? Was she your patient too?" Along with practically every other woman in Columbia and Sweetwater?

She nodded. "And I can tell you this now, since it all came out at the trial this week anyway. She was suffering from postpartum depression. The fact that her body was less firm, that she had stretch marks and couldn't wear a bikini, that she was a mother instead of a young, attractive, adored wife... it all combined to make her resent the baby. She was so busy trying to regain her figure to be attractive for her husband that she neglected to take care of little Oliver."

Mother clicked her tongue. Audrey shook her head sadly. She's as tall and angular as mother is short and soft. They were both wearing black and white: my mother elegant slacks and a silk shirt topped by a soft knit jacket with a belt, while Audrey had on a severe dress, black stockings, and four inch heels with polkadots. Her dark hair was cut in a crisp wedge and her lipstick was fire engine red, while mother's champagne colored hair curled softly around her face and her makeup was understated and lovely. Mother has never worked a day in her life—outside the house—and Audrey owns and operates the most exclusive boutique in Sweetwater. They've been friends since childhood, and in their late fifties are still as close as ever, in spite of their differences.

Denise Seaver by comparison still looked quite earth-motherly. She had tamed her long tangle of grayish hair with a barrette at the nape of her neck, and although the sack like dress still had the same waving hemline, it was a sober gray color, and was topped not by a white lab coat, but a nubby black cardigan. She'd exchanged the plastic clogs and ankle socks for black flats.

"I feel for the young woman," she said now; a little piously, I thought, "and I'm sure she didn't plan to hurt little Oliver, but we all have to live with our actions, don't we? Even the poor ones." She shook her head sadly. Mother and Audrey murmured agreement. I excused myself and moved on.

It had been a long day, and a longer week. With mother and Audrey occupied with Dr. Seaver, Dix still in conversation with Todd, Tamara Grimaldi back in Nashville, and Abigail and Hannah being entertained by Cole, Annie and Robert McCall, under the watchful eye of my sister and brother-in-law, there seemed to be nothing much I had to do. I felt a little disconnected from everything because of the pain killers, it was hot and crowded inside with so many people hanging around, and the atmosphere was depressing. I headed for the outside for some fresh air. And it was while I stood on the front steps, between the two-story white pillars, with my arms wrapped around myself against the chill in the air, that I saw Marley Cartwright again.

She was down the circular drive a bit, leaning against the side of a white Jeep, smoking a cigarette.

When I got closer, I saw that it wasn't her first. The ground around her was practically littered with butts. Five or six, at least. Mother would have a fit when she saw them. Then again, several of the cars were parked half off the drive, tearing up the grass, and that would probably make her even angrier than the cigarette butts.

Marley Cartwright looked up when I stopped a few yards away. For a second we just looked at one another. She had tear tracks on her cheeks, I noticed.

"Are you all right?"

She shrugged thin shoulders inside the dark coat. Stupid question, I suppose. It was a funeral; most of us would probably say we weren't all right.

She dug in her pocket and pulled out a pack of cigarettes, which she held out to me. I shook my head. "No thanks. I don't smoke."

"I didn't used to." Her voice was scratchy. "These days I do a lot of things I didn't do before."

I could imagine. If she'd started smoking since her baby disappeared, she probably drank, too. She might abuse drugs, illegal or prescription. Chances were good she had a doctor who kept her liberally supplied with antidepressants and sleeping pills and medicine against panic attacks. If I'd killed my child and was on trial for murder, I'd need all of those, and more.

"How did you know Sheila?" I asked. Dix had told me they'd had exercise classes together, but I wanted to talk to her, and it seemed an innocuous enough beginning to the conversation.

She coughed and dropped what was left of the cigarette on the ground and put her foot on it. "I met her at the gym. She was pregnant with Hannah, I was pregnant with Oliver."

"I'm her sister-in-law, Savannah. She's... she was married to my brother."

Marley nodded. "I know who you are. She talked about you."

"Really?" I blinked. "Why?"

"Just about how you'd solved some kind of mystery up in Nashville this fall. That you found a dead body?"

"I did, as a matter of fact. In early August. A colleague of mine."

"And you figured out what happened to her?"

"I had help," I said. "And I wasn't really trying to figure it out. I just kept stumbling over information, you know?"

Marley nodded. "Sheila thought a lot of you."

"She did? Wow. I had no idea." I'd assumed Sheila shared mother's opinion of me, that I was meddling in things that didn't concern me and that were unbecoming a gently-bred Southern Belle. To learn now—when she was dead—that she'd valued the parts of me that I'd assumed she deplored, made the whole situation even sadder.

And then I realized something. "Wait a second. Brenda's death was just a few months ago. I didn't realize you and Sheila were still friends."

Marley's mouth twisted. "Just because most of my so-called friends abandoned me when Oliver disappeared, doesn't mean everyone did. Sheila believed me."

"That's..." *Nice? Severely misguided? Stupid of Sheila?* "I'm sorry," I said, "I really don't mean to be rude, but how did Dix feel about that?"

Marley shook another cigarette out of the nearly depleted pack and lit it up. Her hands were shaking. "She didn't tell him. He wouldn't have understood."

She was probably right about that. Dix would have been worried, and with reason. According to Todd, Marley Cartwright was dangerous, and a cold-blooded killer.

Then again, a voice at the back of my head reminded me, Todd said the same thing about Rafe. And yes, granted, Rafe *is* both dangerous and has killed people, but that didn't mean I wasn't safe with him. And in any case, Todd might not be the best person to listen to when it came to this. It was his job to prosecute Marley, and I supposed he had to believe she was guilty.

"Sheila called me," Marley said, gazing at me with those ravaged eyes. "The day she died."

"Last Friday?" Tamara Grimaldi had told me Sheila's call records had shown a call to a friend in the afternoon on Friday. But she hadn't mentioned the friend's name. I kicked myself for not having asked. The fact that Sheila had called Marley Cartwright of all people might be significant.

Marley nodded. "We had lunch together the day before, after her doctor's appointment. She told me about the baby. And I was in with my lawyer all day Friday, preparing for the trial. My phone was turned off. I really wish I could have spoken to her one more time." Her eyes overflowed, and tears rolled down her thin cheeks.

"I'm sorry," I said. "But it wasn't like you could have known she wouldn't come home."

And if Marley had been with her lawyer all day, at least she had an alibi for the time of Sheila's murder. I was getting as bad as Todd when it came to assigning blame to people, I realized. Even if Marley smoked and probably drank and quite possibly had a supply of all sorts of drugs in her medicine cabinet, of course she'd had nothing to do with Sheila's death. Why would she kill the one person who still believed in her innocence?

Unless she was lying about that, and Sheila had found proof that Marley was guilty—

"What did she say when she called?"

"Here." Marley fumbled in her purse again. "You can listen to it."

She pulled out a cell phone and began manipulating buttons and icons. After a few seconds, she held the phone out in front of her. I glanced at the display—the message had been received from Sheila's phone at 2:04 PM last Friday—and then Sheila's voice started. "Marley? Hey, it's me. I'm sure you're probably in with the lawyer all day, but give me a call when you get this. It's important. I'm in Nashville right now, but I should be back in Sweetwater in a couple of hours. Call me!"

There was the sound of the disconnect, and then nothing. I blinked away tears. "She sounds so... alive."

Marley nodded. "That's why I can't bring myself to delete it. It's all that's left."

"It sounds like she was planning to drive back to Sweetwater after her appointment. I wonder what changed her mind."

"Not me," Marley said. "I told you I didn't talk to her."

"I believe you." If she had, there wouldn't be a message. "Did you play this for the detective from Nashville who called you?"

"Sure," Marley said with a shrug. "I don't have anything to hide."

So Grimaldi already knew that little tidbit of information. She hadn't shared it with me. Then again, there was no reason why she should. And obviously something had happened to change Sheila's mind. Maybe she'd made her call while leaving Dr. Rushing's office, and the doctor had called her back inside. Maybe that's why she'd never gotten into her car and driven back to Sweetwater.

"Would you mind giving me your number?" I asked. "Just in case I want to hear Sheila's voice again? You're not the only one who misses her."

Marley looked apprehensive for a second, but she gave it to me. After that we just stood in mostly companionable silence until I excused myself to go back inside. Marley got in her Jeep and went home.

Nineteen

"No," Tamara Grimaldi said when I called her that night, "I didn't make that connection. That's interesting."

I'd waited to call until late, since I knew she had that appointment with the kid's parents in the afternoon, and I didn't want to interrupt. And besides, I'd had things to do myself. The wake, or post-funeral get-together, went on for quite a while, and then we had to clean and straighten and pack up the leftover food and send the excess home with people. Mother has a cleaning crew that would be coming in to take care of any deep cleaning, but we had to live in the mansion until they could come on Monday, so at least we had to set everything back to rights again. And once that was done, I was so exhausted that I needed a nap. By the time I woke up, it was almost six, and I was afraid I'd have a hard time catching the detective on a Friday night. Luckily, she picked up right away, and I could tell her about my conversation with Marley Cartwright.

"Yes," I said, in response to her statement, "isn't it?" And I wasn't surprised she hadn't made the connection between Sheila's friend she'd spoken to earlier in the week, and the woman who was on trial for murder in Columbia. Columbia is an hour from Nashville, and Grimaldi wouldn't necessarily be up on the cases and trials going on two counties over. "Marley didn't kill Sheila, though." Accused murderess or no. "She was closeted with her lawyer all day and night."

"I'll have to check with him or her to confirm that. When I first spoke to Marley on Monday, I didn't realize it would be an issue."

"Why would Marley kill Sheila?"

"No idea," Grimaldi said. "I don't necessarily think she did. But I have to confirm her alibi if there's a chance she might be involved. When she was just a friend Sheila left a message for, it didn't matter, but now that I know she's on trial for murder, suddenly she's coming across as a person of interest."

"You can't be serious."

"Women kill each other, Ms. Martin," Grimaldi said. "You should know that."

I did know that. However— "She seemed really distraught that Sheila was dead. It seems Sheila was the only person who believed that Marley didn't kill little Oliver."

"So maybe Marley didn't kill her," Grimaldi said. "Maybe Marley asked Sheila to pick up some drugs while she was in Nashville. Maybe that's what she was doing in that parking lot."

"She wouldn't!"

"Are you sure?"

I wasn't, actually. Marley had told me herself that she was doing a lot of things now that she wouldn't have done two years ago. Drugs could be part of that. And while I didn't think Sheila would agree to do anything she knew was illegal, she might not have realized what she was doing. Maybe Marley had asked her to meet someone to pick up a package—"since you're going to be in Nashville anyway,"—and Sheila had shown up in the parking lot in good faith. But why had the person she was meeting killed her?

If it was a simple exchange of money for drugs, there would be no reason to kill the messenger.

"I don't know," Grimaldi said when I offered this thought. "But rest assured I'll ask Marley about it. As soon as I can."

"How did it go this afternoon? Did you talk to the parents of the kid in the picture?"

"Very nice family," Grimaldi said approvingly. "Cute kid. Little boy named Owen. No proof at all that he was adopted. Birth certificate—which they showed me—said he was born at St. Jerome's, to the people who are bringing him up."

"That doesn't mean anything," I answered. "David Flannery's birth certificate says he was born at St. Jerome's to Ginny and Sam, and he wasn't. Someone at St. Jerome's has a contact at the state department, and they're pushing through fake birth certificates."

"I'm aware of that, thank you. The way this is headed, we'll have to investigate all of St. Jerome's Hospital and all of the Tennessee Department of Health before we're done." She sighed.

I gave her a sympathetic moment of silence before I asked, "Were Owen's parents any help at all? Do you think they had anything to do with anything?"

"No," Grimaldi said. "They said they didn't go to St. Jerome's on Wednesday night, and they offered as alibis four hundred of their closest friends. They were at their weekly Wednesday night Bible study. Their alibis check out, the documentation for their child is in order, and unless I discover otherwise, there's absolutely nothing I can do."

"So why remove the picture? It doesn't make any sense."

"I know," Grimaldi said. "I'll keep digging. If anything else occurs to you, or if you learn that Sheila spoke to anyone else about what she was doing on Friday, please let me know."

I promised I would. "Any news from Atlanta?"

"Not today. You want me to ask him to call you?"

I hesitated for only a moment. "No. If he wants to call, he'll call. If he doesn't, there's no sense in forcing him."

"How do you feel?"

"Physically, not too bad. The bleeding has almost stopped. I have an appointment with the gynecologist on Monday, and we'll see if everything is getting back to normal. Emotionally I'm a bit of a wreck."

"I'm sorry this happened," Grimaldi said.

My voice caught. "I really wanted this baby. Now that I've lost it, I can't believe I considered getting rid of it."

"You would have made the right choice. You had that pill sitting in your apartment for days, and you didn't take it. You had weeks to decide what to do, and you never chose to terminate the pregnancy. If this hadn't happened, you would have had the baby and loved it no matter what anyone else thought."

"I wish I could be sure of that," I whispered.

"*I'm* sure of it." Her voice was strong. "There's no part of you that could terminate a pregnancy. Especially one where the father of the baby was Mr. Collier. I've seen the two of you together, and there's no way you'd willingly part with his child."

"I think I'm in love with him," I admitted.

"Took you long enough to figure that out," Detective Grimaldi responded, and severed the connection.

I spent Saturday with Dix, Abigail and Hannah, preparing for Christmas. With the big day just a month away, we went shopping for presents, and got them each a new dress for the big day. Abigail wanted satin and pink tulle with tiny white pearl embroidery; Hannah red velvet with a black, white and red tartan skirt and a huge bow in the back. I scraped the bottom of the savings account and bought myself a white blouse with ruffles around the neckline I could wear with several skirts I already owned. After the shopping was done, we went back to Dix's place and watched Disney Princess movies until the girls fell asleep. I spent the night in the guest room, and went with them to church in the morning; the same church where I was christened as a baby and married to Bradley at twenty three.

I don't consider myself particularly religious. In Nashville, I rarely go to church. In Sweetwater I'm used to it, since I was brought up that way. That doesn't mean I get a whole lot out of it. I go because I'm supposed to go, because a properly brought-up Southern girl goes to church on Sunday morning, does good deeds, and helps those less fortunate. It's a way of life more than a matter of faith.

This time I found myself praying. Or maybe bargaining is a better word. *Dear God, I'm so sorry I even thought about aborting my baby. If you'll just give me another chance—with Rafe and with another pregnancy—I promise I'll do better next time. Please take care of him, God, because I don't know what I'd do if something happened to him. And God, if you'll just make him forgive me and give me another chance, I promise I'll never worry about what anyone else thinks of me ever again! Oh yeah, and if you can help Tamara Grimaldi figure out who killed Sheila, so Dix and the girls can get some closure, that'd be great, too. Amen.*

I should have realized mother was planning something, but I didn't catch on until we walked through the doors of the Wayside Inn for the weekly family Sunday brunch that I usually miss because I live in Nashville, and I saw Todd and Sheriff Satterfield waiting at a table for twelve.

I stopped dead. "Oh, no."

"You have to face him sometime, darling," mother murmured next to me, taking my elbow in a grip that belied her dainty and elegant stature.

"I'm not afraid of facing him," I told her out of the corner of my mouth. "He's the one who doesn't want to see me."

"Nonsense, Savannah," mother said, towing me forward. "Todd adores you."

I dug my heels in. "Todd adored me before he found out that I've been sleeping with Rafe. Now he thinks I'm something that crawled out from under a rock."

Just my luck: both the men in my life, as incredibly different as they were in every other way, looked at me the with that same expression in their eyes.

"You're being silly, Savannah," mother said.

"I'm not! I saw him at the funeral, and he wouldn't even look at me. At least let me sit on the other end of the table."

Mother hesitated. "I'm sure he just needs a push in the right direction, darling." She reinforced her grip on my arm and moved us both forward. I sighed and followed.

"Todd." Mother beamed up at him. "Bob." She simpered at her current beau, who grinned back.

Sweetwater's sheriff is a grizzled man around sixty. He looks a lot like his son, only older, with crinkles at the corners of his eyes and gray hair. He's been sheriff almost as long as I can remember, and deputy sheriff before that, and apart from the fact that he's always been a little too quick to assume Rafe guilty of any little crime that comes along, I have nothing against him. We've always gotten along well. I'm sure he was almost as upset with me as Todd was—both on his son's behalf, and on my mother's—but he hid it well enough.

"Morning, Savannah." He bent and bussed my cheek.

"Morning, Sheriff." I shot a glance at Todd under my lashes. "Morning, Todd."

"Good morning," Todd said stiffly.

I glanced at mother. *See?*

She pressed her lips together. "Be a dear, Todd, and make sure Savannah gets situated comfortably." Her voice brooked no argument.

She transferred me expertly into Todd's unwilling hands. "She's still suffering the ill-effects of the recent tragedy."

She stepped away, leaving me to deal with Todd, and him with me. He looked acutely uncomfortable, as if having to touch me brought him physical pain. Yet when I tried to twitch out of his grip, he held on. A true Southern gentleman to the last. He didn't let go of me until I was seated, with the chair pushed under my posterior.

"Thank you," I said.

"A pleasure," Todd answered, while his voice, which sounded like it was squeezed out between two stones, said the opposite.

"Won't you sit?"

Todd hesitated. The appropriate response would be to do so, just as my invitation had been the appropriate response to his helping me to my seat, but he clearly didn't want to. In the end, good manners won out and he took the chair next to mine. We sat in silence for a while. I was toying with an apology, but part of me didn't want to apologize for having fallen in love with Rafe, since I wasn't actually sorry it had happened, and I couldn't bring myself to tell Todd that I was sorry for not having told him it was going on, either. Rafe's and my relationship was private, and none of Todd's business.

At the same time, I supposed I did owe him something. He'd proposed to me in good faith, and although I hadn't precisely led him on, I hadn't been as stand-offish as maybe I should have been, either. I'd let him take me to dinner and the theatre. I'd let him kiss me, and I'd told him, over and over, that there was nothing going on with me and Rafe. I'd even told him that if I were to marry anyone at all, I'd marry him, Todd. It was just that I wasn't ready to get married...

And instead the truth had been that I was head over heels for Rafe, and although I never seriously thought there could be anything between us, I still couldn't bring myself to get engaged to someone else. Back in September, when he had to hightail it to Memphis after Perry Fortunato's death, he'd told me not to get engaged before he got back, that he had plans for me. I guess when it came right down to it, I'd wanted those plans more than I wanted to be married to Todd.

And that was my right, and my choice, but I did owe Todd an explanation, if not precisely an apology. I was just about ready to open my mouth when Todd spoke. "How do you feel?"

I switched gears. "Better, thank you. I'll be seeing Dr. Seaver tomorrow, and probably get a clean bill of health."

I'd been through this once before, of course. I knew my body's functions would be back to normal within one to two weeks, and that my next cycle would probably be normal. I knew I'd have to wait another week or so to have sex, just to be safe. That hadn't been a problem when Bradley and I were married—he wasn't that interested in sex, at least not in sex with me—and it wouldn't be an issue now either, with Rafe gone.

"That's good," Todd said stiffly.

We spent another minute in silence.

"I spoke to Marley Cartwright on Friday," I said. "How's the trial going?"

Todd shrugged. "We've presented our case. It's the defense's turn."

"Denise Seaver told me she testified. That Marley neglected her child and was a bad mother."

"That's what she said."

"Doesn't it strike you as odd that Sheila would be friends with her?"

Sheila had been a great mother. She'd doted on Abigail and Hannah. And I found it hard to believe that she'd develop, let alone continue, a friendship with someone who was neglectful of her own child.

"Maybe she didn't know," Todd said.

"I don't mean then. I mean now."

"Now?"

"I spoke to Marley on Friday. She said she and Sheila were still friends. That Sheila didn't believe Marley did anything to Oliver."

"That doesn't sound like Sheila," Todd said.

I wanted to ask him if he'd known Sheila well enough to make that determination, but the truth was that I hadn't known Sheila well enough myself. She'd been married to my brother for seven years, and we'd always gotten along reasonably well when we saw one another, but that was only rarely, and we were both brought up as Southern women: effusive and warm on the outside, cool and watchful below. We tend to be mistrustful, cautious, and slow in developing attachments, especially to other women. There's a very catty, competitive sort of attitude to being a woman in the South. Below the surface, at least.

On the other hand, once we do get attached, we stick like molasses. If Sheila stood by Marley Cartwright, it could only be because Sheila truly believed that Marley hadn't hurt little Oliver. And if Sheila thought so, I wanted to know why.

"Sheila knew Marley. If she believed Marley was innocent, don't you think there might be something to it?"

"That isn't my call, Savannah," Todd said. "The county makes the choice to prosecute and I do the job, that's all. It doesn't matter whether I believe it or not."

Yet another reason I wouldn't have made it as a lawyer. In my mind there's always a right and a wrong, and I wouldn't feel good about prosecuting someone I honestly believed might be innocent.

"Surely you don't want her to go to prison if she isn't guilty."

"That's not up to me," Todd said. "A jury of her peers will determine her guilt or innocence. All I do is present the prosecution's case. The defense has the opportunity to present their own. I don't make any determinations beyond that."

"But..." I stopped and shook my head. It wasn't worth it. Sometimes I felt like Todd was speaking a different language; that he understood my words but not my meaning. I suspected he felt the same about me. "So how do you feel that things are going?"

"No way to know," Todd said, "until after the defense has presented its case next week."

"Did you feel like you made your case?"

"We can't prove she did it," Todd said, sounding annoyed by that fact, "but on the other hand, they can't prove she didn't. Dr. Seaver's testimony had an effect on the jury, I believe. Nobody likes a bad parent."

True. Although he didn't have to sound so pleased about it.

"Along with the fact that her husband divorced her after the baby disappeared, it's a strong indictment."

"It doesn't prove she did anything, though. Just that he might have thought she did." I thought for a second and added, "Maybe *he* did it. If he was planning to divorce her anyway, and he didn't want her to get custody of Oliver, he could have stolen the baby and given him to his new girlfriend to keep. Or his mother. Or somebody else. And then, when he'd divorced Marley, he took the baby back."

"I think we would have known if Oliver was alive and well and living with his father, Savannah," Todd said, with what I can only describe as a patronizing little smirk.

"Have you checked?"

Todd admitted that he hadn't.

"Then how do you know?" All right, so I didn't seriously think that Mr. Cartwright had kidnapped his own son and left his ex-wife to go to prison for murder, but did Todd have to be so condescending about it? If Sheila believed in Marley's innocence, there had to be a reason.

"There's no sign of Oliver, Savannah," Todd said. "Dad checked everywhere when he disappeared. The child dropped off the face of the earth. His mother killed him and hid the body."

"What if she didn't?"

"Then the jury will find her innocent and she'll be released."

I squinted at him. "Do you believe that?"

"I believe she did it," Todd said, "and I believe the jury will agree with me. And I hope Marley Cartwright ends up spending the rest of her life in prison."

Well, then. There didn't seem to be anything I could say after that, so we sat in silence. Dix and the girls, along with Catherine, Jonathan, and their three kids, came through the door shortly, and Todd excused himself to go greet his best friend. They sat down together, and Todd didn't return to the chair next to mine. I spent the meal helping Abigail with her scrambled eggs and hash brown casserole instead.

On our way outside after lunch, Dix pulled me aside. "I thought you'd like to know," he said, his voice low, "that Sam Flannery called me this morning."

My heart jumped. "Is everything OK? David hasn't run off again, has he?" Jumped a bus to Atlanta to try to find Rafe? Now *that* would be bad.

"Everything's fine," Dix said. "They called to tell me they've decided to go ahead with the DNA test."

Oh. "That's great. You can finally settle Elspeth's estate." And prove once and for all what we all already knew to be true, that Rafe was David's father.

Dix nodded. "I'll get her DNA from a hairbrush or something at her house. I wanted to ask about your boyfriend."

I made sure my voice was steady. "What about him?"

"Will he want to have his DNA matched? There's not much need, when everyone knows the truth already, but it would make it legal."

"You'd have to ask him," I said. If I had to guess, I'd say he'd probably want to, but it wasn't my place to make that kind of decision on his behalf.

"I don't know how to get in touch with him," Dix said. "I thought you would."

I shook my head. "He always just comes and goes. If you call Tamara Grimaldi, she can probably get a message to him."

"I'll do that," Dix said, but he sounded dissatisfied. "Thanks, sis."

He walked off.

Twenty

Mother drove me to Denise Seaver's office on Monday. My car was parked outside my apartment in Nashville, and I was getting royally sick and tired of not having my own mode of transportation. But Sheila's car was still in the impound lot, because Dix hadn't made arrangements to pick it up, and there were no other empty cars sitting around. So when mother informed me that she'd be coming to the gynecologist with me, it wasn't like I could say no.

I did draw the line at the waiting room door, though. She was welcome to drive me to the doctor's office, and if she wanted to talk to Dr. Seaver after the examination, she could feel free to do so, but it was *my* appointment, *my* body, and *my* miscarriage, and I was damned if I'd let my mother into the examining room with me while the doctor poked at my female parts. So mother took up station in the waiting room, sporting a dog-eared copy of Southern Living and a long-suffering attitude, while I went into the clinic with the nurse.

"Everything looks good," Denise Seaver said after checking me out and telling me I could sit up again. "Just a little bit of discharge that should go away in the next few days. Any discomfort?"

"Only occasionally. If I spend a lot of time on my feet, I bleed more and there's a little pain."

She nodded. "Be sure to get enough rest. It's been less than a week; you'll probably feel it for a few more days. Do you have pain medication left, or do you need a new prescription?"

"I have a couple of pills left," I said. I'd been taking them sparingly, only when I felt I really needed them, and there were still a few rattling around the bottom of the glass. They made me feel all floaty and nice when I took them, but they didn't only take away the physical pain, they made the grief easier to handle too, and because I knew I'd be dealing with the emotional ramifications of this for a while, I didn't want to get used to medicating the symptoms.

"Let me know if you need more."

I promised I would. "I don't suppose you have any idea why this happened? Was there anything in the file from the hospital?"

"I'm afraid no one can tell you that," Dr. Seaver said apologetically. "Most of the time, with a first trimester miscarriage like you had, it's because the baby wasn't developing properly and your body rejected it."

"But this was my second miscarriage. Is it possible there's something wrong with me?"

"It's possible," Dr. Seaver said, "but unlikely. Studies show that one in four pregnancies end in miscarriage. If you include loss that occurs before a positive pregnancy test, some estimates say that 40% of all conceptions result in loss. Every year, more than a million women miscarry. Some don't even know it."

"But I've had two miscarriages," I said.

"About one in thirty six women will have more than one. It doesn't usually mean anything other than chance. Your sister-in-law had two as well, and after having two healthy children. There was nothing wrong with her."

That made me feel a little better. At least until I remembered that Sheila was dead, and would have no more babies.

"If it happens again," Dr. Seaver said, "we'll have to do some tests. But for now, I don't think you have to worry. Especially since you're not in a permanent relationship."

"Right," I said. "Um... I think my mother wants to talk to you. She's out in the waiting room."

Dr. Seaver nodded. "Just come out and join us when you've finished getting dressed."

I said I would, and she left the room, hem flapping, and shut the door behind her. I slid off the examining table and went to exchange the paper gown I had on for my own clothes again.

By the time I made it out to the waiting room, mother and Dr. Seaver were deep in conversation, their heads together over my file. I arched my brows, but didn't comment. It was probably too much to expect Denise Seaver not to share her findings with my mother, doctor-patient privilege or no. They'd known each other as long as mother and Audrey, even if they weren't as close. And mother already knew everything anyway. Everything important. The one piece of information I'd been most eager to keep from her was Rafe, and that ship had sailed.

And now it appeared it had sailed as far as Dr. Seaver was concerned, too. When I approached, she looked up at me, a tiny wrinkle between her brows. "You didn't mention that the man you've been involved with was Rafael Collier, Savannah."

"I didn't think it was important," I said, when what I was thinking was, *I didn't think it was any of your business*. Of course I couldn't actually say that. Especially with mother here.

"I was there when he was born," Dr. Seaver said; I guess in an attempt to explain why she was interested. "One of my first deliveries. He almost killed his mother during labor."

Mother clicked her tongue. I rolled my eyes. It isn't as if you can blame a baby for being born, after all, is it? Even when the baby is Rafe

Collier, who'd always been blamed for everything that went wrong in his vicinity.

Dr. Seaver continued, "When LaDonna was pregnant, I did my best to talk her into giving the baby up for adoption. The Bog wasn't a place where one would want to see an innocent child brought up. Especially to a girl who was just a child herself."

Mother nodded in agreement.

"She refused, though. Insisted on keeping him. Said the baby's father would be back to marry her." She shook her head. "Of course, he never came."

"He couldn't," I said. "He was dead. Old Jim shot him when he realized that Tyrell was black. And if you ask me, it took a lot of guts for LaDonna to keep her baby. She was only fifteen. And it wasn't like having a colored baby was easy back then."

"It wouldn't be easy now," mother murmured.

I glanced at her. "Easier than thirty years ago. Maybe not in our family particularly, although we're not as bad as Old Jim Collier. But society as a whole is a lot less prejudiced these days."

Dr. Seaver nodded. "I realized once I saw the baby that it was for the best. It would have been hard to place a baby like that for adoption. If no one wanted him, he might have ended up in a children's home, and there's no way to know whether that would have been better or worse than what he had."

"His mother loved him," I said. "And he loved her. I don't think he fared too badly."

He'd grown up to be a hell of a man, pardon my French. And between LaDonna and the Bog, and a children's home somewhere, I was pretty sure I knew what his choice would have been. He might not wish his own childhood on anyone else, but I doubted he would have traded it, either. I felt the same way about it. I hated the fact that he'd suffered, but growing up the way he did, where he did, made him who he was, and I liked the person he'd become. If his life had been different, he might—would probably—have become someone else.

"It's a lot easier these days," Denise Seaver said. "The Swedish supermodel syndrome is still in effect, of course—"

"Swedish supermodel syndrome?"

She glanced at me. "Blonde, blue-eyed babies, especially boys, are most in demand."

Of course.

"But with the world a more inclusive place these days, it's become easier to place minority and mixed race children. Just look at..."

"David Flannery," I finished when she trailed off.

"Exactly. One couldn't wish for more devoted adoptive parents." Dr. Seaver smiled and got to her feet. "If there's nothing else I can do for you, I guess you're ready to go. You should be back to normal within another week, Savannah. If you have any problems, call me. If not, I'll see you at your regular check-up."

I nodded. "Before you go, doctor..."

"Yes?" Dr. Seaver said.

"The other day, at Sheila's funeral, you said that Marley Cartwright had neglected her baby. That she was an unfit mother."

Denise Seaver nodded. "I testified to that at her trial last week."

"Are you sure?"

She just stared at me, and I added, "See, she and Sheila were friends. And Sheila was a fabulous mother. I have a hard time believing she'd remain friends with a woman who neglected and killed her child."

"Maybe they weren't friends anymore," Denise Seaver suggested.

"They had lunch together last week after Sheila's appointment with you. And she called Marley from Nashville the day she died."

This piece of news seemed to shock both Dr. Seaver and mother. "Oh, dear," mother murmured. Denise Seaver shot her a look before focusing back on me.

"I can only speak to what I saw, Savannah. When Marley brought little Oliver with her for her postpartum appointments, she was having trouble adjusting to life as a mother. She told me more than once she felt out of her depth with the baby, that she was concerned about not being able to take care of him properly."

"But isn't that usual for a new mother? Babies don't come with instructions. Don't we all worry about doing something wrong?"

Mother nodded, a faint smile curving her lips. I guess she was thinking of her own experience with Catherine, trying to figure out motherhood for the first time. Rather nice of her, to tacitly admit to having vulnerabilities. It's not something I get from my mother a lot.

"A lot of women have what we call the baby blues," Dr. Seaver agreed, "but this was more severe. Marley had trouble sleeping. She stopped eating. She had feelings of guilt and inadequacy. She felt sadness and hopelessness, and suffered from low self-esteem. I prescribed antidepressants." She sighed. "I'll never forgive myself for not realizing that the postpartum depression had segued into postpartum psychosis. I should have seen the signs, but I didn't. If I had, perhaps things would have turned out different."

We sat in silence for a moment. It wasn't that I didn't believe her exactly, but this still didn't explain why Sheila, consummate mother that she was, had remained friends with Marley after Marley supposedly killed Oliver.

"I think I'll have to talk to Marley again," I muttered.

Both mother and Dr. Seaver looked at me.

"The trial is still going on," Dr. Seaver reminded me. "She'll be in court."

"I guess it'll have to wait until tonight. Any idea where she lives?"

"Still in the same house where she lived when Oliver disappeared," Dr. Seaver said. "And if that doesn't tell you what kind of person Marley Cartwright is, I don't know what will. To stay in the same house where she murdered her baby..." She shook her head, her lips tight.

Unless she didn't murder her baby.

I didn't say it. Dr. Seaver clearly knew in her own mind what had happened, and I didn't think there'd be any sense in trying to change her perception. Not that I necessarily even wanted to. She'd known Marley; I didn't. Chances were she knew what she was talking about. I just wanted to understand why Sheila and Marley were still friends after what had happened, because it didn't compute with the Sheila I knew.

The doctor disappeared back into her clinic, and mother and I went outside and got in the car. "What did the two of you talk about?" I wanted to know as soon as we were alone and mother's Chrysler was purring along the road back to Sweetwater.

Mother glanced at me. "Just your health, darling."

I thought about reminding her that I was almost twenty eight and that my gynecological health was my own business, but I bit my tongue. She wanted to know because she cared, even if she sometimes had a funny way of showing it, and griping would only make me sound like the little girl she still treated me as.

"What does Rafe Collier have to do with my health?" I asked instead.

Mother flushed beneath the expertly laid makeup. "Oh."

"Yes?"

She squirmed. "Denise mentioned him. I assumed you'd told her he was the father of the baby."

"No," I said, "I didn't think that was anyone's business but my own." I had mentioned Rafe's name a couple of times, so I wouldn't have been surprised if Dr. Seaver had drawn her own conclusions, but I hadn't come right out and told her.

"I'm afraid I accidentally let it slip," mother said.

She must have wanted someone to commiserate with. Someone who already knew the details. A woman, not Dix or Sheriff Satterfield.

"I guess you haven't been able to bring yourself to tell Audrey, have you?"

Mother shook her head, her cheeks pink. I took pity on her. She can't help being who she is, prejudices and all, any more than the rest of us can. And she's my mother; I love her.

"Did Dr. Seaver say anything interesting?"

"Just that she was surprised," mother said.

I'd assumed that. "Anything else?"

Mother glanced at me. "What would she say, darling? As you pointed out, it's no one's business but yours, really."

"I thought maybe she'd mentioned Elspeth Caulfield, or something. She was Elspeth's doctor too, back when Elspeth was pregnant."

"Oh," mother said. "Yes, in fact. She did. She mentioned how you had tracked down Elspeth's son—"

"David."

"—and how the boy had gotten adopted by a well-to-do interracial couple who couldn't have children of their own, and how he's doing very well. Much better than he would have been had his mother been allowed to keep him."

"That may be true," I conceded. "But Elspeth was seventeen, and if she wanted to keep her baby, I think she should have been allowed. Instead, the hospital told her he was stillborn and gave him to someone else. Elspeth probably spent years thinking her baby died."

And as someone who'd just gone through a miscarriage, I couldn't imagine carrying a child for nine months and then having it ripped out of my arms when it was born. Or even worse, carrying it for nine months, giving birth to it, taking care of it, and then having it disappear, like Marley's Oliver.

I glanced at mother. "What do you think about Marley Cartwright? If Sheila was friends with her, is it possible she didn't do anything to little Oliver?"

Mother hesitated. "Bob believes she did."

"But that's his job. It doesn't mean you have to agree. You're allowed to have your own opinion, even if your boyfriend doesn't share it."

Mother flushed delicately at the idea that she had a boyfriend. Still, she stood by her man. "I don't know Marley, darling. I have no way of knowing whether she's guilty or not. But if Bob says so, I'm inclined to believe him."

Of course.

"I'll just have to talk to her myself," I said, and settled back into the seat.

Instead of going home, mother drove into Sweetwater, to the square, and we ended up having lunch with Audrey. While we were sitting there, Bob Satterfield stopped by for a sandwich, and that may have been the reason mother wanted to eat at the Café on the Square in the first place. She'd kept her relationship with the sheriff a secret for a while—at least from me; the others had had their suspicions, being around more—and she was in that stage where she blushed prettily every time the two of them met in public. I wouldn't be surprised if she went out of her way to haunt places where she thought he might show up.

At any rate, when he saw us there, at a table for four, he came over to sit with us while the kitchen put together his roast beef on rye to go. He greeted mother with a wink, Audrey with a smile, and me with a polite nod. It was obvious he was upset with me, probably on Todd's behalf, and although he treated me cordially and correctly, it was without any of his usual jovial warmth.

I didn't let it stop me. "How's the trial going, sheriff?"

The sheriff allowed that as far as he knew, the trial was going well.

"Todd said the prosecution finished their case last week and now it's the defense's turn?"

Bob Satterfield nodded.

"Would you have any idea whether the defense planned to call Sheila to testify?"

"Sheila?" Sheriff Satterfield said. "Why?"

"They were friends. Sheila called Marley the day she died. I just wondered whether it might have something to do with the case." And whether—although it was far-fetched—the trial might have something to do with why Sheila was killed. If, for instance, someone wanted to keep her from testifying...

But no, that didn't make much sense, did it? What could she say, after all, that was explosive enough to kill her over? She had no proof that Marley didn't kill Oliver. If she did, the defense would have presented it already, and avoided the trial altogether. It would be different if Sheila was testifying for the prosecution, and she had proof that Marley *did* kill Oliver. That might be worth killing for. For Marley, anyway. But Todd would have mentioned it, if so.

"No idea, darlin'," the sheriff said. "I didn't interview her back then. Knew she knew Marley, but didn't think she knew anything about what happened. If she did, she never said."

"If she and Marley stayed friends, Sheila must have believed that Marley was innocent, don't you think?"

"Suppose so," the sheriff said. "Course, that don't mean nothing, darlin'. Just that Sheila was a good friend who was loyal to the people she cared about. Doesn't mean Marley isn't guilty."

I realized that. Sheila hadn't been stupid, though. If she believed that Marley was innocent, it was either the truth, or Marley was a truly superior actress. And that wasn't the impression I'd gotten. To me, Marley Cartwright had come across like a woman on the ragged edge of sanity.

"You investigated the case, right? What made you think she did it?"

"Well, now, darlin'," the sheriff said and leaned back on the spindly chair, "it wasn't like that. At first we thought the baby was kidnapped. We went door to door in the whole subdivision. We looked at hours of video surveillance, and talked to anyone who'd talk to us. Place was gated, and the only people going in and out were the residents, plus a few domestics. Cleaning and lawn crews, mostly, it being summer when it happened. We investigated all of 'em. Nobody saw nothing, everyone came out smelling like roses."

"No criminal records? No sex offenders?"

Mother clicked her tongue, and the sheriff glanced at her, but chose to answer my question. "There's a couple in every town, darlin'. Even in Sweetwater. But nobody that had anything to do with this."

"So what happened? Why did you decide to focus on Marley herself?"

The sheriff scratched his head. "Not sure I rightly remember, darlin'. Reckon it mighta been that doctor, Miz Seaver, coming in to say Marley was some kind of psychotic. Think that mighta been what started us looking more seriously at her."

"Interesting," I said. "Dr. Seaver told you that?"

"Reckon she did, darlin'. Why? Is it important?"

"I don't imagine it is," I said. "Just interesting."

Everywhere I turned, I found myself fetching up against Denise Seaver. She'd been Elspeth's doctor back when Elspeth was pregnant, and she'd been Sheila's doctor now. She'd been Marley's doctor, and she was mine. She'd even been LaDonna Collier's doctor thirty years ago, and had helped deliver Rafe. She'd known Dr. Rushing, Sheila, Marley, Elspeth, me... Sheila had called her the day she died, and Dr. Seaver had testified at Marley's trial. She knew all of us, and it seemed that of everyone, Denise Seaver would be the one who should be able to put together whatever was going on. Of everyone, she must be the one with the most knowledge about the situation. But even if she had the knowledge, with that damned doctor-patient confidentiality I'd counted on to cover my own buttocks, I didn't stand a chance of prying any information out of her.

My train of thought derailed when the waitress brought Sheriff Satterfield's sandwich and he prepared to leave. "Dinner at the Wayside Inn tonight?" he inquired of my mother, who blushed prettily and glanced at me.

"Don't mind me," I said, "I'll be fine on my own." And if I got tired of the mansion and my own company, I could always visit Dix.

Or Catherine and Jonathan. Or someone else. Like Marley Cartwright.

"You can have the car," mother told me, "in case you decide to go out. You'll pick me up, won't you, Bob?" She fluttered her eyelashes at him.

"'Course," the sheriff drawled back. "What kinda gentleman would I be if I didn't?"

He winked. Mother giggled—actually giggled—as he sauntered out, and she and Audrey put their heads together and stared after him like a couple of school girls.

Twenty-One

After mother headed off to the Wayside Inn with the sheriff, I took the Chrysler to Dix's house, where he and the girls were eating grilled cheese sandwiches and watching Pippi Longstocking. He gave me directions to Marley Cartwright's house. "Around the corner, three blocks, left on Warwick, right on Arundel Court. It's the house with all the curtains drawn." He wiped Hannah's face and added, "Why are you going to see Marley Cartwright?"

"Sheila thought she was innocent," I said. "I want to know why."

"How do you know that Sheila thought she was innocent?"

"Marley said so," I said. Dix just stared at me. "I know that's just Marley's word. But they stayed in touch. They had lunch together just before..."

I glanced at the girls, both of whom were staring up at me with wide, unblinking eyes, and reworded my statement, "last week, and on Friday, she called Marley from Nashville."

"What about?" Dix wanted to know.

"Nobody seems to know. Marley didn't pick up, so Sheila left a message. I heard it, but all it said was for Marley to call about something important."

"And she didn't?"

"I guess by the time she did, it was too late."

Dix thought for a second. "Do you want me to come with you?"

"Of course not," I said. "You guys are watching a movie. I'll be back in an hour or so, I'm sure."

"If you're not, should I call the sheriff?"

"He's having dinner with mother. If I'm not back in an hour, feel free to call my cell. Or drive over there. But I'm not worried."

"She's on trial for murder," Dix said.

"Sheila thought she was innocent. Maybe she is."

Dix shrugged. "Be careful."

"I'm always careful," I said. And if it wasn't entirely true, I'd never gone looking for any of the trouble that seemed to find me.

Nonetheless, after I'd wound my way through Copper Creek and was sitting in the driveway outside Marley's house, I rifled through my purse and pulled out what looked like two matching lipstick cylinders. I'd bought them a couple of months ago, after Tamara Grimaldi told me it might be a good idea to get some protection. One 'lipstick' contained a tiny dispenser of pepper spray, the other a 1.25" serrated blade. It wasn't long enough to stab anyone in the heart, at least per the expert in the weapons store, but I could use it to slit someone's wrist if they were incapacitated, and I could certainly use it to buy myself a little time to get away. Any amount of blood tends to be distracting, even if the knife isn't too big, and what it lacked in length it made up for in sharpness. I slipped both into the pockets of my cardigan, one on each side, before I exited the car and headed for the door.

Like Dix's house, and all the other houses in Copper Creek, Marley's home was a big brick McMansion. All the curtains were pulled across the windows, just as Dix had told me to expect, and there was no sign of life. Under normal circumstances, I'd have thought the place was empty, but because I'd been warned, I knocked and waited. And waited some more. And knocked again.

"Who is it?" Marley's voice said eventually, from inside.

I introduced myself. "We spoke at Sheila's funeral last week. Remember?"

"Of course I remember," Marley said, irritated, and opened the door. "I'm not stupid."

She looked rather the worse for wear, with her makeup smudged and her hair done à la bird's nest, dressed in a pair of oversized sweatpants and a faded T-shirt that hung from her shoulders. The arms visible below the sleeves had passed slender and edged into bony more than a few pounds ago.

"Sorry." There was a distinct odor of alcohol emanating from her. I pretended not to notice. In her position, I might have felt the need for a stiff drink or two myself. "Can I come in for a minute?"

"Are you sure you dare?" Marley asked, but she swung the door open. "Aren't you afraid I'll take a kitchen knife to you?"

I blanched, and surreptitiously felt for the pepper spray in my pocket. "Do you plan to?"

"Of course not." She tossed her head, and for a second I caught a glimpse of the woman she must have been before all this happened. Beautiful, spirited, and disdainful. "People act like they think I will. They go out of their way to avoid any contact with me. I have to drive to Franklin to go grocery shopping so people won't point and whisper."

She closed the door behind me with a thud, and flicked the lock. I shot a nervous glance at it over my shoulder.

"You coming?" She padded barefoot across the bamboo floor toward the family room in the back. The setup here was the same as in Dix's house, so I knew what to expect.

"Sure." She didn't ask me to take my boots off, so I didn't, just followed her down the hallway and into the combination eat-in kitchen/great room at the back of the house.

The TV was on, but the sound was muted, and a bottle of tequila was sitting in the middle of the table. Unlike at the front of the house, the curtains were open on the big picture window overlooking the backyard. I could see the outline of trees against the midnight blue sky.

"No neighbors back here," Marley said in explanation. "Out front they keep looking at me. But back here there's no one. Just a bunch of trees and a little creek—" Copper Creek, presumably, "—and then another row of houses on the other side. Drink?"

She lifted the bottle.

I shook my head. "No thanks."

"That's what Sheila said last time she was here." She sloshed a bit of tequila into a glass and took a sip. "You pregnant, too?"

"I was." I sat down in one corner of the sofa without waiting for an invitation. "I had a miscarriage last week."

"Sorry." She tossed back what was left in the glass.

"Me too. When was Sheila here?"

"I told you. Day before she died."

"Of course." Sheila had said she had plans. That's why she couldn't go anywhere with me when I asked. "She came here after her doctor's appointment."

"Right." Marley filled the glass again. "Bitch."

"Excuse me?"

"Dr. Seaver. She testified at the trial last week. Said I was a danger to Oliver. That I was taking medication for depression. And that I was psychotic."

"Wasn't it true?"

She shot me a look. "If I'd been thinking about hurting my baby, don't you think I would have asked for help?"

"I thought you did," I said. "From Dr. Seaver."

Marley snorted. "I wouldn't ask that woman for the time of day."

I must have looked surprised—Denise Seaver had been Marley's doctor, hadn't she?—because she added, "I was overwhelmed, OK?

My husband had left me—he was catting around the whole time I was pregnant, and as soon as Oliver was born, he moved out. Bastard." She drank a little more tequila. "So yeah, I was struggling. I was on my own with a newborn, and no help from anyone. Oliver had colic, so he didn't sleep much. Neither did I. And I was worried about not being able to take care of him, you know? I had no husband to support us. I thought I might lose the house, and we'd have to move, and I'd have to get some kind of job, and I was scared."

I nodded. Given the circumstances, I would have been scared, too. "But you didn't think about hurting Oliver?"

"Of course I didn't think about hurting him! I loved him!" She drained the glass and slammed it down on the table. "I wasn't psychotic. I have no idea why Dr. Seaver would say I was." She shook her head. "She was always stopping by to see how we were doing, and commenting on how tired I looked. How difficult it must be to have the responsibility all alone. How I looked like I was having a hard time coping."

"She seems very concerned with child welfare," I said lamely. Denise Seaver had tried to convince LaDonna to give up Rafe, and she had referred Elspeth and the Caulfields to St. Jerome's, where someone had arranged David's adoption. In both cases, it was because she thought the children would be better off with someone other than their biological parents.

Something tickled the back of my brain—something about Dr. Seaver and David, or Dr. Seaver and the Flannerys—but it disappeared before I could hang on to it.

Marley scowled. "She tried to convince me that Oliver would be better off with a mother who was healthy."

That hadn't been very nice of Dr. Seaver. Especially under the circumstances. Poor Marley had had enough on her plate without that.

"You and Sheila were friends back then, right?"

Marley nodded. "We met at the gym. She was almost ready to give birth to Hannah when I got pregnant with Oliver, and we talked a lot.

After Oliver was born, she came over sometimes to see how I was, but I was so angry about everything that I wasn't very nice to her."

"I'm sure she understood," I said.

"She did. She was a nurse, you know? She said that it's normal for mothers whose babies have colic to be exhausted and irritable and to cry a lot."

"I'm sure it is."

"That bitch Seaver didn't think so. She told the jury at the trial that I was suffering from fatigue and depression and delusions."

"Delusions?"

"She was always here," Marley said, her voice becoming shrill. "She'd stop by every day, sometimes more than once. She'd tell me my baby would be better off with someone else, and that I wasn't a good mother. I felt like she was hounding me."

"Was she really here more than once a day?"

"She lives just over there," Marley said, pointing through the trees. "So she'd stop the car on her way to work in the morning, or when she came home in the afternoon. Or both. Or she'd knock on the door when she was out walking at night, just to see how I was doing." Her voice twisted on the last half of the sentence, taking on a solicitous, unctuous sort of quality I assumed she thought she'd heard in Dr. Seaver's voice.

"Eventually I stopped answering the door, and then she started looking through the windows. She said I thought she was out to get me."

"And was she?" Judging from the closed curtains and her earlier remarks, Marley believed people were staring at her now too. Then again, after what had happened, they probably were.

"It felt like she was," Marley said, sloshing more tequila into her glass. "You sure you don't want some of this?"

"I'm positive, thanks. I'm taking pills that don't mix well with alcohol."

"Oh," Marley said and lifted the glass to her lips. "More for me."

"Knock yourself out." I thought for a moment. "I'm not trying to be insensitive, but would you mind telling me what happened the day Oliver d... disappeared?"

She sent me a jaundiced look. "It's OK if you believe he died. Most people do."

"Sheila didn't."

Marley shook her head.

"I'd like to understand why."

"She said she just knew. She knew I'd never do anything to my baby." She took another sip of tequila.

"So what happened?"

"It was a Wednesday," Marley said and leaned back in the sofa. "August, so it was warm. Sunny. We'd had a rough night. Oliver had been crying a lot, and neither one of us had gotten a lot of sleep. I was supposed to go to the gym for an aerobics class, but I couldn't drag myself there. Sheila stopped by afterwards to see if we were OK, and I told her I wished I'd never had a baby."

A tear leaked out of the corner of her eye and rolled down her thin cheek.

"I wouldn't let her come inside. Oliver had finally fallen asleep, outside on the back deck in a swing we had sitting there, and I didn't want her to wake him. I left him there while I went inside and took a shower. It was shady out there, and private, and it was only going to take a few minutes, but when I came back outside he was gone."

Tears were running down her cheeks now.

"What did you think had happened?" I asked.

"I had no idea." Marley dashed at her cheeks with the back of her hand. "I knew he couldn't have gone anywhere on his own—he was just a few months old—but I looked in the yard. Under the bushes and through the flowerbeds. Like I thought he might have crawled out of the swing and hidden." She gave a slightly hysterical hiccup of laughter.

"I ran through the house calling his name because I thought maybe I really was losing my mind, and he hadn't been outside at all, he was upstairs in his crib."

"But he wasn't."

She shook her head. "He wasn't anywhere. Not in the house, and not in the yard."

"So then you called the police?"

"I called Sheila first," Marley said. "And asked her if she'd taken my baby. She said of course she hadn't. She came over and helped me look, and she was the one who called the sheriff."

"And then what happened?"

The sheriff had already told me that they'd gone door to door and talked to people and checked video surveillance cameras and the like, but I wanted to hear Marley's take.

She twisted her hands together. "They looked for him. Everywhere. And when they couldn't find him, they started thinking that I'd done something to him. They said that because I wouldn't let Sheila in that morning, Oliver was already dead."

"That's ridiculous," I said, although a small part of me wondered if it might not be the truth. Her explanation made sense, but so did theirs. It all depended on the point of view.

"Dr. Seaver came by and gave me a prescription for something to calm me down, and said that I should clean the house, to keep busy and because if they found Oliver, they wouldn't give him back to me if they saw that I kept my house looking like a pigsty."

"She actually said that?"

Marley shrugged. "So I cleaned. All night long. Everything. Walls, windows, closets. And then it turned out that that was the wrong thing to do, because the police thought I'd been trying to hide evidence."

"I'm sorry," I said.

"They never found him anyhow. And now I'm probably going to jail for murder."

She sounded exhausted.

"Not necessarily," I said bracingly. "How's the trial going?"

"Not well." Marley leaned her head back against the sofa and closed her eyes. "My ex-husband came back to testify that I have a bad temper and that I threatened to hurt him."

"Did you?"

She opened her eyes again. "I was eight months pregnant, as big as a house, my feet were swollen, my back hurt, and my jackass of a husband told me he'd been sleeping with someone else since I started showing, since pregnant women didn't turn him on. He called me fat, the bastard. So I told him I'd cut off his Johnson if it happened again."

"But you didn't."

She shook her head. "A week after Oliver was born, he told me he was leaving. That I was a psycho. He said I killed Oliver to get back at him."

"This was at the trial?"

She nodded.

"Then what?"

"The jury believed him," Marley said. "Dr. Seaver said the same thing. And she's a doctor, so she should know, right? And some of the neighbors testified that they heard the baby crying all the time, so they made it sound like I was abusing him. And the sheriff testified that the police had talked to all the neighbors and checked everyone who went in and out of Copper Creek that morning, and there hadn't been anyone here who shouldn't have been. Nobody had seen anyone but me at the house."

"Someone could have come through the backyard, right?"

"Must have," Marley said. "The gate to the front was locked. And I know nobody came through the house."

"Those people over there," I pointed through the trees, "are they part of Copper Creek, too?"

She shook her head. "Different subdivision. Gated, as well. But there's a road from here to there. Dr. Seaver drives through Copper Creek to and from work."

Right. She had said Denise Seaver lived over there, and used to stop by. A little chime tinkled in the back of my head. "Was Dr. Seaver here the morning Oliver disappeared?"

Marley shook her head. "She wasn't here that day. Not until late. After everything had happened. That's when she told me I should clean the place up, so I would look like I had it together for when they found him. Does it matter?"

"Probably not," I admitted. "I was just thinking..."

"Yes?"

"Is it possible that Dr. Seaver might have taken Oliver?"

"Why?"

"Because she thought you weren't taking care of him properly. Because she thought he'd be better off with someone else."

"That's crazy," Marley said.

It was. Denise Seaver was a respected doctor with thirty years experience and a good reputation. She had taken care of my female health since I reached puberty, and she had helped deliver every child in our family for the past thirty years. My mother trusted her with her private parts, as well as with her children.

In spite of all that, my spider senses were tingling. Every thread seemed to go back to Denise Seaver. Somehow, she was connected to everyone and everything that had happened, from Elspeth and David twelve years ago, to Marley and Oliver two years ago, to Sheila now.

"What if..."

"Yes?" Marley said. She was sitting upright now, her eyes wide awake. In spite of her statement that it was crazy to suspect Dr. Seaver, she was clearly paying attention.

"What if she walked through the trees that day, and saw Oliver on the deck? That might have been the thing that sealed the deal for her, that you'd left him there and gone inside."

Marley nodded.

"She picked him up and took him back to her house and put him in the car and drove him to Nashville." Sheriff Satterfield had said that no one had been in Copper Creek who shouldn't have been; that only the people who lived there, and a few domestics, had come and gone. But Denise Seaver was a resident, she wouldn't set off any alarms.

"Why Nashville?" Marley wanted to know.

Because of St. Jerome's Hospital. Dr. Rushing seemed to have been running some sort of behind-the-scenes adoption agency out of St. Jerome's, so he probably knew of someone who was praying and hoping for a white baby boy.

"What did Oliver look like?"

Marley got to her feet, left the room, and came back a few seconds later with a picture in a frame, that she handed me. Baby Oliver grinned out, toothlessly, waving a stuffed lamb. He had a head of fuzzy hair, big eyes, and a cute, elfin-like face with a pointed chin.

"He looks like you," I remarked.

Marley nodded. "That's what everyone said. So you think Dr. Seaver took him to Nashville?"

I placed the photo on the table. "She would have dropped him off to a friend at a hospital up there, and then she would have turned around and come back. It wouldn't have taken but a couple of hours. Plenty of time to stop by later that night and tell you to clean the house really well. She might have already decided that she was going to try to make it look like you'd done something to Oliver. If you cleaned and sanitized the house, it would look like you were trying to hide evidence."

"What happened to Oliver?"

"If I'm right," I said, "someone adopted him."

Marley gripped the edge of the table, her knuckles white. "Who?"

"I have no idea." And no way of knowing, since St. Jerome's didn't seem to have kept records of the biological parents of the children they placed. "Although..."

"Yes?" Marley said.

"There was a photograph missing from Dr. Rushing's cork-board last week."

"What?"

I shook my head, too busy trying to get things straight in my mind to take the time out to explain. "Sheila was there on Friday. She tried to call you, but you didn't answer. What if she recognized the boy in the picture?"

"What boy?"

"It was a picture of a little boy. Two years old, give or take. Sitting on a pony."

"OK," Marley said. She must have come to the conclusion that it was easier just to let me prattle on, and I'd get around to explaining everything in my own time.

"Maybe Sheila recognized Oliver, and she called you—maybe Dr. Rushing left the office for a minute or two, to get something, maybe—and when he came back Sheila told him she'd recognized Oliver and that Oliver was kidnapped, and she was going to call the Sweetwater sheriff and tell him, and Dr. Rushing panicked and hit her over the back of the head and killed her."

"OK," Marley said again.

"He waited until after dark and dumped her body in the river and thought everything was fine. But then Rafe and I showed up on Monday, and started asking questions about David..."

"Who?"

"It's a long story. Another adoption that St. Jerome's facilitated twelve years ago, when the mother was told her baby was stillborn."

"Wow," Marley said.

"I know. But it doesn't matter right now. Other than that it sort of shows a history of doing sneaky, underhanded things. David was adopted by a nice family who had no idea that his mother didn't give him up voluntarily, and the same thing probably happened to Oliver."

"So Oliver is still alive?"

"If he is who I think he is," I said, "my friend Tamara Grimaldi with the Nashville police talked to his parents on Friday. The people who adopted him."

Marley had scooted up to the front of the sofa and looked ready to jump off. "Where is he?"

"I don't know that. Tamara Grimaldi would know. I'll find out tomorrow."

"Could I get him back?"

I hesitated. That might be trickier. First of all, the boy in the picture might not be Oliver. And even if he was, we'd still have to prove it. A DNA test would settle the question, but only if his parents agreed to do it, or if a judge ordered it done. And honestly, with Marley on trial for murder, a judge might think twice about pandering to what would probably look like a desperate attempt to shift blame before the verdict came down. And if Marley got convicted, even if the boy in the photograph was Oliver, she'd have to appeal and wait for another trial to get out of jail. And while all that went on, Oliver would get older and older, and more and more attached to his adoptive parents. At some point, like with David Flannery, it would come down to a choice between what the biological parent wanted and what was best for the child.

"He's my son!" Marley said.

"I know that," I answered, "I just don't know how difficult it would be to prove it..."

Marley glanced out the window into the darkness of the backyard. "I'm gonna kill Dr. Seaver. If she stole my baby, I swear to God, I'm gonna kill her."

"Don't say that where anyone can hear you." My cell phone rang, and I stuck my hand in my bag to dig for it. It was Dix. "I have to take this," I said. "Would you excuse me a second?"

Marley nodded. I headed out of the room into the hallway, and lowered my voice. "Hi, Dix."

"Everything OK?" my brother inquired, his voice normal.

"Everything's fine."

"Why are you whispering?"

"I just don't want her to know that we're talking about her. She's a little..." I hesitated before I could utter the word 'paranoid,' and substituted, "sensitive."

"You still in one piece?"

"Of course I'm in one piece. I told you not to worry."

A sound from the family room had me glancing over my shoulder, but I couldn't see anything. Marley wasn't coming toward me.

"You sure she isn't sneaking up behind you with a kitchen knife?"

"I'm positive," I said, but not without another look in the direction of the family room. There were no new noises. I headed back in that direction, slowly.

"So there's no need for me to run to the rescue, right?"

"Absolutely none. You enjoy spending the night with your girls." I reached the doorway to the family room and was just about to tell Dix goodnight when I realized the room was empty. "Damn."

"Excuse me?" Dix said.

"Sorry. But..." I looked around, and held the phone away from my mouth for a moment. "Marley?"

"What?" Dix said.

I put the phone back to my ear. "She's gone. The back door's open. She must have... Damn!"

"What?!"

"Nothing. I've got to go. I think she went to find Dr. Seaver."

"Why?"

"Long story. Just..." I stopped, before I could tell him to call the sheriff. If Marley had gone off the deep end and was heading through the trees to kill Dr. Seaver, I didn't think I wanted the sheriff's help. He thought Marley had killed Oliver anyway; he didn't need to arrest her on another murder charge. Or shoot her because he thought she was a dangerous criminal on a rampage. It would probably be better to handle it on my own. I was armed, after all. "I'll call you later, OK? I'll have to try to catch her."

I hung up before Dix had a chance to answer, and headed out through the back door into the dark yard on Marley's heels.

Twenty-Two

It was a rough few minutes fighting my way through the band of trees. The ground was soggy because of the recent rains, and I couldn't see where I was going. I kept splashing into little puddles that I was sure were ruining my suede boots, and naked branches kept snagging on my cardigan and whipping me across the face. Every once in a while I'd stop and listen for Marley ahead of me, so I'd know which direction to go.

I thought she'd be slower, since I knew she was barefoot and probably cold, in just her T-shirt, but by the time I had fought my way free of the trees on the other side of the little copse, she was far ahead, flitting toward a house in the distance.

"Marley!"

The slim figure hesitated for a moment, and I'm sure she glanced over her shoulder at me, but she continued forward. I put on a burst of speed, ignoring the complaints from my still-healing body, and got to the house just about a minute or so after Marley. By then, the back door was standing open—the glass was broken, a terra cotta pot lay in pieces on the tile floor inside, and Marley must have stuck her hand through the broken window and unlocked the door. Considerately, she'd left me a trail of blood and mud to follow: I assumed she must have cut her hand on the door or her foot on the glass on the way past. It wasn't much blood, just a drop here or there, so I knew she wasn't in danger of bleeding to death.

I entered into a sort of combination mud room/laundry, with a washer and a dryer positioned up against one wall and a pair of muddy rubber boots in a corner, under a slicker hanging from a hook. The tile continued through the doorway to the left and into the next room, from whence I could hear their voices. I crept that way, careful not to jostle any of the little pieces of terra cotta on the floor.

Dr. Seaver's voice was higher than usual and a little shrill; I could hear the fear in it. "Put the gun down, Marley. You don't want to do this."

Gun? That didn't sound good.

"Oh yes, I do!" Marley snarled.

"Don't you think you have enough problems without adding attempted murder of a witness to the list?"

If Dr. Seaver was trying to talk Marley out of using the gun—and where had she gotten her hands on a gun, anyway?—she was going about it all wrong. Reasoning with her wasn't going to do any good; just like any other normal person waving a deadly weapon, Marley was beyond reason. And given what she'd just found out, it was understandable. I hoped she wouldn't shoot the doctor, because she'd only complicate things, but I could understand the temptation.

"You stole my baby!"

There was a beat of silence, then— "You're talking crazy, Marley."

"No, I'm not! You walked through the backyard and took him, right off the porch."

"Now, why would I do that?" Denise Seaver said reasonably. "I know you're worried about the outcome of the trial, Marley, but accusing me of taking Oliver won't help your case."

"This isn't about my case," Marley shrieked. "You stole my baby. I know you did. And you had no right! He was mine!"

"You're imagining things again, Marley. Just like you did before Oliver died."

"He's not dead!"

Dr. Seaver ignored her. "Now, be a good girl about this. Put down the gun, and I'll get you some medicine that'll help you."

I heard a scuff, as if from a foot, and then a shot and a scream. When my ears stopped ringing, I heard Marley's voice again, edging into hysterical. "Stay where you are."

Uh-oh. Inching forward, I risked a glance around the door jamb into the kitchen to assess the situation.

Marley was standing on one side of the island, with a gun in both hands, pointed squarely at Dr. Seaver. Her face was pale, but her hands were steady. Her knuckles showed white where they gripped the handle.

Denise Seaver must have been making dinner when Marley barged in, because a whole green pepper lay on a chopping block with most of a julienned red pepper next to it. Over on the stove, something sizzled and popped. As I watched, Marley removed one hand from the gun and reached down to snag a big knife off the chopping block. She pulled it closer to herself. I surmised Denise Seaver might have been trying to reach for it when Marley shot her.

She was on the other side of the island, as far away from Marley as she could get, with her back up against the kitchen sink. She was pale and looked frightened, trying to wrap a kitchen towel around her right arm but not having much luck, possibly because her hands were shaking. When the removed the towel to try again, I saw a nice, neat groove skimming her forearm, oozing blood, and for a second my mind slipped sideways and I heard Rafe's voice—"It's just a scratch,"—before he peeled his T-shirt up and over his head to show me the damage done when a bullet from Perry Fortunato's gun had graced his side on its way toward me. He hadn't died then, or from the bullet that had lodged in his shoulder a month later, so I doubted Denise Seaver was mortally wounded now. I'm sure she knew it too, but her voice shook when she exclaimed, as if in disbelief, "You shot me."

"You shouldn't have reached for the knife," Marley said.

There was no arguing with that, so Dr. Seaver didn't try. "You'll go to jail for sure after this."

"Not once I explain what you did." Marley's voice was calm. "How you stole my baby and took him to Nashville and gave him to someone else to raise."

Dr. Seaver hesitated. "How do you know that?"

"Savannah told me," Marley said. I shrank back against the wall, but she didn't go on to say that I was right behind her and would be coming through the door at any moment. Maybe she didn't realize I'd followed her. I thought she'd reacted to my yell earlier, but it had been dark outside and hard to see; maybe I was wrong.

"Of course." Denise Seaver sounded displeased. "Did she tell you to come see me?"

Marley shook her head. "I did that on my own."

It could have been my imagination, but I thought this revelation brought on a lessening of tension in Denise Seaver's voice. "Why don't you put the gun down, and we'll talk. I'll need some bandages to wrap this. You don't want me to bleed to death, do you?"

Marley hesitated, and I didn't blame her. Not only was it one of those 'are you still beating your wife?' kind of questions, where you're damned if you answer yes and equally damned if you answer no, but the truth was that part of her probably *did* want Dr. Seaver to bleed to death. I know I would have.

"No," she said eventually, although she didn't sound like she meant it.

"That's a good girl. I'm just going to open this cabinet over here, next to the microwave—" I heard another scuff of feet, the sound of a cabinet door opening, and then a clang, and bang, and a sort of muffled thump. Then Denise Seaver's voice.

"Idiot."

Uh-oh, I thought. That didn't sound good, either.

It was probably worth risking another peek into the kitchen, so I curled myself carefully around the doorjamb.

The situation had changed radically from the last time I checked. Marley was now out for the count, crumpled on the floor, her dark hair fanning out across the Mexican tile. Denise Seaver stood over her with the pan from the stove in her hand, breathing hard. As I watched, she put it carefully back on the burner and turned off the heat, before stepping over Marley and scooping up the gun that had fallen from Marley's lax hand. She turned it on the unconscious woman.

"Dr. Seaver."

The words had left my lips before I was aware of opening my mouth. But really, it wasn't like I could stand there and let her shoot Marley, was it?

Dr. Seaver swung around, and for the third time in a few months, I found myself faced with a gun.

"I got here as fast as I could," I said, and with the gun pointed at my chest, I didn't have to pretend to be catching my breath as if I'd been hurrying. There's something about a loaded gun in your face that makes your breath go all on its own. "Oh, my God, are you OK?"

Ignoring the gun, as if I thought she'd just forgotten to lower it, I stepped closer to peer at her arm. She hadn't done anything to wrap it, and the furrow the bullet had punched in the skin was still oozing blood. My stomach turned over, but I swallowed down the nausea. I'd gotten quite good at that over the past two months, and now it came in handy yet again.

Unfortunately, it was the left arm Marley had hit, not the right, where it might do some good. The gun was still held steady in Dr. Seaver's right hand. She did lower it an inch or two, from my heart to my stomach. If she shot me there, it probably wouldn't be fatal. Especially since there wasn't anyone else in there anymore who might be harmed if she did.

I looked around. "Do you have something I can use to help you wrap that? Have you called 911 yet? Is someone coming? I've got a phone, if—"

"They're on their way," Denise Seaver said. Lying through her teeth. I'd been standing right outside the whole time, and she hadn't called anyone.

I glanced at Marley, prone on the floor. "I can't believe she'd do this. We were just sitting there talking, having a drink, and I knew she was distraught, but I had no idea..."

I glanced up at Dr. Seaver, doing my best to look horrified and confused. "I got a phone call from my brother, just making sure I was all right, you know? He was a little worried about me going over to Marley's alone, so he called to make sure she hadn't gone off the deep end and tried to hurt me. And I didn't want her to hear me talking to him, so I excused myself to go out into the hallway, and by the time I got back to the family room, the door was open and she was gone. I tried to follow her, but it was dark and she knew the way and I didn't, and I lost her somewhere in the trees..." I trailed off, pleased that all of this, at least, was true. I'm not a good liar, and every time I'm able to avoid lying, I consider it a victory.

"She burst in here a few minutes ago," Denise Seaver said, and finally she lowered the gun to where it wasn't pointed at me anymore. "This is hers. She tried to shoot me with it. So I hit her with the frying pan and took it away from her."

"You should probably put it down. You're messing up her fingerprints."

I glanced around the kitchen without waiting to see whether she took the advice. "Nice place. Have you lived here long?"

"Five or six years," Dr. Seaver said, keeping hold of the gun. "As long as the subdivision's been here."

"I had no idea you lived so close to Marley. Or to Dix and Sheila, for that matter." I put my hands in my pockets. Dr. Seaver watched me, but when I didn't bring either of them back out with a weapon, she moved her attention back up to my face.

"What were you and Marley talking about?"

"Before my brother called, you mean? Just... things." I shrugged, to show how unimportant they'd been. "Sheila dying was difficult for her. For some reason Sheila thought Marley hadn't killed Oliver. Sheila was pretty much the only person who did, from what I understand, and I guess Sheila dying pushed Marley off the deep end."

"So you didn't talk about me?"

"You?" I blinked. "I guess we might have. A little. Marley said the trial wasn't going well. You'd testified that she was psychotic back then, and she said that it seemed like the jury believed you. And she said you'd been hounding her when Oliver was a baby. That you came by all the time to see how she was doing."

"I was worried," Dr. Seaver said.

"Of course. And with reason, as it turned out." I glanced at Marley's still form. She hadn't so much as twitched, but at least her chest was rising and falling. Hopefully Dr. Seaver hadn't cracked her skull with that heavy cast iron frying pan. "Poor thing. I don't understand how a mother can kill her own child, do you? But I guess maybe she wasn't responsible, really. Postpartum psychosis is something like temporary insanity, isn't it? She did sound pretty paranoid when I spoke to her earlier. She keeps all her windows covered because she says people are staring at her, did you know that?"

"She's off her rocker," Denise Seaver said bluntly. "She came in here screaming that I'd stolen her baby."

"That's crazy." I looked up, aware of how narrowly she was watching me. "Is it possible that she doesn't remember what she did? You know, total break with reality? Maybe she doesn't remember killing Oliver, and she really believes that someone kidnapped him?"

"Anything's possible," Dr. Seaver said. "She said you told her that I did."

"Me?" I blinked innocently. "Why would I do that?"

"I can't imagine," Dr. Seaver said dryly. "Could it have something to do with your visit to Emil Rushing's office?"

I blinked for real this time. "What do you mean? We just wanted to talk to him about..."

David Flannery, I was about to say. But suddenly something that had troubled me earlier fell into place. When I first asked her about it, Denise Seaver had told me David was stillborn, and I'd assumed Dr. Rushing and the staff at St. Jerome's had lied to her, just as they'd lied to Elspeth. But mother had told me earlier today that when she and Dr. Seaver talked, Denise Seaver had described David's adoption by the lovely, interracial Mr. and Mrs. Flannery. Details she wouldn't have known if she hadn't been aware of David's survival until I told her a few days ago. So she'd lied. And if she'd lied about that, might she not have lied about other things, too?

I kept coming back to Dr. Rushing's office and the pictures on the cork-board.

Sheila might have seen Dix's picture of David, the one from Elspeth's house, at the office sometime. If so, she might have recognized David in the picture on Dr. Rushing's cork-board. If she asked about him, it might have put the wind up Dr. Rushing. But if she had, she would have called Dix on Friday afternoon. And she hadn't. She'd called Marley. And Marley didn't know or care about David.

So what if Sheila had seen someone else instead? What if that missing picture, the little boy on the pony that Detective Grimaldi had tracked to Mt. Juliet, was Oliver Cartwright?

Had Sheila confronted Dr. Rushing with her suspicions, and he'd killed her and dumped her body in the river?

But wouldn't he have taken the picture of Oliver off the cork-board on Friday, then? Why wait three more days, until Sheila's body was discovered, until a full-fledged homicide investigation was underway, and until Rafe and I had had time to stop by St. Jerome's? That didn't make any sense.

Unless...

I turned to Dr. Seaver. "It was you. When Marley didn't pick up the phone, Sheila called you."

Denise Seaver smiled, but it wasn't her usual kind, earth-motherly smile. Instead, it was edged and sharp. The gun was back up and pointing at me again. "Figured that out, did you?"

"I knew all along," I said. "Her phone was gone, but the police checked her call records. She called Marley, and then she called you. You told Detective Grimaldi that it had been a follow-up after her appointment. And instead... what?"

"It *was* a follow-up to her appointment," Dr. Seaver said. "We talked about Marley and Oliver and the trial. She wanted to be like you, and solve a mystery." She chuckled.

Oh, my God. This was because I'd figured out who killed Brenda Puckett? If I hadn't, Sheila might be alive?

"When she called me on Friday afternoon," Dr. Seaver said, "I told her to sit tight until I could get up to Nashville so we could talk to Emil together. I said she should make sure not to tip anyone off by going back inside, but to find an out-of-the way place where she could stay and wait for me. She spent a couple hours in her car, sitting in the back of the parking lot outside the hospital."

My heart was beating hard. "What happened when you got there?"

She crossed her ankles and leaned back against the island. "By then it was dark. And Emil had left. I told Sheila I knew where he lived, and for her to follow me. Instead, I drove to a parking lot near the river in Donelson, and when she stopped the car, I hit her over the head and threw her in. I tossed her purse in after her, left her car there, and drove home."

Her voice was chillingly unemotional.

"So two years ago you took Oliver off Marley's back porch, and you drove him to Nashville and dropped him off to Dr. Rushing, and he handed him off to the new parents. St. Jerome's arranged for a new birth certificate, and everyone probably got paid handsomely..."

"I didn't do it for the money," Denise Seaver said coldly.

Of course not. And that must be how she managed to sleep at night.

"It's hard to argue about David," I admitted. "Elspeth Caulfield would have made a horrible mother, and Rafe wasn't in any position to be a father. And God knows poor LaDonna wouldn't have done any better. David is happy and healthy and has two parents who love him. He's better off than he would have been otherwise. But you shouldn't have lied to Elspeth."

"It was for her own good," Denise Seaver said.

"Yes, but..."

I broke off without finishing the sentence, and shook my head. I'd seen this kind of blind conviction before, in—ironically—Elspeth herself, and I knew there was nothing I could say that would convince her she'd done anything wrong.

"Oliver, though. He was Marley's son. She was an adult. And she was doing her best. Her husband had left her and she was struggling with post-partum depression and a colicky newborn, but she loved her baby. And you stole him. That's a crime."

"I did it for Oliver," Dr. Seaver said.

"Why didn't you call children's services, if you were concerned about his welfare? They could have helped."

"They never do anything. Take a child away for a couple of months, and then give her back to the parents. Right back into the same untenable situation." She shook her head. "Much better to make a clean break. Find new parents who care."

It sounded like she spoke from experience. "Did you grow up like that?"

"I grew up in the Bog," Denise Seaver said. "With Wanda."

"Wanda?"

It took me a few seconds of rifling through the archive in the back brain to connect the dots. Then I remembered. Wanda Collier was Old Jim's wife. LaDonna's mother and Rafe's grandmother. She'd died long before he was born.

"Are you related to Rafe?"

"Distantly," Dr. Seaver said. "Second cousins twice removed, or something like it. Not a connection I've ever wanted to pursue."

Good thing. Not that Rafe's family tree wasn't already full of criminals. He might not mind the addition of another.

"What about Dr. Rushing?" I asked.

Dr. Seaver smiled. "That's your fault."

"Excuse me?"

"If you hadn't gone to St. Jerome's last week and put the wind up Emil, I wouldn't have had to kill him. He knew about Sheila, of course, that she was dead, but he had no reason to suspect that I'd had anything to do with it. So he called me as soon as you left, and told me you'd been there asking questions about David Flannery. He was worried that your boyfriend was planning to cause a stink."

"Rafe didn't say a word about being David's father."

"Emil said they looked exactly the same." Dr. Seaver shook her head in exasperation. "It's those kinds of things you just can't predict. Like Emil being stupid enough to put Oliver's picture on his wall, and Sheila being stubborn enough not to believe that Marley killed him."

"So you drove up there again?"

"I didn't have a choice," Denise Seaver said. "Emil waited for me in his office, and after he was dead, I removed the photograph of Oliver from the wall and the paperwork from the filing cabinet."

"Why didn't you remove David's? That's why he called you, wasn't it?"

"David isn't important," Dr. Seaver said. "Too many people know about him already. And there was no crime committed there. The elder Caulfields signed the adoption papers, and it was their idea to tell Elspeth the baby was stillborn. Someone will take the fall for falsifying the birth certificate, but it won't be me."

No, and unless I could figure something out, she wouldn't take the fall for any of the rest of it, either. Slowly, I lifted my hand out of my pocket. Her eyes narrowed, watching it.

"Lipstick," I said, showing her the cylinder.

She relaxed a little. I was feeling pretty good, until I twisted off the cap and realized I'd pulled out the wrong canister. Pepper spray in one pocket, tiny knife in the other. I'd wanted the spray; this was the knife.

I managed a weak smile. "Wrong color."

I dropped it back down, and fumbled for the other one. Denise Seaver watched me narrowly. "See?" I pulled out the other cylinder and untwisted the cap. "I'm just going to..."

I lifted the tiny can of pepper spray and took aim, desperately trying to make it look like I was getting ready to touch up my lips. She caught on about a second too soon, and the spray hit her face at the same time as she pulled the trigger on the gun. Maybe one was a result of the other, or maybe it was a reflex. I'm not really sure. I threw myself sideways, hoping to avoid the bullet, but as it turns out, it's hard to guess where someone's aiming. Either that, or I didn't move fast enough.

Granted, it could have been a lot worse. At first, all I felt was a sort of punch to the shoulder. It took a few seconds before it started to hurt. But then it *really* hurt.

I didn't have time to worry about it, though. Denise Seaver had dropped the gun and was clawing at her face, keening. The gun was on the floor a few feet away, and I threw myself at it, skidding right into Marley on the way, sending her sliding across the tile. She ended up bumping her head again, this time on the stove. But the new injury on top of the old one elicited a weak moan, so at least I knew she was still alive.

I scooped up the gun one-handed, and turned to face Dr. Seaver, and that's what I was doing when the back door exploded inward and a group of men burst through. In the lead was Cletus Johnson, one of Bob Satterfield's deputies, and right behind him was my brother. The third man stepped across Marley's prone body and gathered me in his arms. "You're safe now. I'm here. I'll take care of you, Savannah."

Twenty-Three

"And that's what happened," Todd said two hours later, after explaining to me that Dix had called him and he'd called Cletus and all three of them had gotten to Denise Seaver's place as fast as they could considering that Dix had had to make arrangements for Abigail and Hannah before he could leave home.

By this point I was in the hospital. Again. For the second time in a week.

A different hospital this time, and for a very different reason.

And guess what? Painful as the miscarriage had been, physically speaking, being shot was worse. I felt like my shoulder was on fire, and according to Cletus Johnson, who'd been shot once himself, I was actually lucky, because I already had some painkillers in me. If not, I would have felt worse.

He'd called for an ambulance and waited for it to arrive before taking Denise Seaver off to jail. The ambulance took Marley and me to the hospital, where Marley was diagnosed with a concussion—from being hit with the frying pan and then shoved headlong into the stove—while I ended up on the operating table so the doctor could dig the bullet out of my shoulder. That's when I learned I'd been lucky yet again: the bullet had avoided shattering any bones, so healing wouldn't be as God-awful as it might have been otherwise.

I came away from the experience with a whole new admiration for Rafe, and that's saying something, when I practically worshipped the ground he walked on. But he'd been shot in the shoulder two months ago, just about in the same spot where I'd been shot now—if we ever got back together, we'd have matching scars—but where I felt pretty certain I was at death's door at the moment, he'd seemed absolutely fine when it happened to him. He'd turned a little pale when Wendell poked at his shoulder, but he hadn't punched him. And that's what I wanted to do to anyone who came too close to me.

Dix had carefully refrained from touching me when he leaned in to tell me he had to head back to the girls. "Jonathan's with them. But he wants to go back to his own family. And Abby and Hannah need me. Things are scary enough for them right now, without daddy disappearing too."

I nodded. "Go. I'm fine. Thank you for coming when you did."

"I'm just sorry it took so long," Dix said.

"It's all right. I had it under control."

"So we saw." He grinned. "Anything I can do for you before I leave?"

I had to concentrate hard to get my brain to cooperate. The pain and drugs and everything that had happened had combined into a sort of stew up there. "Could you call Tamara Grimaldi? She'll want to get her hands on Dr. Seaver, too. I'm sure two murders in Nashville trump a couple of attempted murders and a kidnapping down here."

"Sure. I have the number; I'll give her a call." He leaned in and pecked me on the forehead. "Rest up, sis. I'll be back in the morning."

I nodded drowsily. "Keep mom away until then too, if you can."

Dix promised he'd try, and left. I leaned back against the pillows and closed my eyes.

I hadn't given Todd another thought; if anything, I guess I just assumed he went home with Dix. That's until I opened my eyes again a little later, and found him sitting next to the bed.

"Oh." I tried to sit up, realized it made my shoulder feel as if someone had jabbed a red-hot poker into it, and slumped back down. "Hi, Todd."

"Savannah." He looked uncomfortable. "How do you feel?"

"Like someone shot me," I said.

Todd grimaced. "I'm sorry."

"That's all right. It wasn't your fault. But thanks for coming to my rescue."

He nodded. We sat in uncomfortable silence for a few seconds, both of us no doubt trying to come up with something to say. I was rather amazed that he was here at all, since the last time I'd seen him, he'd given me the brush-off.

"How did that happen?" I asked eventually. "Dix was too busy to get home to give me any of the details."

"Oh," Todd said, his face lightening in relief, "let me tell you." He went through everything from his point of view, and ended with, "And that's what happened."

"Thank you."

He shook his head. "When we heard the shot, I thought we were too late."

"I had it under control," I said, in spite of the bandage over my shoulder and the pain I was in.

Unlike Dix, Todd didn't smile. Instead he looked deeply into my eyes as he reached for my hand. "I thought I'd lost you."

I let him take it and hold on, but I kept quiet. There was nothing to say. He'd lost me a long time ago, and not to a bullet, but it wasn't like I could say that. So I just smiled. Politely.

Todd continued, stroking the back of my hand with his thumb. "I'm sorry for the way I acted yesterday. And last week."

"It's OK," I said. "I understand."

"I just..." He shook his head. "You told me there was nothing going on between the two of you."

"There wasn't." Then.

"You got pregnant!" Todd said.

Right. "It was a mistake. I should have been more careful." Should have thought about what I was doing, and the consequences I might be dealing with later, instead of being so overwhelmed with what I was feeling that I didn't think at all. "It won't happen again."

Except it already had. We hadn't used protection the second time either. But I'd already—still—been pregnant then, so it wasn't like that encounter could result in another pregnancy.

"I was hoping you'd say that," Todd said, and I came back to myself with the realization that we seemed to be talking about different topics. A quick look back over the conversation told me what the problem was—I'd been talking about protection, he'd been talking about my sleeping with Rafe in the first place—but again, it wasn't like I could tell him. So I smiled, a little stiffly, and remained silent.

"Savannah..." Todd said, squeezing my hand.

Uh-oh.

"Todd." Better to grab the bull by the horns before he could propose again. "Listen. It's not that I don't appreciate it. I do. I'm honored that you care so much that you want me to become your wife. But I'm not planning to marry anyone. No time soon."

Todd sat back and let go of my hand with an impatient huff. "I'm here, Savannah. Next to your bed, pouring my heart out. And where is he?"

"Not here," I said.

"Right. Did you call him?"

No. And I didn't plan to.

"He might never come back," Todd said. "He got what he wanted from you, and now he's moved on."

Quite possible. Likely, in fact. "I know that. Can we stop talking about him, please?"

"I just want you to understand—" Todd began.

I overrode him. "I understand, believe me. All he wanted was sex, and now that he's gotten it, he won't be back. He didn't sign on for fatherhood, and once he figured out I was pregnant, he ran as fast and as far as he could. He might never come back. I know. And I don't want to talk about it. Is that OK with you?"

I didn't wait for Todd's murmured agreement before I continued, "So you'll drop the charges against Marley, right? Now that you know that she didn't do anything to Oliver?"

"It isn't quite as easy as that," Todd demurred, but he added, "We'll have to work something out, I suppose."

"I would hope so. You can't send her to jail for murder when the person she's supposed to have killed is alive and well and was, in fact, stolen from her."

"No," Todd admitted, "I guess we can't. I'll take care of it tomorrow."

I lay back against the pillows. "Thank you. How *is* Marley?"

"Resting," Todd said. "I haven't been in to see her, but the doctor said she'll be fine. She got hit pretty hard."

"It was a cast iron frying pan. Enough to give anyone a concussion." My eyes were drifting shut even as I struggled to keep them open. "But at least I stopped Dr. Seaver from shooting her."

"Too bad she shot you instead," Todd said.

I tried to shrug, but it hurt too much. "It happens."

Todd said something else, but I was already half asleep, and I missed it.

When I woke up again, it was morning, and my hospital room was full of people. Todd was still there—or maybe he was back; his clothes looked different, but it's hard to tell one navy blue suit and white shirt from another, really—and Dix was there too, leaning against the wall next to the window. The girls were with him, peering nervously at me. I guess maybe they'd wanted to make sure for themselves that I was all right. Having their aunt get shot right on the heels of their mother dying must be scary for them. I smiled and twiddled the fingers on my good arm in their direction. Abigail waved back, but Hannah was too busy sucking her thumb.

Mother sat in a chair next to the bed, and looked positively haggard. "Savannah."

"Hi, mom." I tried for a sunny smile, but it fell flat.

"Are you all right, darling?"

"I'm fine," I said. "My shoulder hurts, but the doctor said it should be fine in a few weeks. And I caught her."

"You sure did." The voice came from over by the door, and when I looked in that direction, I saw Tamara Grimaldi in the opening. She was carrying a bunch of flowers, and was smiling. "I guess congratulations are in order. You've done my job for me. Again."

I smiled back. "No offense, detective, but I wouldn't want your job for all the money in the world. Have you talked to her?"

She shook her head. "I came here first. Didn't want the flowers to wilt on the way."

Dix moved to take them from her, and she gave him a smile too. He blinked. She added, "You know you shouldn't do things like that, Ms. Martin."

"I had to follow Marley," I said. "I couldn't let her go over there alone. She was talking crazy, saying how she wanted to kill Dr. Seaver. And then I had to stop Dr. Seaver from shooting Marley instead. She had the gun pointed right at her. It wasn't like I had a choice."

"No," Detective Grimaldi answered, "I imagine not. You never seem to have a choice, do you?"

I shrugged. It still wasn't easy to do. My shoulder was stiff and painful, and I grimaced.

"How do you feel?" the detective asked.

I gave her the same answer I'd given Todd last night. "Like someone shot me."

As opposed to Todd, Tamara Grimaldi grinned. "You'll feel better in a few days. Good as new in a couple of weeks. Just take it easy and don't try to lift anything. Don't do any pushups for a while."

"I never do pushups. You sound as if you're speaking from experience."

"It's a job hazard," Grimaldi said. "You want to tell me what happened? I got the basic information from your brother on the phone last night, but he didn't have all the details."

"Sure." I launched into a description of the events of last night, complete with shocked sound effects from mother and winces from Todd and Dix. When I got to the end, Tamara Grimaldi shook her head.

"You did a good job, Ms. Martin. But please don't do anything like that again. I'd hate to have to explain—" She stopped.

I bit my lip. "Have you spoken to him?"

She shook her head. "Wanted to talk to you first. Thought you might not want me to."

"I don't." If Rafe came back, I wanted it to be because he wanted to, not because he had to. Or felt he had to. Or because I was hurt.

Grimaldi nodded. It must be what she'd expected to hear.

"What about Marley?" I asked. "Will she get her baby back?"

"He's not a baby anymore," Grimaldi said. "But yes, once we've ascertained that he's her son, she'll get him back. I've got a judge working on a court order, just in case the adoptive parents make a stink."

Mother clicked her tongue. Todd looked guilty, probably because he'd been the one prosecuting Marley.

"This sucks for them, doesn't it?" I said. "If they adopted him thinking everything was legal and above board..."

"They didn't," Grimaldi answered. "If nothing else, they knew there were no adoption papers. I don't think I can get them on conspiracy to commit kidnapping, although I'd like to try. That's none of your concern, though. We'll handle that, along with rooting out Emil Rushing's contact in the Department of Health. You just focus on getting better."

"I just feel so bad for Marley. Two years of hell, just because Denise Seaver decided she didn't deserve to keep her child. And then the trial on top of losing Oliver in the first place..."

"He's still small enough that the transition will be pretty easy for him," Grimaldi said. "In another year, he probably won't remember any of this."

"Marley will."

"There's nothing I can do about that. But she's getting her child back. She'll be fine."

"Have you spoken to her?"

Grimaldi shook her head. "She's my next stop. Then I'm off to the sheriff's office to see Denise Seaver."

"Are you taking her to Nashville with you?"

"Eventually," Grimaldi said. "For the time being, I'm just going to leave her here. We'll file charges for murder up in Nashville once we get our ducks in a row. In the meantime, Sheriff Satterfield has everything he needs to hold her for attempted murder and kidnapping here. She'll be busy for a good long time either way."

She reached out and put a hand on my shoulder for a second. My good shoulder. "Take care of yourself, Ms. Martin. And let me know when you're ready to come back to Nashville. I'll pick you up and drive you home, if you want."

I smiled. "I might just take you up on that."

I wanted to go home. To get back to my regular life. Trying to rustle up real estate clients during the day and reading romance novels and eating ice cream at night. No more murders. No more unsuitable boyfriends, either. Just me, by myself.

"Don't mind if you do," Grimaldi said. She straightened up and glanced around the room. "Mrs. Martin." She nodded to mother, who nodded back. "Mr. Satterfield." Todd nodded too, if a little stiffly. "Mr. Martin." She hesitated for a moment before she held out her hand. Dix took it. "I know it won't bring your wife back, but Dr. Seaver will pay for what she did. I swear."

"Thank you," Dix said, and it sounded like his voice might have been a little froggy.

Tamara Grimaldi turned to the girls. "It was nice to meet you both. You take care of your daddy, OK?"

Abby nodded solemnly. Hannah took the thumb out of her mouth to ask, "Will you come back and visit us?"

Grimaldi glanced at Dix, then glanced at me, before turning back to Hannah. "I might."

"Good," Hannah said, and stuck her thumb back in her mouth.

ABOUT THE AUTHOR

Jenna Bennett writes the *USA Today* bestselling Savannah Martin mystery series for her own gratification, as well as the *New York Times* bestselling Do-It-Yourself home renovation mysteries from Berkley Prime Crime under the pseudonym Jennie Bentley. For a change of pace, she writes a variety of romance, from contemporary to futuristic, and from paranormal to suspense.

FOR MORE INFORMATION, PLEASE VISIT HER WEBSITE:
WWW.JENNABENNETT.COM

Made in United States
North Haven, CT
25 November 2022

27215287R00171